FIERCE

- A FARWAY HIGH FAIRYTALE -

SCARLETT KOL

FIERCE
Copyright © 2026 by Scarlett Kol
All rights reserved.

ISBN: (ebook) 978-1-7776350-8-4
Print: 978-1-7776350-9-1

Edited by Laura Koons at Red Adept Editing
Proofread by Vonda at Red Adept Editing

Cover Art by Sanja Gombar

Published by Vicious Pixie Press

*To those who believe in fairytales
and trust their instincts.*

"He never raised his eyes to her, but nearly all day she felt him at her side without ever seeing him."

- Andrew Lang,
The Twelve Dancing Princesses

THE RED FAIRY BOOK
(LONGMANS, GREEN AND CO., 1890)

1

----

nce upon a time, the Lions came to play. But whoever tried to take them down just got blown away. Go Lions!

"Go Lions!" I shouted from the side of the gym, my voice disappearing into the roar of the crowd. Feet pounded the bleachers, and the booming sound rumbled through my chest. Energy, pure and electric, pulsed through every cell of my body and shook me awake, as if I'd spent my entire life asleep until that moment.

Captain Kate tipped her head back and laughed at the crowd's attention. She drank it in, savored it, as it fueled her megawatt smile. She popped up on her toes toward the rapt crowd and cupped her hands around her mouth. "Who's number one?"

"We are!" the mob shouted back.

She glanced back over her shoulder at the three straight lines of cheerleaders behind her. Astrid rolled her eyes at the drama, but Kate simply winked at her and turned back to the bleachers.

"I said," Kate yelled, and the rest of the cheer squad joined her. "Who's number one?"

The audience responded louder and more desperately than before. "We are!"

"Woohoo!" Kate whooped as she shook her pom-poms over her head and spun around to face her squad. She stomped one sneakered foot on the glossy gym floor as she thrust her hands to her hips. She nodded. The squad nodded back in unison.

We are the Lions. The mighty, mighty Lions...

I mouthed the words as my arms instinctively mimicked the precise choreography. Like a worn-out song on my playlist, every note and inflection was committed to my memory, except I wasn't the one who got to sing it. They were the exalted ones, and I was just the alternate.

If high school were a kingdom, Kate and the girls on the squad would be royalty. Twelve perfect princesses who drew the envy of all the other peasants. Even the muscular clones of the football team in their purple-and-gold jackets couldn't outshine the cheerleaders. They might be the reason for the pep rally after barely squeaking into the playoffs by taking down their longtime rivals, the Bartlett Bears, in a last-minute Hail Mary play that scored us that one extra touchdown, but they still weren't the stars. They couldn't be. The Faraway High Cheer Team owned more real estate in the school trophy case than any other sport in the school's history. A legacy of champions—and one I so desperately wanted to be a part of. *One day.*

The cheering subsided, and the real show began. High kicks, roundhouses, back handsprings. Perfectly toned bodies flipped and twisted across the gym floor. The crowd hollered, amplifying the energy of the tumblers on their passes. They leaped higher, flipped faster, and landed every trick tighter than I'd ever seen.

"Go Lions," the squad cheered as they broke into their next formation.

Piper, Melody, and Joy strutted to center stage, tossing their heads to the side so their flawless ponytails swung in time to the clapping of the audience. Sydney joined the trio and hoisted herself onto Piper's and Melody's shoulders as they grabbed hold of her right foot. She rose in the air like an impossible gilded flower, beautiful and graceful, blooming as her arms pulled away from her chest, every movement precisely timed for maximum showmanship. Without wavering, she balanced on her right leg as she threw her left behind her and clutched the tip of her sneaker. When her grip locked around her toe, she turned to the crowd and beamed a wide, rehearsed smile, as she flaunted her impeccably executed scorpion position.

Shouts and whistles echoed off the gym roof.

The bases pushed on Sydney's foot, and she popped up higher, dropping her leg and clutching her chest again. She tucked her arms tight to her sides as her body rotated into a full twist. Three hundred and sixty degrees of weightlessness. Of unrestrained falling.

I bit my lip, waiting for her to steady herself. To regain control.

Her arms flung out into a T as she fell into the last half twist, dropping into the cradle of her teammates' arms below.

Except she didn't stop.

Piper's eyes widened as Sydney slid through their grip. Shoes squeaked across the floor as they tried to recalibrate.

I gasped and clamped my hand over my mouth.

Sydney's body sank closer to the floor. Her head dropped back, and I lunged forward as if I could reach her from my place on the sidelines. The rest of the squad froze and stared. My stomach clenched, but instead of Sydney crash-landing on the ground, her golden hair whisked across the floor as Joy yanked her up at the last second.

Sydney stumbled forward and regained her balance. Melody placed a hand on her shoulder, but she shrugged it off and clapped her hands.

"Go Lions!" she shouted, as her fake smile slid back in place and a telltale red crept up her neck into her cheeks.

I stepped back against the wall and watched as the last of the routine played out in front of me. Each move seemed tainted now, the earlier energy held back as all eyes stayed glued to Sydney, but she kept going.

Finally, the cheerleaders all struck their final poses, waving their pom-poms over their heads as Principal Andersen stepped up to the narrow wooden podium near the bleachers.

"Wow. That was amazing. Let's give a big hand for Kate Fleming and the fantastic Faraway High Cheer Team."

He applauded along with the students for a few moments then raised his open palm over his head. The room silenced. He was likely relishing the power he wielded as his thin lips contorted into a smirk. If he only knew what people said behind his back.

"This concludes the first of what I hope to be many playoff pep rallies this year. Our team has been working hard all season, and I expect to see each and every one of you in the crowd tomorrow showing off your Lion pride. You are all officially dismissed. Go team!"

He ended his speech with an exaggerated fist pump then stepped back from the podium and rushed toward the side door to usher everyone out. The line of teachers along the far wall followed as the thunder of over four hundred sets of feet thumped their way to the exit.

I backed away from the horde and watched as it passed by. The football princes with their arrogant smiles as the rest of the varsity athletes clipped behind on their heels. Sydney storming through the crowd with a death glare as the rest of the cheerleaders hung back to give her space. Then, as usual, the senior class, along with a few popular juniors who'd somehow made the cut, followed by the juniors, sophomores, and freshmen. All in a hurry to take advantage of being able to leave a whole twenty minutes early from last period.

"Hey, Melina, want to come with us to Bean There for a mocha on the way home?"

I peeled my eyes off the escaping parade and turned around. My day-one crew—Jaida, Hailey, Isaac, and Leo— loitered by the back wall, watching me watch everyone else instead of bolting for the exit. I'd honestly expected them to be halfway out of the school by now.

Jaida crept closer then wrapped her arm around my shoulder and started leading me toward the door. "Sounds like they've released the white chocolate peppermint flavor early this year. I know it's your favorite."

I slipped my hand in hers then spun myself around

until I was no longer in her grasp. "I'd love to, but I have to clean everything up here and then set up for practice. But thanks for waiting for me."

Isaac pushed himself off the wall and slung his backpack over his shoulder before coming to join us. "Ugh. That sounds boring. Are you sure you don't want to just blow it off? It's not like—"

Jaida glared up at him, her dark eyes compressing to sharp, narrow slits. His shoulders tensed, and he eased back a step, probably afraid she'd unleash some crazy sort of torment on him. Jaida might be just over five feet, but her fiery side could topple giants.

Hailey slipped in between the two of them and leaned back against Isaac's chest. "It's okay. Allyssa couldn't come either. Maybe we can go at lunch tomorrow?"

I nodded. "Sounds good."

Hailey tugged on Isaac's arm and pulled him out the door with Jaida close behind.

I sighed as they crossed into the hall, leaving me in the gym. A white chocolate peppermint mocha would be so amazing right now. I closed my eyes and imagined the hot deliciousness sliding down my throat, my chest warming at the memory of my last one. Had it really been a year already?

"Do you need any help?"

A weight fell on my shoulder. I jumped and snapped my hand back, grasping someone's fingers before they slipped out of my reach. As I whirled around, Leo raised his open palms in surrender, an amused grin breaking across his lips.

My heart pounded out a pop song against my ribs as I swatted his arm. "Don't sneak up on me like that."

"Like what?" Leo rubbed his bicep as his smile widened. "I was standing here the whole time. You were the one spaced out in a totally other world. Where were you anyway?"

"You know me, just hanging out in my own brain. It's nice there. You should come visit once in a while."

He frowned. "No thanks. Who knows what bizarre stuff you have going on in there?"

I responded with a playful sneer then headed toward the front of the makeshift stage. Pieces of metallic purple and gold foil sprinkled across the performance space while heaps of shiny pom-poms lay scattered in pairs between them. I picked up the first set of pom-poms, tucked them under my left arm, then proceeded down the row, snagging the abandoned balls like a convicted felon collecting trash on the side of a highway for community service.

Leo started on the back row, picking up the pom-poms and smashing them against his side with a lot less care.

I winced as more strands fluttered to the floor from his rough handling. "You know, you don't have to stick around here. If you hurry, I'm sure you can catch up with Isaac and the others."

He shrugged. "It's no big deal. But honestly, why do you keep doing this? I mean, don't most squads put away their own gear? It kind of feels like they are taking advantage of you." He swooped his long arm just above the gym floor and snatched another metallic ball in his fist. "You're an alternate, not the team servant."

"It's not taking advantage if I offer to do it. I'm just trying to make a good impression, you know? Ainsley made her way onto the squad as an alternate when Amelia's family moved away, and I'm just hoping that maybe I'll get the chance one day."

He clapped his open hand against the pom-pom, and it popped out of his grip back onto the floor. "It doesn't seem very fair to me."

"Then it's a good thing it isn't up to you." I bent down and reached forward, but the metallic strands slipped through my fingertips. Leo crouched in front of me and held the pom-pom in his hand. I grabbed for it, but he tugged it away at the last second, and I tipped forward, nearly falling on my face.

"Gotta be faster than that, Lina." He held the pom-pom out again and flashed a crooked smirk.

"And to think I was going to thank you for helping me." I pushed on his shoulder, and he faltered, landing on his butt.

He tossed his head back and laughed. "You're welcome."

I extended my open hand and turned my face away to hide the grin teasing its way across my lips. His fingers wrapped tightly around mine, and he yanked me closer as he rose to his feet. The pom-poms were crushed between us as the warmth of his chest prickled across my bare arm.

"Now I have to thank you," he whispered, his green eyes holding mine for a breath before darting away.

"No problem." I flexed my fingers against his palm until he released his grip, then I stepped back and shook my head. "Next time, don't be so clumsy, and I won't have to save you."

I gathered all the poms together, then piled them in

the corner of the gym. I dropped to my knees and unzipped a large purple duffel bag and stuffed each of them inside.

Leo's shadow loomed behind me. "The other reason I stayed behind was because I wanted to talk to you about the game on Friday night. Did you maybe want to do something after?"

I pulled the opening of the bag closed and zipped it shut. "Uh, yeah. We always go out together after every game. It's a tradition."

"Yeah, but I don't think everyone else can come this time. Allyssa said something about a gaming marathon. Hailey and Isaac are working on a project for their Business Innovations class."

Tossing the bag over my shoulder, I stood up and straightened my cheer skirt. "What about Jaida?"

"She said… What was it again?" Leo turned his face toward the ceiling. "I don't remember, but she said she had something going on."

"That's so odd. I swore everyone said they were coming to the game. Maybe I should just check." I grabbed my backpack off the floor and fished around the front pocket for my phone. Streams of group chat message bubbles filled the screen as I flicked back through our texts. "See, right here." I held my phone up to him. "Jaida said—"

"Oh, for sure everyone is coming to the actual game." Leo pushed my hand out of his face. "I just meant afterward. They all have other plans later."

"That's strange. No one said anything to me."

He shrugged. "Yeah, super strange, right? Maybe they

just didn't want to bother you with the whole pep rally thing today."

"Maybe."

"It's gotta be. Did you want me to carry that?" He reached for the duffel bag, but I tugged the straps closer to my chest.

"Nope. I'm fine."

"Good. As long as you're good." He ran his fingers through his hair then shoved his hands in his pockets as he walked beside me toward the door.

"What is with you today, Leo? You're so…" I waved my hand in a circle toward him as I scanned him over. "I don't know… fidgety. Like you drank three energy drinks at lunch or something."

"I'm fine." He stopped walking and rocked back on his heels, his head hanging down as if the toes of his sneakers had suddenly become the most interesting things in the room.

I flopped my head to the side and leaned over, forcing him to look at me. "Are you sure?"

"Of course." He scoffed and looked away. "Totally fine. Just trying to make a plan for Friday night. Maybe it's you who's off today?"

"Whatever you say." I pulled the bag tighter over my shoulder and continued across the gym floor.

Leo's steps thumped close behind me. "Seriously, though, after the game it looks like it's only you and me left. So, are you wanting to bail, or did you still want to do something, just us? I mean, not just *us*, but like out in public with other people. But only if you wanted—"

A loud, hollow smack echoed through the gym as Kate charged in, smashing her palm against the door. Astrid and Sunni, her usual lap dogs, followed close on her determined heels.

"Sydney is driving me completely insane," she yelled as she whirled around, her arms open wide and borderline flailing.

Leo glanced at me, his eyes asking questions his lips were smart enough to avoid. I shrugged and leaned back, as if that might somehow hide me.

Kate continued. "We've practiced that routine about a million times, and she's supposed to do a torch, not a scorpion. It's always been a torch. I should know. I choreographed it. But no, she had to show off."

"Calm down, sweetie. No one knew the difference. It's fine." Astrid grabbed Kate's hand and sandwiched it between her own.

For a second, Kate's head drooped, but she quickly ripped her hand away and slapped it on her hip. "It's not fine. She's lucky she didn't get dropped on her head today, and all because she can't follow simple instructions. She's been undermining me for weeks. Always telling me how to deal with the squad. Contradicting my decisions. Doesn't she realize that I'm the captain, not her?"

"Of course she does," Sunni said. "Maybe just try talking to her, and you can work all this out. Or you could —" Sunni's dark eyes widened as she caught sight of Leo and me standing motionless near the corner. "Um, hey, Melina."

All three girls turned to stare. I tugged Leo's sleeve and raced forward, making a wide circle to their left.

"Just finished cleaning up," I said, as I patted the duffel bag and beelined for the door. "See you all at practice."

Their heavy stares weighed down on my shoulders,

pushing my feet to move faster. I was one hundred percent sure Kate wouldn't have wanted me hearing everything she'd just said. Everyone loved her too much—or maybe feared her. It's not like she didn't have a bit of a reputation for being a tough captain, but she wouldn't want people gossiping about her either.

I could almost breathe the hallway air when Kate's voice rang out behind me.

"Melina, wait."

My sneakers squeaked on the floor as I halted in the doorway. Leo rammed into my side and stopped, but I shook my head and nudged him out in front of me.

"Thanks for taking care of everything today. You're always such a massive help to the team," Kate said.

I cleared my throat as the compliment stole my voice. "Yeah, of course. It's no big deal."

"Keep it up and we might have to think about giving you a more important role."

Astrid and Sunni glared at each other then looked over at Kate. She plastered on her carefully curated smile as her rigid stance softened.

I nodded. "Thanks."

"Just be ready," Kate called after me as I slipped out into the hall.

2

———

I turned the knob and fell against the door, pretty much tripping into my house. My exhausted arms didn't respond to me anymore as they flopped down by my sides. Kate's anger toward Sydney had fueled her to push us through the hardest, most grueling practice ever. Most of the girls thought she'd gone over the edge because of competition season looming on the horizon, but I knew the truth. She was super pissed.

The scent of tomato sauce and spices washed over me. Garlic mixed with something. Oregano? Maybe thyme? Either way, my mouth watered like a hungry dog's. I wiped the back of my hand across my lips as my stomach rumbled loudly to make sure I got the message.

"What's for dinner? It smells great." After stumbling through the front hall, I rushed into the kitchen expecting a table of familiar faces—and maybe a scowl from Mama for being late—but the dishes and the room had already been cleared.

My shoulders drooped, and I shrugged out of my jacket then flung it over the back of a chair. I'd told everyone I had practice after school. What was the point in telling your whole family if no one remembered to wait for you anyway? I tugged at my skirt, wishing I'd taken the extra ten minutes to change, my bare legs tingling as the warm air sank into my cold skin.

"Great, you're home." Marco slipped in from the living room, his stare glued to his phone as he swiped his thumb across the screen. However, I doubted he could even see anything with his greasy hair dangling in his face and his hood up, his eyes almost completely covered.

I stepped in front of him, blocking his path as he rushed through the kitchen. "Where is everyone?"

He sidestepped, but I pivoted with him, back and forth, until he gave up and leaned against the counter. "Papa took Matthew to basketball practice, and Mama is holed up in her office on a client call, something about a missed shipment or something. What's with the outfit? Did they actually let you on the team?"

"I'm already on the team and this is my uniform." I stuck my nose in the air and twirled around. "And I've been at practice learning some very demanding routines while you did what? Played on your phone?"

"Then how come I didn't see you at the pep rally today?" His lip twitched as he fought a smile, already knowing the answer but waiting for me to say it out loud.

I crossed my arms and stood up taller. "I was there. Surprised you didn't notice me."

He rolled his eyes then smacked his palm against his forehead. "Of course. I did see you there. Weren't you the one holding up the wall while everyone else did the cheering? All that practicing sure paid off."

"Not funny, Marco. I need to be ready to step in at any time."

"I'm not trying to be funny, Melina, but there's only ever been twelve spots on the team. When are you going to realize that you're gonna be standing on the sidelines all year unless something happens to one of those perfect little cheerleaders? Plus, those girls are so cliquey, they still might not even pick you next year."

I glared at him as I dug my fingernails into my palms, masking the sting of his completely wrong opinion. "You don't know anything."

He shrugged and swiped his hair out of his face, his focused stare fixed on mine. "Maybe, but I don't want to see you get hurt either." As quickly as the shot of empathy hit him, it disappeared, and he slid around me and headed toward the door.

"Melly, Melly," a tiny voice squeaked.

I spun around. Big, wide eyes looked up at me as two chubby hands reached for attention.

Bending down, I rested my palms on my knees. "Hey, Tommy. How are you doing, buddy?"

Tommy lunged at me. "Melly, up."

His arm hooked around my neck, and I swooped him up against my hip as his silky curls tickled against my bare shoulder.

"And what did you do today, big guy?"

He giggled as I bounced him up a little higher. The arm around my neck tightened, and his other hand smacked against my chest. A sticky pink glob smeared across the light-gold stripe of my uniform.

"Ew. Tommy. What is that?"

Marco laughed behind us. "Probably applesauce."

"But it's red." I swiped at the substance, and it spread even farther.

"Yeah, it's strawberry flavored. Matthew gave him some after dinner."

"Strawberry! That'll stain." I leaned over to put Tommy down, but his bottom lip stuck out and his eyes welled with tears. Pulling him close again, I thrust him toward Marco. "Here. Take him."

Marco threw his open hands in the air and backed up into the front hall. "Nope. Not happening. I've had toddler duty for the past hour."

I followed after him, Tommy's wailing ringing in my ear. "Seriously? Can you please just take him so I can go change?"

"Sorry, I gotta go. Oh, and you're going to need to babysit tomorrow because Mama and Papa are going up to see Miguel at college."

"I can't tomorrow. It's Friday. Game night. Why can't you do it?"

"I'm working. That trumps *maybe* being a cheerleader."

"Very funny. Take him, please."

He shook his head.

"Marco!"

"Already late." He shot back a snarky smirk as he twisted his feet into his sneakers, not bothering to untie them first, then ripped open the door and slipped out. "Bye, sis."

The door slammed behind him, and the hollow sound reverberated through my chest, or maybe it was just my cringe at how easily he just abandoned me.

I stared at the closed door as if Marco would suddenly grow a conscience and come bursting back in to help me. One second, two seconds, three. A car door clunked closed outside, and lights danced in the small window transit as he disappeared down the street. Tommy rested his head on my shoulder as he choked back sobs. The house fell silent around us. Empty and forgotten. The strawberry stain started to bleed through the fabric, just like the dread in my chest about what Kate would say if I didn't get the mark out.

With a deep sigh, I tilted my head against Tommy's and hugged him closer. "I guess it's just you and me, buddy. Let's go get cleaned up."

A QUIET CALMNESS fell over my brain as my bedroom door clicked closed behind me, shutting out the rest of the world. Mama had emerged from her office just in time to bathe Tommy and put him to bed, but I'd still wasted most of my night in the kitchen hoping someone would come home to save me. Except, no one came. At least she agreed to call Mrs. Danley from the next street to watch Tommy and Matthew tomorrow night. Fingers crossed she said yes.

I held out my cheerleading uniform. After scrubbing until my hands were red and raw, the applesauce stain seemed to have disappeared except for a hazy line around the outside, taunting me. I looked closer and blinked. The line vanished. I rubbed my palm over my face. Maybe I was just seeing things? Kate and the squad would not tolerate a dirty jersey.

My phone vibrated in the pocket of my sweatpants. I flopped onto my stomach across my bed and pulled it out. Our group chat had gone off while I'd been babysitting and scrubbing. Streams and streams of messages flowed across the screen as I scrolled toward the bottom. It didn't look like I'd missed much. Jaida was bingeing old sitcoms while trying to study for her biology quiz. Isaac hated listening to his sister practice her oboe. Allyssa won some weapon thing online that I didn't really understand, but I hearted the message anyway. No chaos or crises to worry about.

Me: Anyone have any big plans this weekend?

Jaida: Melina! You're alive! Thought Captain Kate might've made you do cartwheels until your arms fell off or something. We haven't heard from you all night.

Me: Ha! Nope. Just got stuck watching Tommy again. And Kate's not that bad.

Hailey: As long as you stay out of her way…

Me: Harsh.

Hailey: You know what I mean. Mrs. Lochlann is the teacher advisor for the squad and even she's too afraid to confront Kate. She just lets her run everything like a pretty little dictator.

Me: Mrs. Lochlann is also like a hundred years old and barely leaves her classroom.

Allyssa: Or does Kate have something on
her? You don't get that much power
without exploiting others' weaknesses.

Jaida: You play too many video games, A.
She's a mean girl, not a final boss.

I hovered my thumbs over the keys, except I couldn't think of the words to respond. She wasn't wrong. Kate's bossy reputation wasn't a secret, and it wouldn't be the first time someone had called her mean; however helping spread that news somehow felt like a betrayal, and I couldn't really afford to be on her bad side. Besides, it wasn't like she went out of her way to be mean to people or anything. She just expected the best from her team. Nothing wrong with being driven, right?

Rolling onto my back, I started typing as another message popped up.

Leo: I think what she's saying is that we
don't want anything bad to happen
to you.

Hailey: Yeah, that's it. Thanks, Leo.

Staring at the screen, I deleted my response and sighed.

Me: It's fine. Thanks for worrying. Talk to
you all tomorrow.

Jaida: WAIT! We still on for mochas at
lunch?

Me: Yep. Goodnight.

After flipping my phone to silent, I slid it back into my pocket. Grabbing onto my left calf, I rolled forward and up onto my feet. Why did I let things like that bother me? I shouldn't really. They just didn't understand. I wanted to be part of the team more than anything, and if kissing up to Kate and the rest of the squad was the way to do it, I would. Cheerleading wasn't just a sport to me. It was a way out. A new life. Colleges handed out scholarships to the cheerleaders in this town like candy at the Main Street Christmas Parade. They were the golden ones. They were winners.

I carefully folded my uniform then placed it in the gym bag sitting on my desk. Bright purple letters spelled out "Success" on my wall in all capitals, and I traced my fingers over the paper cutouts as if doing so would give them power. Amplify their intention or something new-agey like that. I'd created my vision collage at the start of freshman year and it had grown a lot over the past two years, every time I found something new to inspire me. Brochures from colleges I'd love to attend. Photos of places I wanted to visit. Paris. London. Rome. Places far away from Faraway. And of course, quotes and phrases that made my heart long in hopeful and painful ways every time I read them. I closed my eyes and read them over in my mind, no longer needing to see the words anymore to know what they said.

Downstairs, the front door slammed, and I flicked my eyes open, forcing myself out of my own thoughts. I tapped my open palm on the inspiration board and nodded as an invisible weight pressed down on the top of my head. *One day.*

But nothing came without hard work.

Stretching my arm behind me, I bent my left leg up and grabbed the top of my toe until a pleasant tingle rippled through my quadriceps. After a few seconds, I released my hold and switched to my right leg. I wavered a bit but regained my balance and tugged my toe closer to deepen the stretch. My legs were stiffer than they should be. Hopefully, I wouldn't feel it in the morning. With a deep breath, I tipped my head back and closed my eyes, letting the release flow through my body. Except something felt off, almost sticky on my flesh. I let go of my foot and scanned the room, but nothing seemed out of place.

I marched over to the closet and ripped open the doors. "I swear, Matthew, if you are spying on me again, you are in so much trouble."

But Matthew wasn't there, just rows of my shirts and skirts hanging in perfectly straight lines. I sighed and closed the doors again, returning to my empty spot on the floor.

Okay, Melina, get it together.

As I raised my arms in a wide V over my head, I straightened my spine and planted my feet on the floor.

"We are the Lions. The mighty, mighty Lions," I whispered as I moved through the choreographed motions. Right K, left K, bow and arrow, touchdown pose. I pushed harder and harder, making each movement sharper than the last, but the eerie sensation of being watched never faded; instead it slithered across my skin, leaving a trail of goose bumps behind.

"C'mon, Lions. Fight. Fight. Fight." I finished the routine and dropped my arms to my sides, listening closely, but only the sound of my own pulse echoed in my head.

A bead of sweat broke across my brow, and I swiped it away with my sweater sleeve. I opened the window, letting the late-fall chill blast against my burning cheeks. Dead leaves skittered down the quiet street, and a thickness hung in the air that threatened this year's first snowfall. In the distance, the glorious round moon lit a path from its perch in the sky down my street and across the lawn until it rested in a faint glow on my windowsill. Leaning farther out, I drew my upper body deeper into the night and let the light wash over my face as I wondered what might be at the end of the beams if I followed them. If I let myself run away.

A howl split through the darkness. My grip on the windowsill slipped, and I lurched forward, my head tipping down. The naked bushes in the garden bed below threatened with their pointed, empty branches, but I slid back into the warmth of my room. The howl rang out again. Probably just a neighbor's dog, except it sounded like something larger than the golden retrievers I'd seen parading down the sidewalk. Much less tame. I shuddered and pulled my arms close to my chest. The cold seeped into my bones and slowly, silently, the unnerving sensation of the unknown stare returned. Slamming the window shut, I backed away and drew the curtains tighter until the last slice of moonlight disappeared.

I shook my head and stumbled across the room, rubbing my arms until the chill started to subside, letting exhaustion creep in instead. After turning off the lights, I rushed toward my bed and jumped onto the firm mattress. I curled the soft comforter underneath my chin and slid my phone out of my pocket, placing it on the nightstand. The screen lit up as my fingers brushed the top. A single message notification appeared.

Leo: Are you sure you're okay?

I flipped the phone face down and ignored it. Of course, he'd be the one to notice something was off with me. I'd never successfully managed to keep a secret from him since the day we became friends on the monkey bars in second grade. But I couldn't talk to him about cheerleading. He wouldn't get it. And even if he did, I honestly didn't know the answer to his question.

3

———

The stadium lights burned bright in the inky night sky, like lucky stars that would hopefully guide our team to a win and the next round of the play-offs. Or maybe the entire crowd would have to wish on them really hard for that to happen. Most of Faraway and at least half of all the towns in a twenty-mile radius had braved the late autumn cold to pile into the stands for tonight's game. The biggest crowd I'd ever seen, or at least the largest I could remember.

I lugged the crates of water bottles out into the stadium and lined them up along the edge of the field near the bleachers in a straight line, each one carefully positioned so the Lions sticker faced out and each cheerleader's name was visible at a glance.

"You are always so particular, Melina. I'm impressed." Ainsley appeared on the field beside me, hefting the bag of pom-poms onto a bench and pulling open the zipper.

"Thanks. If I were in charge, I'd just want everything

to be exact, you know?" I reached into the bag and helped her pull out the gold-and-purple poms. "Besides, maybe I'll get a shot like you and finally get to be on the actual squad instead of being a glorified equipment manager."

Ainsley snorted, and her high ponytail bobbed as she laughed. Then she stopped and covered her mouth with her hand, like anyone around could hear her with all the noise. "It's not all that great. Trust me."

"Thanks, but you don't have to try to make me feel better. You complained every day when you were an alternate like me. Now look at you." I waved my hand and stood back to do just that. She was everything we'd both hoped for back in August. The flawless cheer bow. The front row spot right next to Kate. Every set of eyes on her. Wishing they could be her. Just like I did. "You're practically a goddess around here. And you totally deserve it. I don't know anyone else who has as much school spirit as you."

Her cheeks flushed, and she looked down at her white sneakers. "Thanks, but seriously, Melina. If I knew…" She crossed her arms over her chest and turned around, heading back toward the dressing room.

"If you knew what?"

She shook her head. "Nothing. Don't worry about it. Just enjoy where you are now. You might wish for it one day."

A chill rippled along my skin as I watched Ainsley walk away. I clenched my jacket sleeves tight in my fists and pulled my arms closer to my rib cage. Must be getting colder than I'd thought.

As Ainsley reached the edge of the bleachers, Sydney

barreled around the corner, nearly knocking her to the ground. She grabbed onto her forearms and shouted in her face, but Ainsley only looked away.

I chucked the pom-pom bag to the ground and sped toward them. As I came closer, Sydney's face sharpened. Tears glazed her eyes, and running black mascara drew crooked lines down her cheeks.

"Is everything okay?" I asked as I sidled close to Ainsley. Even though we were on different levels now, I still wasn't going to let some diva yell at her.

Her hands left Ainsley's arms, red marks replacing Sydney's fingers across Ainsley's skin.

"Melina. Thank goodness it's you. Please tell me you've seen my bracelet. I can't find it anywhere." Sydney pulled my hand into hers and clenched it.

"I don't think I've seen any bracelets around, but maybe I can help you find it. What does it look like?"

Sydney's expression darkened, her forehead dropping as a storm whipped up in her hazel eyes. "My cheer bracelet. The only one that matters." She grabbed Ainsley's elbow and pulled her arm up in the air between us. The gold-stranded friendship bracelet laced around Ainsley's wrist slid down an inch as the tiny purple beads in the weave shone under the lights. The same one Kate had. The same one every girl on the squad had. Every girl except me. "I need to find it. Fast."

I put my hand on her shoulder, and her body trembled beneath my grip. "Don't worry. We'll find it, and if we can't, we'll get you a new one."

She ripped away from me. "You can't just get me a new one. I need *my* bracelet. Please help me find it."

"Okay." I nodded at Ainsley, but she wouldn't meet my eyes, her face suddenly pale. "Where did you last see it?"

"I don't know. Last night, I think." Sydney placed her palm across her forehead and swayed back and forth as if trying to conjure the memory or maybe just trying to stand up straight. "Just after practice, maybe?"

"All right, let me check through the rest of the gear. It could have fallen off when you were putting your poms away. Did you try the gym locker room?" I raced back to the pom-pom bag and dropped to the grass as I dug through all the side pockets. Nothing there.

Sydney paced behind me, and the small hairs on the back of my neck prickled as she scrutinized my every move. "Of course I checked the locker room. I've looked everywhere. The gym. My car. I flipped my entire house upside down. It's like it just disappeared. Give me that." She reached around me and tore the bag from my hands then flipped it upside down, shaking it hard enough for everything inside to tumble out onto the grass.

Athletic tape. Pens. Packages of bobby pins. But definitely no bracelet.

"Um, Sydney…" Ainsley pointed at Sydney's face as she backed away from us.

I glanced up from the mess on the ground. Red dripped from Sydney's left nostril. She stroked her hand across her skin and held it out, gazing at the crimson smear of blood on her fingertips.

Pushing myself up, I grabbed the bag from Sydney's grip and guided her to a nearby bench. "Are you okay?"

"I'm going to get help," Ainsley called as she ran off the field and disappeared beneath the bleachers.

I fished through my backpack until I found a package of tissues and handed it to Sydney. Her hands shook as she slipped out a few sheets and held them to her nose. Her tears flowed again, widening the black makeup rivers on her face.

"Everything hurts," she said, her voice low and muffled. "My whole body feels like it's broken, and I can't make it stop."

"Here." I wrapped my arm around her back and gently tried to help her back to her feet without pushing on her too hard. "You should probably go home."

"I can't. The game."

"They will be fine without you for one night. You need to get better."

She lunged forward and bolted toward the exit. I chased after her, but her long legs kept her just a few steps ahead.

"Sydney," I yelled as I turned around the corner of the bleachers and stopped short, nearly toppling over my own feet.

Sydney crouched with her head hanging over a metal trash can, the sound of her retching loud enough to hear over the stands full of fans above me. She finally gave up and slowly slid down to the grass, her right fist still gripping the top edge of the can. Her body wavered and shook as she swiped the back of her free hand across her mouth, a red line tracing across her ashen skin.

I rushed to her side and swung her arm over my shoulder, helping her to her feet again. "Let me drive you home."

She nodded, her hazel eyes rolling unfocused in their sockets.

"There you are." Kate stood poised with her hands on her hips, Astrid at her side and Ainsley hiding behind them. "We were so worried."

Kate reached out to Sydney, but she flinched in my grip, pulling away.

"You're a mess, Syd." Kate's pretty pink smile deflated to a pout, but she stopped pushing. "I think you should skip this game."

"Don't worry, I was just taking her home." I eased in closer and adjusted my hold around Sydney's waist. We turned toward the school parking lot and hobbled a few steps forward.

"But you can't go, Melina," Kate called from behind us.

I turned my head but kept walking. "I'll just be a few minutes. Everything is already set up."

Kate circled around and stopped in front of us. "That's not what I meant. We need you to cheer tonight."

"What?" I gasped.

"You are the alternate, aren't you? If Syd can't cheer, we need you to do it." She took Sydney's arm and peeled it off me. "Astrid, go tell Sunni she's flying tonight and that Melina is taking her place on the floor."

"Got it." Astrid nodded and rushed back toward the school.

Kate turned to me again. "You do know the cheers, right?"

"Of course. But…" I glanced over at poor Sydney but couldn't find the words to say more.

"Ainsley," Kate called. "Go find Mrs. Lochlann or some other teacher to take Sydney home. We need to get Melina ready for her debut."

"Kate, don't—" Sydney's body tensed as if she were

going to argue, but instead she buckled over and coughed. Tiny dots of red splattered the toe of Kate's sneaker.

"Ew." She wrinkled her nose and patted Sydney on the shoulder. "Maybe it's best if you take a break from cheering for a while."

4

We don't care where you've been. Now you're in the Lions' den.

I shouted the words loud enough that they echoed in my head, even though they disappeared into the noise of the crowd. The buzz of the stadium's energy set me on fire, blazing through my veins, pushing every jump higher, every arm movement longer and more precise.

On the field, the Friday night lights failed to work the same magic with our team, who were down by three with only a minute and twenty left on the clock. This was the moment we needed to cheer harder than ever to get the fans to push our players to their brink, but I wanted to watch just as much as everyone else.

I kicked my leg high and clapped along to the last few lines of the cheer then hung back with my hands on my hips, looking out onto the field. A circle of broad purple-jerseyed shoulders clustered near our forty-yard line. My heart pounded like a marching band drum as the importance of this next play vibrated in the air.

I leaned close to Ainsley. "Is it just me or does cheering make football seem absolutely thrilling?"

"It's just the adrenaline," she shouted back, her glittery lipstick sparkling. "Trust me, you'll get over it as soon as that buzzer sounds. Especially if they lose, which they probably will."

"I don't know. For some reason, it feels like a lucky night."

Ainsley rolled her eyes and raised her left arm in the air, the gold foil catching the stadium lights. "Whatever, Melina. One person's luck is another person's misery."

"What is that supposed to mean?"

Except my words fell flat as Ainsley ran toward the bleachers and scooped up her water bottle. She tipped her head back and squeezed a huge gush into her mouth then stared past me out to the field.

As I glanced over my shoulder, the Lions' huddle broke, and the teams lined up, waiting for the snap. Our quarterback, Alex Chase, shuffled back, looking for an opening, then pulled his arm back and let the ball fly. The wide receiver snagged the pass and ran. He burned past the forty-yard line... the thirty... twenty... ten ... touchdown! Screams erupted around me. The volume in the stadium cranked higher as the vibe of excitement hummed in my chest.

"Go Lions!" I yelled as I tossed up another high kick and shook my pom-poms above my head.

The other girls joined in the celebration, hollering and doing handsprings to keep the crowd entertained as the rest of the clock ticked down, but the Central Wildcats didn't stand a chance now.

Fans rose to their feet, stomping and shouting in

support or simply filing toward the exits as a faint chorus of "let's go, Lions" rippled through the din. I scanned the stands to the top left corner of the bleachers. Jaida, Leo, Allyssa, Hailey, and Isaac waved their hands in the air, laughing and screaming along with the crowd. I'd strategically avoided eye contact with any of them while I cheered to try to keep my nerves calm—as if I could really keep myself calm anyway. But now, after managing the full four quarters without falling on my face and with the team seconds from pulling out a win, I wished someone would just look my way. But no go.

The buzzer sounded, and the sideline players rushed the field, attacking their teammates with awkward hugs and ill-timed fist bumps as the excitement in the stadium hit fever pitch.

"Looks like you might get another chance to strut your stuff, rookie." Sunni yelled near my ear. "You did pretty good for a first-timer. The fans loved you."

"You really think so?" I shouted back.

Sunni nodded, her glossy black ponytail bobbing along. "Now, give them more of what they want."

She gave a graceful high kick then smiled at me. "Way to go, Faraway High."

"Woohoo!" I added and waved my poms over my head again, watching as rows of fans still followed our every move even though the game was over. The power rushed through my limbs. Going from hiding on the sidelines to the spotlight made everything more exciting. More visceral.

Behind me, the team and coaching staff slowed their celebration and started packing up, enjoying the last glimpses of victory and likely hoping they could hold on to it for at least a few more games. They paraded off the field as hometown heroes—at least for the next week, unless they could pull out another win. The quarterback hung behind the rest of them, shaking hands with Coach Beaufort, then pulled off his helmet and swiped his fingers through his sweaty, slicked-back hair, letting it flop lazily across his brow. His stare laser-focused on the exit as he quickened his pace, the victory seeming to roll off his shoulder pads as he kept up a stern, almost stoic, expression.

I cupped my hands around my mouth and yelled, "Lions rule!"

He glanced up and locked eyes with me through the crowd, his serious demeanor cracking as a broad smile broke across his lips. He tipped his hand toward me in a polite wave. I waved back, and he laughed, the lightness complementing his features far better than his more somber tone. He waved again, and I moved forward as if he'd tugged some invisible string but stopped short when Kate appeared in front of him, her hand on his shoulder.

He wrapped an arm around Kate's waist and swung her up close to his chest. She tossed her head back, her ponytail rippling in icy waves behind her and her ruby lips curling into a smile as she playfully pushed him away and giggled. An unsettling thickness caught in my throat as I watched them from the outside. High school royalty gravitating toward each other like pretty magnets. A different echelon than the rest of us. The confident ones.

He tipped his head closer to hers and whispered in her ear before placing her back on the ground. She splayed her hand across his chest and turned away, holding his gaze until the last second before strutting back toward the squad. A mischievous grin graced his lips as he watched her walk away, then he shook his head and rushed off toward the locker room.

"Melina!" a voice called behind me.

I blinked, breaking free of the enchantment of the beautiful people, then turned toward the bleachers.

My friends stood on the top row, waving their arms at me. They all shouted in unison. "Hey, Melina!"

I chuckled and waved back then swerved through the rest of the cheerleaders to the edge of the turf. Jaida bounded down the stairs to the field, jumping over the last few, and raced toward me. She rammed right into my chest, nearly knocking me to the ground, but I braced myself and stayed standing.

"You, my friend, were amazing. Why didn't you tell anyone you were cheering tonight?" she said as she squeezed me tighter and hefted my body a few inches off the ground.

The rest of the crew followed up behind her. Isaac with his arm over Hailey's shoulders, Allyssa with her headphones around her neck peeking out from the collar of her jacket, and of course, Leo, standing behind the group with a crooked grin.

I placed my forehead against hers. "I'm sorry. I didn't know it was happening until the absolute last minute. I swear."

"Well, we'll forgive you this time," she said as she released her iron grip and stepped back. "But I can't wait to hear all about it."

She glanced back over her shoulder. Hailey's eyes widened, and she looked at Jaida then shot a glare at

Allyssa. Allyssa responded with a shrug, and Jaida shook her head at Leo.

"What's going on?" I asked.

"Oh, nothing. Just wish we all weren't so busy tonight so we could go out and celebrate with you, but of course, we all have stuff." She turned her face away. "Really important stuff that just can't wait."

My shoulders dropped. In all the excitement, I'd forgotten that everyone was bailing on our postgame plans. "That's okay. I understand."

"Call me later, though. Okay?" Jaida jerked her head toward the stadium exit, and everyone shifted to leave. She patted Leo on the shoulder as she brushed past him. "Trust me. I want to hear all about your night."

His smile disappeared as he slipped his hands deep into the pockets of his wool peacoat. I couldn't remember the last time I'd seen him wear it, and since it still looked impeccable, without even a speck of lint, I doubted it was often. But he really should. Especially with his hair carefully styled and swept back like tonight. If he hadn't shown up with Jaida and the others, I might've thought he was some hot college guy back to relive his high school glory days. My cheeks flushed as I continued to scan him over. Did my brain just call Leo hot? Must be the adrenaline. Maybe more grown up, instead. A more polished and put-together version of the Leo I saw every day.

I tugged on his lapels and smoothed my hands down his sleeves. "A little dressed up for a football game, don't you think? Are you ditching me for a big date or something?"

"No, of course not." He pulled my hands away and backed up. "I just thought I'd try something different."

"I'm just teasing. You look good." I nudged him with my shoulder and he seemed to relax. "You also look very cold, but still good."

He rolled his eyes, but the stiffness in his shoulders eased. "Thanks a lot, Lina. I can go home and change if you want?"

"Don't be silly. I need to take care of the cheer gear, then we can get going." I swung my hand behind me, pointing toward the benches, and backed away. "Unless you just want me to meet you over at Twisted Top?"

"No, it's fine. I can wait."

"Okay, then. I'll be right back."

"Actually, hold on. I was thinking…" He grabbed the back of his neck and looked up at the scoreboard still lit with the winning score. "Maybe we might want to go somewhere else this time? Somewhere a little more exciting than ice cream?"

"Galileo Vincent Moretti, do not tell me you suddenly have a vendetta against ice cream."

He winced. "Please don't use my full name. My skin crawls just thinking about it."

"What is up with you then?" I poked my finger into the center of his chest and stared up at him, trying to catch his stare. Leo had always been a terrible liar. You could tell before he even opened his mouth when he was preparing to hide the truth. He shifted his weight. His fingers fidgeted. And the most obvious tell—he couldn't look you in the eye. Even a lousy poker player would have him marked in seconds. "First you come to a football game dressed like you're going to a job interview. Then you're all side-eye and smirks with Jaida. Now you want to change postgame ice cream. Is everything okay with you?" I slid my palm across his forehead. "You don't feel warm."

He wrapped his fingers around mine and yanked my hand away, drawing it down to my side but not letting go. "I'm not sick. It's just that—"

"Melina." Kate's arm slammed down over my shoulders as she slid next to me. "There's my number one rookie. You did outstanding tonight. Didn't she… um… What's your name again?"

"It's Leo, but I don't think we've ever really met." He dropped my hand and stepped back, creating some much-needed space. However, as much as he held his voice steady, his jaw clenched as he said the words.

"Right. Leo." She slid her arm off me and put her hands on her hips. "Anyway, the football team and the squad are heading to Fat Tony's to celebrate the big win. It's kind of a victory ritual. You want to come? It'll be a blast."

I bit down on my lip to keep from squealing. Me. Hanging out with the squad outside of practice.

"Absolutely," I blurted. Then I realized what I'd done. "I mean… I would absolutely love to come, but I already have plans." I nodded toward Leo.

"Well, that's too bad." Kate's face stiffened, and she let out an exaggerated sigh. "I guess if we somehow manage another win in the next round, you can come with us then."

My fingers found the hem of my skirt and bunched the slippery fabric into my fists. I peeked over my shoulder as the other girls laughed and chatted, getting ready to leave. A knot twisted in my chest as Kate turned and started to walk away.

"She'll go," Leo called after her.

Kate halted but didn't turn around. "Are you sure?"

I leaned closer to him and lowered my voice. "What are you doing?"

"You've been dying to be on the squad for forever. This might be your big shot." He slid his cool fingers against my cheek and pulled my face up toward his. The knot released, and something foreign and warm took its place. "I'll still be here when you're done chasing your dream."

His stare locked on mine, and for a split second everyone else disappeared. I gasped, the intensity shift stealing my breath. Leo's eyes widened, and he dropped his hand, breaking whatever spell the excitement of the night had cast.

"Do you mind if Leo comes with us?" I said as I shook my head and crossed my arms over my chest.

"If he wants, but—"

"No way, Lina. I'm good. I'll just catch up with you later." He nodded, silently nudging me away, but I didn't move. "I'm serious. Go before they leave you behind."

"Thank you. You're the greatest." I pulled him into a quick hug then chased after Kate, who had already rejoined Astrid and Sunni near the bleachers.

I looked back. Leo smiled then turned and walked away. I brushed my hand over my cheek and watched him go, as the odd sensation of his skin against mine rushed through me again like an aftershock. Leo was just a friend. One of my best friends. We'd touched a million times, so with all the excitement of the game my senses must've been a bit heightened. What else could it be?

I let out a deep breath then headed toward Kate and the rest of the squad. Deciphering that moment would be tomorrow's problem. Tonight I had to celebrate.

5

―――――

eep breaths, Melina. You've got this.

I stood on the steps outside Fat Tony's and shook out the last of my nerves. Staying to lock up the water bottles and pom-poms in the gym had pretty much guaranteed that I'd be the last one to arrive, which meant walking into unknown territory. I'd been to this place a hundred times, but never on game night. Our group of friends preferred the less crowded Twisted Top, yapping at our regular table next to the old-timey jukebox. Besides, even if we wanted to change up our routine, Tony's was always too busy to get a table. Except I could really use a friendly face.

I straightened the bow on my ponytail and tugged at the hem of my skirt then opened the door. The warmth of the restaurant wafted out into the autumn night, prickling across my cold cheeks as the heavy smell of parmesan and tomato sauce engulfed my senses. My stomach growled in appreciation.

The red-and-white checkered tablecloths faded into a

sea of purple and gold, as every patron had donned the school colors. The winning school colors. Lion central. The room buzzed, pulsing with the fiery energy that had somehow transferred from the stadium to here. Except I felt like I was watching from the stands instead of in the middle of it all. Like I'd walked into a private party where everyone knew everyone and I had come as a friend of a friend. A sharp pain twinged in my gut, but it didn't seem like hunger. Maybe I shouldn't have come. I'd only cheered for one game, and besides, I'd promised Leo we'd hang out. Leo with his piercing gaze and something to say on the tip of his tongue. I should've at least found out what he wanted before ditching him. Maybe he'd still be up for going out. I slid my phone out of my jacket pocket and started to type as I headed back toward the door.

"Hey, Melina, over here." From the oversized corner booth, Sunni raised her arm and beckoned me. My fingers froze mid-word as the rest of the table swiveled in my direction. I waved back and fought the goofy smile curling on my lips, abandoning my message and slipping the phone back into my pocket.

One more deep breath.

I crossed the floor, darting back and forth to avoid the servers with their wide trays of pizza and breadsticks, but I couldn't shake the heaviness surrounding me. Every table turned to stare as I passed. Conversations momentarily stopped to look up.

Did I have something on my face?

I casually swiped my hands across my cheeks, but only a few golden sparkles flecked my fingertips.

"Lions rule!" someone called out behind me. I glanced

back over my shoulder as a table of juniors gave me an awkward thumbs-up.

What in the world was happening? I'd lived in this little town my entire life, and not once had random people tried to get my attention. Did the playoffs have some unique magic that transported me to an alternate dimension the second I stepped off the field? Or, far more likely, they mistook me for someone else. In my cheer-leading uniform, I could be any one of a dozen girls. It must've been a mistake.

Shaking my head, I turned back toward the corner booth but instead slammed face-first into the solid wall of someone's chest.

"Sorry," I mumbled as I stepped backward, the side of my leg catching on the edge of a nearby table. My feet twisted beneath me, and the uneasiness in my stomach rose in my throat. I flailed my arms out to break my fall, but instead a strong hand gripped my upper arm and yanked me back to standing. After exhaling a relieved breath, I glanced up into the most stunning pair of blue eyes I'd ever seen up close. Deep and endless, like a sapphire ocean disappearing off the end of the world. Or at least what I dreamed an ocean would look like if I ever got to see one in person.

"Easy now. Are you okay?" the eyes said in a deep voice that rumbled low through the noise of the restaurant.

I blinked. Once. Twice. "Um, yeah. Thanks."

"Way to bulldoze the poor girl. Could you be any more clumsy, Alex?" A hulking mass of football jacket-wearing handsomeness slapped his hand on Alex's shoulder.

"Please excuse Griffin." Alex released my arm, casting

his buddy a piercing side-eye. "He's my best friend with the worst manners."

Griffin shrugged, seeming not to care. "Or maybe you just need to get better friends."

I fought the urge to laugh out loud. Griffin Carlisle, the starting running back, could be friends with anyone he wanted at Faraway High. People queued up just to look at him. If some new girl hadn't siren-songed her way into his heart at the beginning of the year, I'm sure I wouldn't even be able to get this close to him on a Friday night for the line of girls who'd be trying to win his attention. He and Alex made such an exhaustingly striking pair that it probably went against some law of nature to have that much good-looking in one place.

Alex shook his head then turned his attention back to me. "And I'm—"

"Oh, I know who you are," I said.

He stood up straighter, his chest seeming to puff up a little as a proud grin formed on his lips. "You do?"

"Um, of course she does. She's a cheerleader." Kate appeared behind Griffin and sashayed her way in front of the boys, knocking her hip into mine. "Knowing who the players are is part of the job. It'd be nice if the team extended us the same courtesy."

"But I do know you." Alex pointed at me. "You're Marco Cardona's little sister, right?"

I choked back the urge to vomit. Of course, the first time people actually noticed me and it was for being related to Marco. Sarcastic slacker Marco. Why couldn't he associate me with Miguel instead? I straightened my stance and stuck my hands on my hips. "Typically, I go by Melina, not just 'Marco's sister.'"

"Whoa. Okay. Definitely noted." He raised his open palms and shifted his weight to his back foot, giving us a breath of distance in the crammed aisle. "Either way, it's nice to finally meet you."

I eased up, trying not to let disdain for my brother ruin my evening. "Thanks. You too. Both of you."

"I saw you cheering your heart out tonight. You did really great." Griffin nudged Kate with his shoulder. "Maybe she's the reason we pulled out that win tonight."

"Oh, c'mon. Are you that superstitious you think you need us to win?" Kate teased back.

"No, I just follow enough stats to know that we shouldn't have won that game, so there must've been something special about tonight. It definitely wasn't Alex's string of incompletes in the second quarter." He laughed.

"You're one to talk, Griffin 'how many fumbles can I make in one game' Carlisle."

Griffin put his hand over his heart. "Ouch, dude. That hurt."

"As much as I'd love to stand here and watch you all insult each other like whiny toddlers, I'm going to take my girl here to celebrate the big win, if that's okay with you?" Kate fluttered her hands in the air, urging the boys to back up and let us pass.

"Of course, Captain Kate." Alex nodded and moved out of our way.

Kate glared up at him as she passed. "C'mon, Melina."

I followed behind her. The heaviness returned at the base of my neck as we passed the last few tables.

Kate pulled me close and shouted in my ear. "Looks

like someone's attracting a lot of attention. How does it feel?"

"Pretty good, I guess." Is this what people like Kate and the other girls on the squad always felt like with all the constant attention? Or did they honestly not realize how the entire world fell into place around them?

"Well, I'm so glad you came." Kate slipped her hand in mine, her soft skin gripping tightly and tugging me along behind her, weaving through the crowd like a pro. Maybe one day I'd have half the confidence in my entire body she had in her one hand.

"You made it," Melody said as we approached the table.

"Sit, sit," Kate said. "I'm so glad you changed your mind about coming."

I looked down at the one empty seat at the end of the booth, the other ten girls crammed in as close as they could possibly get, their elbows practically smashing into each other. "It's okay, I can find another seat."

"Not another word. I insist." Kate slid me into the booth and walked over to a neighboring table, stealing one of their empty chairs with a flawless smile and a flirty wink.

"I can sit there," I said as I pushed to my feet.

A hand pulled me back down hard onto the bench.

Ainsley stared up at me and shook her head so slightly, I doubted anyone else would notice. She leaned close to my ear and whispered, "Let it go. If Kate tells you to sit here, just sit here. Trust me."

Kate placed the chair in front of the table, halfway in the aisle. She gracefully sat with her legs crossed, taking up as much space as her body could consume, almost as if putting herself on display for the entire place to admire.

"So what did you think of your cheer debut?" Kate asked.

"It was incredible," I blurted then leaned back into my seat and tried to temper my excitement. "I mean, I'm glad I could help out."

"Well, you did a great job. Everyone thinks so." Her gaze ran across the booth of faces, and they all responded with nods and smiles. "People definitely noticed."

My cheeks flared, and I looked down, focusing on a cutlery bundle tightly wrapped in a stark white napkin. "I'm sure everyone will be happy to have Sydney back, though. She's definitely a fan favorite. Have you heard how she's doing?"

Kate pursed her lips and cast an odd glance at Sunni and Astrid. Whispers erupted around the table, but I couldn't quite hear the words. "I got a text just after the game, and it looks like she might be out for a little while longer."

"Is she going to be all right?"

"We're not really sure." Kate slipped her phone out of her purse and clicked through a few screens. "But the doctors don't know if she will be back for the rest of the playoffs and possibly even the state cheer championship."

A ripple of heat tingled through my limbs. In my head, I pictured Sydney on her knees, her white-knuckled hand grasping the side of the trash can. She'd looked awful. Pained and broken. And as part of me ached for her, another part kept poking holes in my memory as the excitement of possibly taking her place bubbled through my blood.

I dug my fingernails into my palm to fight the smile

attempting to curl across my lips. "Did they say what's wrong with her? I hope it's nothing serious."

"Who knows? I'm sure we'll hear something soon." Kate shrugged and looked over at Astrid. She nodded in response to her silent question, then Kate turned and placed her elbow on the table, her head perched on her hand. "But if she's still sick, we might need you to cheer for another game or two. If that's okay with you?"

"Of course," I said, digging my nails in deeper to cut the joy in my tone. "But only until she's better."

"Oh yeah. Absolutely." She shook her head and lounged back on her metal and plastic throne. "Now let's get some food. I'm starving."

6

———

"And that's why Sunni is banned from talking to the school mascot," Melody said as she held open the restaurant door, letting us all file out behind her.

"Hey!" Sunni cut in front of the group. "It's not my fault those big stuffed heads are hard to hear through. I know what I said, and I was impeccably polite."

"That can't be true?" I asked.

"I guess only Sunni and Lionel the Lion know the real story." Joy nudged Sunni in the shoulder and shot her a playful wink.

Sunni rolled her eyes as a smirk twisted on her lips. "And I'll never tell. It's going with me to my grave."

The rest of the squad laughed, and I laughed with them, my cheeks aching. I hadn't laughed and smiled this much in… well, probably ever. I'd always dreamed of being part of this group but never realized it'd be so much fun.

"Okay, girls, time to get going." Astrid shimmied her way in front, her hair rippling in thick velvet waves behind her as she raced down the front steps toward the street.

The laughter died, quick and sudden, like someone'd accidentally clicked the mute button on the world's remote control. Everyone nodded or waved silently as they darted in all directions away from Tony's and into the night. Everyone except for Kate.

She lingered on the stairs, slowly descending as if the entire town lay before her, waiting for her arrival. A queen surveying her kingdom.

I pulled my coat tight around my chest, shielding myself against the autumn chill that blew in as the squad thinned out, and rushed toward the sidewalk leading home.

"Hey, Melina, wait a second," Kate called.

She eased up on my right and linked her arm with mine, leading me farther from the building. She glanced over her shoulder then leaned her head closer to mine, her typically booming voice dropping to a near whisper. "I didn't want to say anything inside with the other girls around, but we're having a squad team-building thing tomorrow night and I thought you might want to come."

"Really?" I squeaked then cleared my throat and tried to stand up straighter. I'd never been invited to the team-building stuff before. They were squad only. No alternates. No boyfriends. No one extra. Did this mean I for sure wasn't exiled to equipment duty for the rest of the season? "I mean, if you're sure everyone else is fine with it, I could probably make it."

Kate's crystal-blue eyes shimmered as her lips twisted into a knowing grin. "Only if you're not too busy."

"I should be fine." More than fine. Ecstatic even.

"Great. Wear something comfortable but not too nice." She unhooked her arm, the evening chill settling on my skin as she peeled herself away and marched ahead of me. At the end of the walk, she turned and pointed back. "I've really got to go, but I'll text you the details tomorrow."

I nodded as she spun back around and raced up the street, disappearing into the darkness as she passed out of the hazy glow of the streetlights, leaving me alone in front of the restaurant.

As I dug my hands into my coat pockets, I tipped my head back, watching the steam from my breath swirl against the starry sky. When I woke up this morning, I never dreamed I'd be standing here now. Like someone had given me a gold key and I'd opened a door into a brand-new world. One where I wasn't just a background player, the extra that no one noticed.

"Hey, Not Just Marco's Sister," a deep voice said from behind me.

I jerked my head up, a wave of dizziness rushing over me as Alex swaggered down the restaurant stairs. "Hey?"

"I mean, Melina." His dark-red lips twisted into a handsome smile. "See, I told you I'd remember."

"That's a pretty incredible feat, considering I only left about five minutes ago."

Alex slapped his open palm onto his chest. "Five whole excruciating minutes."

"Wow. Do lines like that actually work for you?"

"Pretty much never." He chuckled and stepped to the side of the walkway, letting an elderly couple pass behind him. "But you aren't running away, so it couldn't be that brutal."

"I guess not."

He slid his hand across the back of his neck and tilted his head down. The milky moonlight laced through his messy dark hair as it flopped across his brow, and my hands twitched at my sides, wanting to swipe it out of his eyes. To see if it felt as soft as it looked. Except I knew better. This was Alex Chase. Quarterback. Senior. And way too gorgeous to be talking to me. His purple-and-gold varsity jacket protected him like armor. Our proud kingdom's finest knight, kindly taking the time to talk to the peasants.

But with a face like his, I'd take the courtesy.

"Congratulations on the game, by the way," I said.

"Thanks. Hopefully, we can get a few more wins in before it's all over."

"Sure would be nice to go out a champion, huh? Be a high school legend or whatever."

"Yeah, right." He tipped his head back and laughed then leaned closer to me. "Don't tell anyone, but I honestly don't care if we win. I'm just hoping that if we go far enough in the playoffs that scouts will start coming to the games. Score myself a one-way ticket out of Faraway."

"Really? No offense, but I kind of pictured you as a lifer."

"No offense, but I can't wait to get out of here." He dug his hands deep into his pockets and glanced back over his shoulder into the night. The humor in his expression faded. "It probably sounds stupid, but it's like there is this huge world that's spinning around me, and I can't find a way to get on and take the ride. To see things. To do things. To experience anything but the same day in and day out in this boring little town."

The last of his smile drooped into a tight frown, the sharp edges of his clenched jaw showing in his cheeks.

"It's not stupid." I put my hand on his arm but immediately yanked it away. "I get it way more than you think. That's one of the reasons why I want to be on the squad so badly. To try to get myself a scholarship."

"Good plan. The cheerleaders are more recognized than our football team. I'm sure you'll be able to go wherever you want now. To be honest, I'm kind of jealous."

Jealous? Of me? Yeah, right.

"Except I'm not really on the squad yet. Sydney is sick, and I was just filling in for her tonight and maybe another game or two." My throat tightened. Even though it was the truth, it hurt to say it out loud. After living in a fantasy world for the last few hours, reality became even harder to face than usual. Besides, I couldn't rely on Kate's invitation for tomorrow to actually mean anything. "Maybe next year."

"Well, you did a good job. It would be great to see you cheering at more of our games." He smiled, and it seemed genuine, but with someone like Alex, I doubted I'd ever really be able to tell. "Assuming there are more games to cheer at, that is."

"Here's hoping." I nodded and rocked back on my heels, searching for something else to say, but my mind came up blank as the excitement of the evening gave way to bone-deep exhaustion. I'd been running on glitter and school spirit for hours, and even though I stood in front of probably the dreamiest guy at Faraway High, I couldn't keep my mouth from releasing a big, dramatic yawn.

"Well, looks like we've both had a long night. I should probably get going." He flipped a silver key ring around his finger then caught it tight in his fist, but he stayed rooted in place. "Are you waiting for a ride or something? I could drive you home if you wanted."

"Thanks, but I'm okay. My house is only a few blocks over from here."

"All right. Be safe, Not Just Marco's Sister. I wouldn't want anything to happen to you." He paused and frowned. "What's your name again?"

I rolled my eyes. "Very funny."

"Goodnight, Melina." He pumped his fist and walked backward toward the street. His laughter echoed on the air, and I couldn't help smiling, even though I tried with all my strength to fight it.

"You're definitely not someone I plan on forgetting," he added before slowly turning around and vanishing behind the row of cars that lined the curb.

My cheeks burned against the cool night air. It didn't mean anything. He flirted with everyone. Didn't he? It wasn't like he even—

"Okay, so what was that about?" a stern voice asked.

I shook my head, snapping back to reality, and placed my palm on my forehead. "What?"

"You and Alex Chase. I didn't even know you knew him." Jaida stood to the left of the sidewalk, her arms crossed, Hailey and Isaac creeping up behind her.

"I don't. Not really." The stillness of the moment dissolved as I tried to put words together. "We just met."

Hailey snickered and glanced over her shoulder in the direction Alex had disappeared. "Uh-huh. That's why he nearly tripped over his own feet staring back at you."

"The boy can run and carry a football with a gang of dudes chasing him, but he's no match for Little Miss

Heartbreaker over here. Way to go, Melina." Isaac raised his open palm, and I high-fived him as the heat in my face cranked all the way up to one thousand.

Jaida shook her head. "Speaking of how amazing our friends are, where's that wonderful Leo guy at? Is he still inside?"

"No," I said. "He decided not to come. But wait, I thought you all had plans tonight?"

Hailey nudged Jaida with her shoulder, and she lurched forward a step.

"Working on a big project or something?" I added. Why did everyone need to be so awkward tonight? Maybe it was me. I held my cool fingers against my forehead and tried to focus my cloudy thoughts. Or had I been so focused on the game that I hadn't remembered the details?

"Um, yeah, we did," Jaida finally said. "But we finished up quicker than we thought. Isaac is going to be a sweetheart and type up the final report for us in the morning, so we figured we'd just..."

"Come out and celebrate with you. We stopped by Twisted Top, but you weren't there so Fat Tony's seemed the next logical place." Hailey nodded at Jaida then slipped past and rushed up the stone steps of the restaurant. "Let's get inside. I'm starving, and they are closing soon."

"Sure. Be right—" My mouth stretched into a massive yawn, and I swallowed the rest of the words.

Jaida wrapped her arm over my shoulder, the sweet smell of her pineapple shampoo sending my tired brain on a tropical vacation. "Hey, you don't have to come with us if you don't want to. I mean, I'd love to hear all about your night, but you look like you might want a nap more than breadsticks."

I straightened my stance. "Of course not. I'm—" Another yawn escaped, betraying me. "Okay, maybe I'm a little sleepy. But I really don't want to just bail on you guys."

She tipped her head against mine and squeezed my shoulder. "It's no big deal. You've had a huge day. Get some rest, and we'll talk tomorrow."

I let myself fall into Jaida, her firm arm propping me up. "Are you sure, J?"

"Absolutely. Go home." She spun me closer and wrapped her other arm around me. "I'm so proud of you, Melina. You never gave up on your dream, and now it's finally coming true. That's incredible."

I held on tighter and closed my eyes. It wasn't exactly what I wanted. Only a temporary situation. A small taste of what I might have one day. *One day.* "Thanks. I'll text Leo on the way home and let him know you're here in case he wants to join you."

"Perfect." She released me and bounded up the steps, disappearing through the main door. I sighed and turned toward the street, taking each step carefully and savoring the stillness of the stars as I headed down the street toward home. As I reached the corner, I pulled my phone out of my pocket.

> Me: Hey. Just ran into Jaida, Hailey, and Isaac. They just got to Tony's if you want to join them.

I waited a few seconds, but he didn't answer. I typed again.

> Me: Thanks for being so cool about
> tonight.

Three dots lit up the screen.

> Leo: Me? Cool? I've never had a
> cheerleader call me cool before. Is this
> what popular feels like?

> Me: Ha. Ha. You could've come with us.
> Just imagine what sitting at a whole table
> of cheerleaders would do for your social
> status.

> Leo: Why didn't you tell me sooner? I
> can't believe I missed it. That's it. I'm
> dropping out of school and moving away.
> The only way to recover is to start over
> somewhere else. Tell the crew I'll miss
> them.

As I read the words, I heard Leo laugh in my head, his deep, wry chuckle when his sarcasm set in. He was probably half-asleep right now, likely curled up in his room watching one of those old spy movies he loved. One of my favorite versions of Leo always appeared in that small window of almost dreaming when his sense of humor seemed to take over. Like the filter he put between himself and the world fell away, or he just didn't have the energy to hold it up anymore. I started typing but stopped and flipped to the phone screen instead, my fingers dialing the numbers without thinking.

"Hey," Leo's drowsy voice said from the other end of the line. "You're calling instead of texting. Is the world ending?"

"Everything's fine for now. Maybe I just wanted to

hear your voice." I laughed, and a warmth built in my chest as he joined in.

"Don't flatter me too much, Lina. I might get used to it. So tell me all about your night. Was it everything you imagined it would be?"

"It was great. I had lots of fun. But I still feel bad about ditching you."

"It's okay. You'll just owe me one. How about we try again tomorrow? You can fill me in on all the football gossip."

"I can't. Kate invited me to some sort of team-building thing." I lowered my voice and scanned the empty street across from me as if someone might hear. As if someone else knowing would somehow make the whole invitation disappear. "How about Sunday?"

"I can't. Gotta work." His voice muffled as he shifted on the phone. "And it's one of those movie marathon days. I'm going to smell like popcorn for a week."

"Could be worse. I happen to love the smell of pop—"

A howl pierced the night. Loud and way too close.

I gripped the phone tighter as a strange sensation settled on the top of my head and a warm breeze rolled across the skin on the back of my knees. My stomach clenched as a haggard breath whispered in the dark. I clutched my house keys in my fist and spun around, my throat tightening as I prepared to scream.

Except nothing was there.

I pivoted in place, swinging my arm out like I could scare away anyone or anything that might be following me.

"What was that?" Leo's voice called in the darkness.

"Uh, nothing." I shook my head as my heartbeat

pounded in my ears. I wrapped my arm around my stomach and dared to look back over my shoulder. Still nothing. "Just someone's dog. But I should probably hurry and get home."

"Okaaay." He seemed unconvinced, but he didn't push. "Talk to you tomorrow."

"Yeah, tomorrow." I hung up and shoved the phone into my pocket.

Another howl rang out but much farther away.

The uneasiness in my stomach returned.

I ran all the way home without looking back.

7

I pulled back the thin lace curtain covering the kitchen window and peered out into the darkness. The combination of my warm breath and dinner cooking on the stove steamed up the glass again, and I wiped it clear with my sweater sleeve.

A set of headlights appeared at the end of the street, and I flexed onto my tiptoes, gripping the curtain tighter in my fist as the car inched closer.

"Dinner will be ready in five minutes, Melina," Mama called from across the kitchen. "Can you please go fetch your father and your brothers to come eat?"

"I can't. My friends are going to be here any minute."

The headlights in the window came closer and closer but didn't stop. They cruised right past the front of the house and turned down Colton Street before disappearing into the night. My shoulders fell, and I collapsed against the wall. Another false alarm.

A shadow lurked in the doorway to the living room. "Haven't you been saying your friends were coming for, like, I don't know, four hours now? Maybe you should just face it. You've been stood up."

"They didn't stand me up, Marco." I shot him my fiercest death glare, trying to mask the harsh truth no one else had the nerve to say out loud. If they even noticed.

Marco shook his head, the hair flopping over his eyes leaving nothing but his snarky smirk visible on his face, then shuffled into the kitchen. "Sure, sure. Whatever you say, little sis." He kissed Mama on the side of her head and then pinched a limp noodle out of the big blue pot simmering on the element.

"Could you please keep your fingers out of everyone's dinner and your nose out of your sister's business?" Mama smacked his hand with the back of her wooden spoon, and Marco dropped the noodle onto the stovetop. "If you're so interested in helping, why don't you help set the table?"

"Fine," he grumbled as the smirk vanished.

As he reached into the cupboard beside the sink for plates and cups, Mama glanced over her shoulder and winked. A warm, sympathetic smile graced her coral lips, but instead of providing comfort, the gesture punched me in the gut.

She slid the forks out of the cutlery drawer and made her way around the table, laying them each perfectly straight next to where the plates would go. She held up one last fork—my fork—and pointed it in my direction as she slipped between me and the table. "However, if I were you, I would ask myself if these new friends are worth waiting for all day," she whispered as she leaned toward the window. Her eyes narrowed as she scanned the street, but nothing new appeared. "Maybe it would be best if you just stayed home tonight and joined us for dinner. It's been a while since most of us have sat down at the same time for a meal. Everyone is always so busy these days."

She swept my hair off my left shoulder and moved to tuck it behind my ear, but I jerked my head away.

"They're coming, Mama. You'll see."

"Something smells amazing in here," Papa's deep voice bellowed as he joined us from the hallway. He slid behind Mama and wrapped a thick, muscular arm around her shoulders and pulled her close to his chest. "You're still here, Melina? I thought you were going to be out for the evening."

"Seriously?" I snapped and stormed down the hall.

Mama shouted after me, "I'll make you a plate!"

"I'm not hungry." I closed the door to my room, trying with every inch of strength not to slam it and garner more attention, although it probably would've felt amazing if I had.

I fell back against the door, letting my head bang against the wood, the hollow thud flowing through my body. My phone screen loomed dark in my hand. The same way it had for hours. I let my fingers flit across the glass and open the chat window, even though I knew I shouldn't. Four short lines from 10:12 a.m.

> Kate: Still coming to the team event tonight?

> Me: For sure.

> Kate: Good. I'll pick you up around 5ish.

> Me: Can't wait.

Then nothing. Hours had passed. Came and went just like five o'clock, six o'clock, and now seven. I should've texted back a while ago to make sure she was still coming, but I didn't want to come off sounding desperate, so I didn't. Then as the time fell away, it made anything I could possibly send sound even more awkward. Maybe Kate was just running late. Being cheer captain probably came with a lot of responsibilities. Or maybe something happened? She lived in one of those big estate-like houses on the outskirts of Faraway. Maybe she'd hit a deer on her way to pick me up. My chest burned as I held my breath and slid down the door until I hit the floor. If something happened to her because she was coming to get me, it would be all my fault. I held the phone tight in my fists to keep my hands from shaking and read the brief conversation again. Or there could be one other explanation. The one I'd been dreading. Maybe she never intended to come for me and all this was some sort of joke. A prank. A way to put me back in my place and show that I never really belonged. I'd always be the alternate. The extra. The forgotten one. The one who—

"Melina, your friends are here," Papa called from the other side of the door.

What? I shook my head and blinked several times until the purple shades of my room came back into focus. Muffled voices floated from the direction of the kitchen. I pushed up onto my feet and pulled the door open a crack.

"My apologies for interrupting your dinner, Mrs. Cardona." The cadence of Kate's polished politeness echoed off the walls, and my heart pumped harder in my chest.

I raced toward the voices, slowing before I reentered

the kitchen and trying to keep my breathing level. Kate and Astrid stood in the front hall, poised and flawless, even in casual gear. Matching white woolen beanies capped their heads, their silky hair streaming out from underneath. Their purple-and-gold *Go Lions* hoodies fit cool and comfortable instead of frumpy like they did on everyone else, and their black leggings with the word *Cheer* in golden glitter font up their left thighs hugged every sculpted curve of their immaculate bodies. A fact that Marco hadn't missed either. I nudged him with my shoulder, and he snapped out of the trance cast by Astrid's hips.

"What?" he said, shaking his head.

Astrid gave a muffled scoff and slid in behind Kate, hiding herself in the corner of the front hall.

"Oh hey, there you are." Kate tilted her head to the side, gazing around Marco at me. Or maybe trying anything to avoid eye contact with him. "Sorry we're late. We went to grab some snacks for later, and it took Astrid way too long to decide which flavor of chips she wanted."

"Hey!" Astrid cast a death glare at the back of Kate's head. "It's not my fault you didn't plan ahead for your own sleepover."

"Oh. I thought this was just an evening event." Mama glanced back at me, a small V cutting deep between her knitted eyebrows. "You didn't mention anything about staying out all night."

"Of course, Mrs. Cardona, I completely forgot to tell her yesterday about staying over. Assuming she even wants to stay. I was just so impressed with her performance at the game last night and couldn't wait for her to officially join the team that I must've forgotten." Kate rolled her eyes and laughed. Astrid joined in, and the playful sound seemed to lift the weight building on Mama's shoulders until a genuine smile broke across her lips.

Except my brain kept tripping over Kate's words. *They want me to join the team. Really? Like a real member of the squad?*

"Melina," Marco whispered.

I'd hoped they would ask, but once Sydney came back they wouldn't need me, would they? Or maybe I really did do that well yesterday. I didn't think so, but I'd tried my hardest, even though I missed the last turn on the third cheer.

"Melina. Anyone in there?" Marco snapped his thick fingers in front of my face.

I shook my head. "Yeah. I'm good. I mean, I'm definitely down for sleeping over."

Kate narrowed her stare and scanned me over but quickly beamed her comforting smile again. "Both of my parents will be home, and I can leave you their number to call them if you'd like." She shifted her crossbody bag over her shoulder and rummaged through it until she pulled out a pad of paper and a bright-pink pen, then she scribbled the phone number. "And Melina, I'd suggest bringing a coat. It's getting quite cold outside. I can lend you something to sleep in."

Kate held the paper out to my mother, and she took it, clutching the sheet in her fist as she remained hypnotized by Kate's charisma. "Thank you. I'm sure everything will be just fine, but I appreciate your cautiousness."

"Of course, Mrs. Cardona. Safety first, right?" She nodded until my mother started nodding along with her.

"Now don't let your dinner get cold because of us. Ready to go, Melina?"

"Absolutely." I scooped up my cheer bag from the hall steps, where it'd been packed and ready to go since noon, then slipped on my coat as Astrid opened the door and headed out into the moonlight.

"Have a great evening," Kate sang as she slipped outside.

I quickly followed behind and shut the door, rushing down the steps to catch up. Astrid climbed into the driver's seat of her snow-white Escalade. Maybe one day I'd have a car like that, but definitely not while I was still in high school. I shook my head. I'd certainly crossed over from reality to a fantasy world. Like I'd walked into a dream.

"Hurry up, Melina, we've got to get going," Kate said as she held open the passenger-side back door.

I glanced back at the house. In the kitchen window, silhouettes of my family crowded around the table, moving in a familiar rhythm, and my stomach rumbled. Pulling my coat closer to my chest to block the growing chill, I rushed ahead and chucked my bag into the back seat.

Before I could jump inside, Kate rested her hand on my shoulder, keeping me frozen in place. "Just one more thing. I'm sure you heard me tell your mother about asking you to join the squad. Well, this is me asking. Are you interested?"

"Of course. I want that more than anything."

"We expect a huge commitment. You will basically eat, sleep, and breathe cheer until you graduate. No exceptions." Kate pursed her impeccably painted lips as her expression hardened. The lightness she'd shown my family vanished in the darkness, and shadows crept in, giving her an ominous stare that matched her tone. Her hand on my shoulder held firm.

I gulped and took a deep breath. "For sure, Kate. I'll do whatever it takes."

"Perfect." Kate nodded, and a gentle grin broke across her face, although the shadows loomed in her eyes. "Then give me your hand."

A shiver rushed over my skin, but I obeyed, extending my arm out in front of me. Kate's warm fingers pulled my jacket sleeve up to my elbow as she reached into her pocket and pulled out one of the iconic cheer bracelets and tied it around my wrist.

"Welcome to the team." She opened the passenger door and eased into her seat, the door still hanging open. "Tonight is going to change your life."

8

———

The shiny purple stones and gold threads on my wrist glinted under the streetlights as we sped down one street after the next. Astrid's heavy foot switched between gas and brake like she was practicing for a career in drag racing, several times almost bringing up the peanut butter sandwich I'd scarfed down as I waited by my kitchen window for them to arrive.

I leaned back against the car seat and flopped my head to the side, watching the passing houses through the window. "Has anyone heard how Sydney's doing?"

"Oh, she's fine," Kate said, still staring forward. "Don't even worry about it."

"Well, that's good. She looked pretty awful last night. I'm glad she's okay." I closed my eyes as the memory of Sydney slumped next to the trash can crept through my brain. The pained expression that tainted her gorgeous face. The blood, like a macabre shade of red-carpet lipstick as it pooled across her lips and splattered onto the grass. I shuddered, and the seat belt bit tighter around my hips as I pushed the horrific images from my mind. "Do you know when she's planning on coming back to the squad?"

Silence.

Kate glanced over at Astrid, and she shrugged.

"She's not," Kate muttered then dropped her head back and sighed. She twisted around in her seat to face me, and I caught the whisper of concern under her practiced facade as it slipped into place. "I mean, it was her choice. We talked about it with her, and she wasn't committed to the team the way she should be. We knew it, and so did she. Besides, her stepping down is the reason we're able to give you a spot on the squad since we only have twelve spaces. Unless you'd rather stay an alternate instead?"

Heat rose up my neck, and I leaned closer to the window to conceal it, the cool glass helping ease the burn. "Nope, I'm good. I'd do anything to be part of the team. Just as long as Sydney's cool with it."

"Yep. She's totally fine." Kate winked and turned forward again. "But enough about Sydney. Tell us more about you."

About me? Uh-oh. I scanned my brain to find something interesting to say, but every fleeting thought was so boring. Ordinary. "Not much to tell, really. Born and raised here in sleepy Faraway. Took dance classes for thirteen years—ballet and jazz. Four brothers. One is at his dorm most of the year, but three are still lurking around being annoying."

"Ha, I'll say." Astrid snorted as she jerked the car to the right to head down Brazier Road.

Kate shot her a dirty look, but she didn't notice, or simply didn't care. "They don't seem that bad. I thought your family was really sweet. Like they care about you a lot."

"Yeah, my parents are pretty great. Except they're always so busy. We almost never get to have dinner when everyone is home." A hollow feeling burrowed in my chest as I thought about everyone sitting around the table at home without me. But there would be other family nights. It wasn't every day I'd get the opportunity to be part of Kate's inner circle.

"And that guy who came down at the end of the game. The tall blond one. Is that your boyfriend?" Kate asked.

"Leo?" I pictured him all dressed up under the stadium lights and an unexpected flutter prickled through my chest. He still hadn't told me what he'd wanted to say last night. I'd have to remember to call him later. Besides, I couldn't wait to tell him I'd finally been given an actual spot on the cheer team. Hopefully, he'd be excited for me. "No, he's one of my best friends. I don't have a boyfriend."

"Well, lucky you. By this time next week, all you'll have to do is snap your fingers and you'll have any guy you want… or girl, or whatever."

"But no one comes before the squad," Astrid said. "We're always priority number one. Like sisters."

"Got it." I nodded. I'd always wanted a sister—I would've traded Marco for one in a heartbeat—but I never thought I'd have eleven. "What about you, Astrid? Do you have any siblings?"

"Nope. Just me. I'm actually adopted, but I can't complain. My parents are almost always traveling, so they buy me pretty things to make up for it." She tapped her palm against the leather steering wheel as her delighted smirk reflected in the rearview mirror. It must be nice to have actual alone time instead of everyone buzzing around your house like irritating bees. But I'd bet it did get lonely eventually. However, I honestly didn't know Astrid at all before cheerleading so I was sure her family had their own issues even if they hadn't been debated in the town gossip. As small as Faraway was, you could still hide if you worked hard enough to stay under the radar.

"And of course everyone knows your family, Kate. I mean, everyone loves your dad. Jackson Fleming is probably the closest thing this town has to a celebrity. That must be so cool."

Kate rolled her eyes and rested back in her seat. "Don't remind me. It's like everyone always wants a piece of him, you know? And seriously, a local weatherman—it's not like he's some A- or even D-list movie star. Don't get me wrong, he's a great dad even when he's being a total dork, but being in the spotlight all the time is tough. Even my mom heads out on a 'retreat'"—Kate turned around again and mimed air quotes—"at least once every few months to get away from people hounding her. But I guess all fame comes with its sacrifices, and it could be a whole lot worse. Besides, everyone would choose popularity over obscurity, right? It's all part of the package."

"Yeah, I guess so." Obscurity hadn't really done me any favors. Even though I'd probably never be considered popular in this town, a little recognition would be nice. The middle child, but the only girl. The good student, but not the brainiac. The cheerleader, but just the alternate. So close to being something. Being seen. Except it always seemed out of reach. Like chasing after the end of a rainbow. However, tonight could be a new start. Maybe I could get closer than I'd ever been before.

The streetlights disappeared as we crossed the town line and kept cruising down the highway. The trees lining the road reached up with their crooked branches, their leafless, near-winter forms like spindly fingers trying to snatch the moon from its sky. I shivered, a chill running across my skin as we continued farther away from town. Normally, people took the highway west toward the interstate and off to Des Moines or anywhere else more exciting than here, but going east the road meandered off into nowhere. The last time I'd gone this direction was for Sasha McKenzie's party, where some girl ended up being taken away by ambulance. Maybe that's why a foreboding vibe settled over me. I glanced out the window again into the darkness, which seemed to grow thicker the longer we drove.

Astrid signaled left and turned off the highway. The car bumped along the gravel road as we wound deeper into the forest. The stars disappeared beneath the thick canopy of the treetops.

"Where exactly are we going? I thought this was just a team-building thing?" I asked as the shadows lengthened around us. Besides, didn't Kate explicitly tell my mom we'd be at her house?

Kate glanced back from the front seat again, her trademark mega-smile plastered across her lips. "Oh, it is. Think of it like a camping trip. There's nothing better for connecting with your team than to get away from all other distractions. No prying parents. No Wi-Fi. Nothing to keep us from getting to know each other on another level."

Astrid nodded as she eased the oversized Escalade into a tiny spot at the end of a line of familiar cars. "Absolutely. Getting back to nature."

Camping? When Kate mentioned a sleepover, I hadn't exactly planned on sleeping outside. I definitely hadn't packed for that kind of adventure. In my head, I'd imagined what the squad might do for these types of events, but most times I pictured movie nights, dance parties, or maybe a soul-baring game of truth or dare. Typical stuff. Not roughing it in the wild. Especially this late in the fall. The crispness of the pending winter had been swirling around town for the past few weeks. I tucked my chin into my jacket as I shivered at the thought of the inevitable chilly night that lay ahead. Here's hoping there would be little sleep and a huge bonfire.

Astrid cut the engine and reapplied her berry lip gloss in the rearview mirror. She blew a kiss to her reflection and opened the car door. The autumn smell of wet leaves wafted into the back seat. "All right, everyone out."

She jumped out of the SUV, her chestnut curls rippling back over her shoulders as her sneakers crunched on the ground. Without waiting for anyone, she circled around the passenger side toward a well-worn path that snaked between a dense stand of trees across from the cars.

My fingers fumbled with the seat belt as I struggled to release the latch, my body rushing faster to follow Astrid than reality would allow. This was it. This was really happening.

As I slipped out of the vehicle into the night, Kate grabbed the edge of my open door and blocked my exit, pinning me between her and the car seat. "Leave your phone and stuff in the car. You won't need it for a while."

"It's okay. I don't mind carrying it. Besides, you said there's no Wi-Fi."

She rolled her eyes up toward her long lashes, her hands sliding to her hips in a wordless demand.

I tugged my bag strap tighter to my chest then eased it off my shoulder and rested it on Astrid's back seat. I attempted to step around Kate, but her hand caught my chest under my throat, holding me in place. She cast her gaze at the cell phone in my hand. I swallowed as my body stiffened under her grip. Her sudden shift in tone hung heavy between us.

"Oops. Sorry." I slid the phone into the front pocket of my backpack, my hand hesitating on the zipper. Maybe they just didn't want anyone taking photos? I doubted anyone would like a terrible picture of themselves on everyone's social media feed on Monday, but it's not like I'd do something like that. I was nothing compared to the power of this squad. Besides, after all I'd done for them, you'd think they would trust me by now. However, in that moment, my trust in them suddenly waned.

"See, that wasn't such a big deal, right?" As if reading my mind, Kate wrapped her arm over my shoulder and led me away from the car, closing the door behind us. "Oh my gosh. You should totally see your face right now. It's like I'm going to bite you or something. You are so cute sometimes. Isn't she cute, Astrid?"

Astrid kept trudging ahead of us, probably rocking her signature eye roll. "Yeah. Totally adorable. Like a baby otter." She fluttered her fingers over her shoulder dismissively without bothering to look back.

Kate squeezed my arm and leaned her head close to mine. "There's nothing to worry about. You're one of us now. We take care of each other and keep each other's secrets. You can keep a secret, can't you?"

"Of course," I said as I eased into Kate's grip. Besides, what could a bunch of high school cheerleaders really have to hide?

9

"Obviously, we will have to work the routines a bit since you're shorter than Sydney and rookies don't typically get to be fliers for stunts, but if you work hard, maybe you can change my mind. Like, you've always worked so hard on the sidelines. It's not like we haven't noticed. You've always..." Kate prattled on. And on. And on. Telling me all about the long legacy of championship cheerleading teams at Faraway High dating all the way back to the 1930s and someone's great-great-great-grandmother's best friend's niece or something. What it meant to be a winner. What she ate for breakfast. Her favorite shade of contour. I absorbed every little detail, nodding and uh-huhing whenever necessary, while making sure I didn't trip as the path below us cluttered with thick brush and felled trees.

Astrid maneuvered around and over the obstacles as if she'd walked this route a million times before—and maybe she had. I peered back into the thick woods behind us. The rest of the world had vanished under the canopy a while ago, and I pulled my hands into my sleeves as the darkness seeped under my skin. In the daylight, this hike probably didn't seem as long and treacherous. Probably less creepy too.

"Hey, Melina, is something wrong?" Kate asked, drawing my focus back to her.

I shook my head and snapped out of my trance. "No. It's nothing. Just feels like it might snow."

"Sure, maybe." She shrugged, the idea of snow not souring her sunny expression. "Now, what was I saying? Oh yeah, we will definitely have to do something about—"

"It's about time. We thought you'd completely bailed on us." Sunni's voice rang off the trees as she appeared up ahead, rushing our way with her hands flung in the air. "You could've at least let us know you were going to be late."

She shot a glare at Astrid as she passed her, but Astrid didn't even look up, still walking in the distance to where the trees thinned and opened up to the starry night sky.

"Take it easy." Kate's arm slid from my shoulders, and I shivered as the icy wind drifted across the back of my neck. She shook her head and sighed, her breath steaming in the air around us. "You should know me by now. If I say I'll be somewhere, I'll be there. Maybe you just need to have a little trust and patience."

"Don't play around, Kate. It's not a good look." Sunni glared at her for a second then instantly dropped it. "Oh, hey, Melina. You came. I wasn't sure if you'd be here."

"Hey," I said, keeping myself a few steps behind Kate. The air thickened like I'd walked into a private conversation, and I definitely didn't want to be caught in the middle of someone else's disagreement. I'd learned that the hard way too many times trying to referee for my pesky brothers. It never ended well.

The three of us filed the last quarter mile in awkward silence as we followed Astrid toward a large circular clearing. As we approached, the familiar voices of the rest of the squad carried on the wind and helped to ease the tension. Unfortunately, I didn't hear the crackle of a campfire, and I regretted not wearing thicker socks, as my toes already tingled from the cold.

Ahead of us, the rest of the cheerleaders lounged around in their matching leggings and sweatshirts. Charlotte, Joy and Piper yapped together near the tree line, Nina and Melody were huddled over what looked like a contraband phone, while the rest—Ainsley, Sheena, and Tessa—slouched on a fallen log to the left of the path. None of them looked too impressed. If I could barely feel my own fingertips, they must've been freezing waiting who knows how long out here in the cold. Plus, if this was supposed to be a camping trip, where were all the tents? Or camping chairs? Or really anything other than just a group of girls in the woods? Or maybe that's why Sunni seemed so distressed? Captain Kate made the rules, so maybe there was some unwritten decree that they needed to wait for her first?

As we approached, Kate sped up, hooking her arm with mine as she passed and practically dragging me along with her.

"Hey, everyone," she announced, commanding attention like a general addressing her well-dressed army. All chatter stopped. Anyone slouching stiffened their posture as they crowded around us, every single girl automatically falling into line. Even my own shoulders rolled back on cue as I stood taller in Kate's grip.

"Me and Astrid asked Melina to join the squad, and she said yes." She squealed next to my ear then tugged my arm, thrusting me forward and putting me even more on display. "Isn't that exciting, ladies? Let's welcome our newest little lion to the pack."

Kate released her hold and clapped her hands, the rest of the girls erupting in matching applause.

I snickered.

She dropped her hands as her expression iced over. "What's so funny?"

"Um…" Lions lived in prides, not packs. They covered that in junior high biology, maybe even elementary. But correcting her in front of everyone probably wasn't the smartest move. Did I seriously need to be such a geek all the time? No wonder it took so long for me to get a spot, and here I was about to completely blow it. "Nothing. Sometimes I laugh when I'm excited. It's fine."

"Okay, weird." Her stare narrowed, scrutinizing me further, but I kept my mouth closed. Eventually, she shook her head and continued. "Follow me."

The squad parted and left open a lane for her to lead deeper into the clearing. I hurried behind her, scanning the crowd for Ainsley, but just as I thought I'd caught her eye, she shuffled in behind Melody.

"Thanks, everyone," I said as I passed the rest of my new teammates. "I'm super pumped to be here, and I'll make sure you don't regret letting me take Sydney's place.

I mean… No one can really take her place…" Heat rose in my cheeks as the confused stares of the other girls bore down on me. What was I even saying? *Get it together, Melina.* "Because she was such an amazing cheerleader… but since she's not here… What I'm trying to say is, I will do my best to fill her shoes, and hopefully, we can win another state championship."

"Oh, we will," Astrid said in her flat, matter-of-fact tone. "It's almost guaranteed."

Kate suddenly turned to face the crowd, and I nearly bulldozed her as I tripped over my feet to halt. "Okay, everyone, now let's have a little fun," she said.

Perfect. I needed something to keep me busy before I kept running my nervous mouth. "Does anyone have the stuff for s'mores? 'Cause I can seriously make the best s'mores you've ever tasted."

"Um, yeah. Sounds great. Very rustic." Kate grinned, but her face squished with distaste. Like the look I gave Tommy when I didn't want to read him a story but he insisted. Did she seriously not like s'mores? Marshmallows and chocolate—what was not to like?

She leaned closer, her voice dropping to a whisper. "Actually, to be honest, this isn't your typical camping trip. The reason we brought you out here is that we have a tradition when someone new joins the team, and since you've agreed to be one of us, it's your turn."

"My turn for what?" I spun around as the rows of cheerleaders moved out around us and assembled into a wide, perfectly formed circle, surrounding me and Kate in the center. The pretty little soldiers filed into formation, their expressions as flat and empty as their movements.

The darkness weighed heavier on my shoulders, keeping me rooted to the spot as a new sense of dread churned in my stomach. "What's going on?"

Kate placed her hand on my arm and squeezed, bringing my attention back to her. "Trust us, it'll all be fine. We've all gone through this."

With a soft smile, she backed away from me and joined the curved line with the other girls. She stuck her hands on her hips as if she were about to lead the squad in a new cheer. Except no one else moved.

"Okay, now I'd suggest you strip down to your underwear unless you want your things wrecked."

"You're kidding, right? It's freezing out here." I laughed, but Kate's lips pressed tighter as her stare hardened.

The wind whistled through the treetops, making her silence all the more terrifying. I spun around, looking from face to face throughout the squad, but no one flinched or even cracked half a smile.

"Like, this is some sort of joke, right?" I crossed my arms, trying to look tough and also to hold myself together. No one knew I was here. No one would know where to find me. They wouldn't do anything to hurt me, would they? Besides, if this was some sort of hazing ritual, the school would be all over it, and the team would never be able to compete, which would destroy Kate. They wouldn't. I bit my lip and fought to slow my breathing as the dense fog of reality clouded my brain. I pointed at each of them in the circle. "You can't make me do anything I don't want to, you know?"

Kate sighed. "We know. But you made the choice to be part of the squad, so just trust us." She paused until our stares locked across the space between us. "You're gonna want to lose your gear quick. You're running out of time."

"Time for what?" I yelled.

But no one answered.

Kate pulled her hoodie over her head and slipped out of her leggings, her matching bright-pink sports bra and boy shorts almost glowing in the dim moonlight.

"What are you doing?" I searched the woods for any sign of light or motion, but only the eerie black stared back at me. I took a deep breath and swallowed. This must be some sort of prank. A test to see how far I'd go. How badly I wanted to be on the squad. But I wasn't going to be the butt of someone's warped sense of humor. I just had to hold out until they gave up waiting for me to break.

Kate ignored me and continued with her ritual as she folded each piece of her clothing into precise squares and laid them at her feet. She slipped out of her shoes and stood on top of them barefoot.

"Are you insane?" I grabbed the sides of my head, twining my fingers through my hair and pulling to make sure I wasn't dreaming, that I hadn't fallen asleep in the back of Astrid's car and in a few minutes they would shake me awake to save me from this strange nightmare. Except the pain surged through my scalp and my body trembled, confirming my fear that this was real.

Kate nodded. Everyone else broke their stances and removed their clothes, placing them in careful piles by their feet. I spun around and around, waiting for the punchline, but it never came. The vibe circling the clearing wasn't funny. It hung thick and serious, bearing down on top of me. Everyone moved in unison, like marionettes dancing on invisible strings pulled by an unknown master. One I didn't feel like meeting.

"Ainsley?" I stopped spinning and walked toward her, my voice pleading for answers. She shivered and cast her head to the side in silence.

"That's it. I don't need this." I marched in the direction of the cars. Or at least the way I thought they were. Even if I had to hike a few miles back toward town, it suddenly seemed safer, and way warmer, than whatever was about to go down.

No one bothered to stop me. Good. I definitely would have made a few enemies if anyone tried to put a hand on me. Might've obliterated my social status in the process, but it was better than hypothermia and inappropriate photos of me in my skivvies splashed all over the internet.

Except as I approached the edge of the circle, my knees locked, and I struggled to shuffle my feet forward. Before I could move again, a surge of energy flowed through me, pulsing wave after wave up my spine and down my limbs, hard and electric, as if I could shoot lightning from my fingertips. I crossed my arms and clutched at my biceps, trying to ground myself as I swayed back and forth on my weak legs. What was happening to me?

I squinted as a hazy fog clouded my vision, and I struggled to make out the shapes of the rest of the squad in the dim light. Each of them twitched and swayed until their puppet master cut their strings and they toppled to the ground like human dominoes, closing the circle tighter around me.

Another pulse ripped through me, as if coming up through the earth and blasting out the top of my head. My knees buckled and collapsed under the weight of my body. I leaned forward on my wobbly arms as everything shifted out of focus.

"Help me!" I screamed into the sky, but only my own hollow echo answered back, my plea lost to the soundless stars.

"Kate!" I shouted as I fought against the pain to turn around and face her. "Make it stop. Please make it stop."

Across the circle, Kate sat hunched on all fours. She raised her bowed head in my direction, and a cruel smirk twisted across her lips. "You said you'd do anything."

She winced, and the expression drained from her face as she slumped onto her forearms. Her back arched then bucked back down like I was watching her do yoga in double time. Loud cracks echoed off the naked trees. Kate folded her head down to her chest as something rippled across her exposed skin. Hair, thick and brown, bloomed in patches along her sides, then over the rest of her body until it blanketed her entirely.

I blinked. Once. Twice. This had to be an illusion. Some sort of trick.

I needed to get out of here.

As I pushed up on my weak arms and squinted through the darkness for any option for escape, another jolt of electricity slammed up my spine. My elbows gave out. My chin smacked the ground. The earthy smell of dirt mixed with a salty metallic tang pooled on my tongue as I dragged myself forward, slithering on my stomach like a snake. The waves kept coming.

Over.

And over.

And over.

Rolling onto my side, I pulled my thighs into my chest and gripped white-knuckled onto my knees to comfort myself against the pain. The cool night air breezed over my damp skin. My limbs were soaked with sweat, and my cheeks caught the streams of tears racing down my face.

Make it stop. Please make it stop.

As I rocked myself back and forth, the world around me floated in and out of focus. Maybe I'd lost consciousness, or maybe reality didn't even exist anymore. I closed my eyes and pleaded with the universe to help, and then, with one last ripple up my spine, the pain stopped. Collapsing on the ground, I lay still for another second, expecting the ache to come back again.

One... two... three...

The snap of twigs echoed around me. Footsteps padded against the hard ground.

Louder.

Closer.

I raised my head, my chest aching as my breath stayed trapped in my lungs. Ahead of me, a pair of bright-yellow eyes stared back, round and bright, like twin moons piercing through my skull and straight into my soul. I scrambled back in the dirt as the beast ahead of me stalked closer, slow and casual, its sandy-colored fur ruffling over its body as it moved. My heart pounded in my head as my blood rushed through my limbs, pushing me to run. I fell back, and the wolf inched closer. I tipped my head back to scream, but my voice had disappeared, replaced by a low, animalistic sound bellowing up from my gut.

"Aooooooo," I howled into the night.

The wolf in front of me stopped and raised its snout to

the sky. She howled loud and uninhibited, until a chorus of raw voices joined her. An itch tickled in my throat as the urge to partake took over. I howled back, stronger and sharper than before, as a deep sting of dread built in the pit of my stomach.

What had I done?

10

The silver moon called me toward it.

A spotlight shining just out of reach to illuminate my path as I raced through the thick brush of the snow-speckled forest. My fur-covered body flowed forward, rolling like waves crashing on a shore—free and wild and unstoppable. The musky scent of the pack lingered on the air, helping my nose guide me deeper and deeper into the night as my ears attuned to the nocturnal songs around me. My massive paws surged forward, each step precise and powerful over the exposed roots underfoot. I didn't know where I was going, but something inside, something primal, refused to stop running.

A sharp pain shot up through the sole of my left foot, sudden and aching, like I'd landed on a pointy rock.

I faltered, but didn't stop.

The pain surged again but harder and out of time with my stride. Once. Twice. Three times.

"Wake up, sleepyhead," a syrupy-sweet voice cut

through the darkness as something thumped my foot again, knocking another dose of agony through my limbs.

I fought to force my drowsy eyelids open as harsh beams of sunlight burned my retinas. Shielding my face with my arm, I rolled onto my back and dared to look up. Three fuzzy figures towered over me and slowly came into focus. Sunni, Astrid, and Kate posed in their matching white beanies and black puffy vests, their makeup glossy and fresh with not one hair out of place, while I writhed my way back into waking existence.

"We can't let you sleep all day. Or at least not on the ground." Kate crouched near my feet, her arms resting on her knees. "Can you imagine the rumors if someone found you out here like this?"

The world spun as I eased myself up into a sitting position. Green trees melted into blue sky and dark, dirty ground as I ripped myself out of my dream world and back into reality. I grabbed the side of my head to stop the spinning, and luckily it obeyed, but not without leaving me a little nauseous. Hopefully, I didn't do something last night that I'd regret.

"Where exactly is here?" I asked as I clutched the gray camping blanket wrapped around me tighter to my chest, my naked arms shivering from the early morning chill. It was still morning, right?

"We're still in Willowgate Park. But here, put these on before some random hiker heads out this way." Astrid tossed a pile of clothes on my lap and stuck her hands on her hips. "Besides, you'll probably get cold soon."

As if responding to her words, my whole body shook, and I dug into the stack of things in front of me. I held up a baggy pink sweater with the words "Chaos Queen" printed in cursive across the chest. "Thanks, but these aren't mine."

"Of course they aren't," Kate said. "You decided not to listen when I told you to take them off, so your clothes are basically scraps now. Fortunately, we thought you might be the stubborn type, so I packed an extra outfit, just in case."

Scraps? I closed my eyes for a moment, and new images flooded my brain. Falling to my knees on the rocky ground. My fingers contorting and twisting into fur-covered claws. Tipping my head back and howling at the moon. Hadn't that all been a dream? It couldn't have been real. Could it?

I gasped and pulled the sweater on, the familiar scent of Kate's magnolia perfume surrounding me.

"What happened last night?" I placed my cool palm against my forehead as heat built in my cheeks. More broken memories filtered through my consciousness, each one falling into place to tell a warped fairy tale. Dead leaves crackling under my gray paws. Every speck of dirt or falling snowflake clearer and sharper than I'd ever seen. A pack of eleven other wolves running untamed under the milky moonlight. My pulse quickened and throbbed at my temples as a fierce animalistic power flooded through my veins. I lurched forward. "What did you do to me?"

Kate placed her hand on my shoulder and looked back up at Astrid and Sunni. "We gave you exactly what you wanted. You're one of us now."

"That's not what I meant. I'm talking about the…" I

scrunched up my face as the words stuck sharp on the end of my tongue. Kate's face disappeared as my memory flashed to her brown snout and yellow eyes staring at me. I shook my head. This made no sense. I cleared my throat and whispered, "Did we or did we not turn into wolves last night?"

Kate shrugged. "Basically, yeah."

"What?" My heartbeat thumped in my ears as the nausea took hold again. I ripped back the blanket, but it caught around my legs, pinning me down as I struggled to move. "That is completely unhinged."

"Relax, Melina. It's not as bad as you think." Kate grabbed the corner of the blanket and easily peeled it back, releasing me.

I yanked on the pair of borrowed joggers and clambered onto all fours. I glanced down at my hands. They were still my hands—human hands—not claws or paws. "Is this some sort of joke?"

"I know it's a lot, but we've all gone through this, and we're just fine. You'll be okay." Sunni held my stare and nodded, coaxing me to nod along with her.

I shook my head, breaking her mental hold. "All of you? This is so messed up. Do you know that?"

Sunni shifted her eyes toward the ground as she ran the toe of her white sneaker through the dirt. Neither Astrid nor Kate looked in my direction either.

I curled my hands into fists. "Will someone just tell me what's going on?"

A loud rumble echoed in the air, and I swung my arm over my stomach to muffle the sound.

"I've got a better idea. Why don't we go get some

breakfast, and then we can explain everything." Kate slapped her palms on her knees and pushed herself up to standing. She extended her hand to me. "Sound good?"

I clasped my hand in hers, her soft skin easing some of the tension rising in my chest. "Yes, please."

11

Bang!

I threw open the last of the three bathroom stalls and peeked inside. Nothing but bits of torn toilet paper dotted the beige tile floor.

"Perfect," I whispered into the empty space as I finally let myself exhale and released the pressure building deep in my chest.

From the moment I'd been scooped off the ground until now, no one had left me alone. I needed a minute or two to process or at least pin down my racing thoughts about what happened last night. Not that any of it really made sense. But at least Kate, Astrid, and Sunni let me go to the bathroom by myself. I couldn't handle another second smothered by their cautious stares and awkward silences. They promised they'd explain everything, but so far none of them had revealed anything, just played their disturbing fantasy game like becoming a wolf was a totally normal thing to do.

I closed my eyes and let myself filter through the

broken memories still trying to piece together in my head. The entire squad circling around me. The pain as I transformed. The howls of the other wolves. And probably the most frightening, a glorious sense of power and freedom I'd never felt before.

But this couldn't be happening. Maybe I'd just banged my head and was still asleep somewhere, dreaming up this vivid nightmare. I yanked up my sleeve and dug my fingernails into my flesh until it stung. My forearm flinched, forcing me to stop. A line of crimson crescent moons carved across my skin, and I swallowed against the thickness in my throat. Yep, definitely awake.

I crossed over to the sink and gripped the smooth porcelain sides then dared to look in the mirror. My reflection didn't seem any different from any other day except for the dark circles under my eyes, but staying up all night and sleeping on rocks would do that to anyone. I leaned closer and traced my index finger over my cheek and down the tip of my nose, and even pulled back my upper lip to expose my normal-looking teeth. No fangs. No fur. Nothing out of the ordinary. Except something new flowed beneath my skin. An electric sensation I couldn't see but that changed how my limbs moved. Lighter. More fluid.

I turned the tap and held my hand under the cold water, letting the icy chill seep into my bones. The only way I'd get answers was to suck up my fear and ask the questions I dreaded. As I cupped my palm under the stream, I leaned over and splashed the cold water on my face before braving the mirror again. Droplets dripped from my eyelashes down my cheeks and off my chin into the sink below. I sighed and wiped away the rest of the water with the sleeve of Kate's oversized sweater, turning it an even more vibrant pink. The wide neck slipped off my shoulder, and I pulled it back into place as I let out a sigh. Whatever was going on, I definitely didn't feel like myself anymore, especially playing dress-up in Kate's hand-me-downs.

My phone buzzed in my pocket.

Kate: Are you okay in there?

I stared at the screen. Nope. Definitely not okay, but I doubted there was an emoji to truly express my feelings. Heck, I didn't even know what I felt. My stomach growled, and I held the phone against my abdomen until it stopped. If I didn't get out of here soon, I might actually starve to death. I tipped my head back and breathed out before typing my response.

Me: Yeah. I'll be right out.

I shoved my phone back in my pocket and stumbled out of the dingy bathroom into the bright, kitschy aesthetic of the Red Dog Diner. The happy doo-wop song blasting from the ceiling speakers poked at the newly created darkness in my chest, but the heavy scent of bacon grease coaxed me into a half-hearted grin. I'd never really been a breakfast kind of girl. Maybe because I preferred my sleep to a bland omelet or unappealing bowl of cereal, especially since Mama refused to buy the sugar-loaded kinds that might have made getting up early more tolerable. But today, the rumbling in my stomach begged for my least favorite meal. I ran the tips of my fingers over the tops of the red vinyl upholstered booths as I strolled toward the corner table where Astrid and Kate peeked over their menus and failed at pretending not to be watching me.

All around, happy families sat around pillars of syrup-soaked pancakes. Truckers hunched over black coffees and daily specials piled high with sunny-side eggs and hash browns. The smells teased my nostrils and strengthened the churning in my empty stomach to near earthquake-level proportions. The neon signs on the wall swirled around my head in glowing streaks of color as my head wobbled back and forth. The music slowed, each note muddled as if I'd dunked my head underwater. My knees trembled. The corner table floated farther away, and each cautious step closer threatened to drop me to the checkered linoleum floor. I smacked my hands out to my left, gripping onto a chair and catching the arm of an older gentleman in a scratchy green cardigan.

"Can I help you?" He glared up at me as he dropped his fork back onto his plate.

The resulting clang broke the time warp. The world sped up again, and I backed up into the booth across the aisle, gathering more harsh stares from the mother I'd jabbed with my elbow.

"I'm sorry," I said to the man in front of me and turned to repeat the same to the woman I'd accidentally assaulted.

Both of them scowled back in response. I turned away and rushed forward, focusing on the black-and-white photo of Elvis Presley hanging over Astrid's head, although the exit sign over the side door seemed pretty tempting too. However, even if I wasn't sure what cheerleading horror story I'd been dragged into, I couldn't leave without knowing what they'd done to me. Besides, Astrid drove us all here, and going home would be a forty-five-minute walk that I definitely couldn't handle in my current state.

I collapsed into the booth next to Sunni and scanned the blue laminated menu on the table. Eggs Benedict. French toast. Each line sounded like heaven, and my mouth watered again.

"We already ordered for you. Figured you probably didn't want to wait." Kate snatched the menu off the table then reached across Astrid and stuffed it back in the silver rack behind the condiments. "And don't worry, it's on us. A little welcome-to-the-team treat."

"About that, I'm not sure if that's a good—"

My stomach growled and gurgled even louder than before. I crossed my arms over my chest and shrank down in the booth.

"Here, drink this." Astrid slid her large glass of chocolate milk in front of me. "It'll help until the food comes."

"Thanks." I raised the cup to my lips and paused as everyone's stares fell on me, but the empty hole in my gut ached to be satisfied, so I tipped it back and guzzled, dropping the empty glass back on the table. A wave of relief rushed over my body, and the fuzziness in my brain eased off a little.

"The first transition is always the worst. Takes everything out of you," Sunni said as she nudged me with her shoulder. "Next time keep a protein bar in your bag. It helps so much."

I ran the back of my hand over my mouth, a few

brown drops of milk staining my skin. "What do you mean, next time?"

Kate glared at Sunni. "Maybe we should start with the basics."

"Yeah, like maybe why the entire cheerleading squad turns into wolves. That would probably be a good place to start," I said.

"Can you keep your voice down?" Kate scoffed as she relaxed back in her seat. "If you hadn't already figured it out, all this is a secret, and it needs to stay that way."

Sunni quickly surveyed the other tables then pinned me down with a hostile stare. "Like taken to the grave, secret. Got it?"

I shivered and nodded back. "But what if—"

"But nothing, it's the number-one rule. We keep our mouths shut and sacrifice our nights to run around the forest in exchange for getting an edge on our routines. A bit of animal instinct, balance, and strength that makes us special. Better than everyone else." Kate leaned her head across the table, and a spark of pride flickered in her blue eyes. "And don't think this is something we made up, either. It's part of a long line of Faraway High tradition. Years of cheerleaders channeling the power of the wolves to excel to greatness. We've always been champions. We'll always be champions."

I scrunched the cuffs of Kate's sweater in my palms and shrank farther down in my seat. Years, really? How many? Were all those shiny trophies in the school's case won because of this… this… whatever this was? "I don't know. Doesn't that kind of sound like cheating?"

"What? Of course not. Every squad does everything they can to be at their absolute best, and so do we. The only thing in the rules about who can be on a squad is that they need to be a student. We aren't using performance-enhancing drugs, we aren't sabotaging the other teams, and we've never tried stunts that weren't in the approved National Cheerleading Association guidelines. Besides, we don't really know that other schools don't do the same thing. Right, ladies?"

Astrid stopped scrolling on her phone, her cluster of multicolored gemstone bracelets clinking as they slid down her arm. "She's not wrong. I'll bet ten designer backpacks that the squad from Harrowwood County are bear shifters. Those girls are always so grouchy, and I swear one of them actually growled at me when we slaughtered them at Divisionals last year. What do you think, Sunni?"

She held Astrid's stare and flashed a quick, comforting smile. "Yep. No rules broken."

"See?" Kate said. "Not cheating. Other schools have fancy choreographers and trainers for their teams that we don't. No one is giving us an advantage like that. We still have to do the stunts and learn the moves. We still make mistakes and fall down all the time."

The words flowed out so effortlessly, so free, like she didn't know how insane it sounded or didn't care. Or maybe she simply had a point. I'd seen the work everyone put into our routines. I'd helped bandage the skinned knees. No matter what kind of spell might be at play, it definitely didn't make the team unbeatable.

"But what if—" The words died on my tongue, and everyone straightened in their seats as our server appeared at the end of the table. He looked familiar. Probably one of my eldest brother's friends or maybe from a few years ago on the varsity baseball team.

"All right," he said, as he balanced a huge tray at his shoulder, "I've got one order of pancakes, two veggie egg-white omelets, and one Red Dog special."

Sunni raised her hand. "Pancakes over here."

He leaned across the table and slid the stack of fluffy golden cakes in front of Sunni, giving her a coy smile. The pungent scent of the food swirled into an intoxicating haze. I closed my eyes and tried to block out the hunger, but the sounds of the diner erupted around me in its place. A noisy mess of cutlery scraping against plates and a thousand foreign conversations layered over the subtler hum of the ceiling fan above us and the bass of Server Boy's heart *thump, thump, thumping* near my face as he distributed our plates while unabashedly flirting with all three cheerleaders. I clamped my hands over my ears, only dulling the cacophony.

"Is she okay?" he whispered to the far side of the table.

"She'll be fine," Kate replied. "She had a rough night."

He snickered. "I'll bet."

I opened my eyes to glimpse his amused smirk before he swaggered back toward the kitchen. However, I honestly didn't care what he thought of me, my appetite winning out over my anxiety.

"We weren't sure what you liked, so we ordered a little of everything," Astrid said as she cut her omelet into precise little squares.

"It's great. Thanks." I shoved my fork into my mouth. The saltiness of the fresh-cut hash browns blended with the creamy, runny egg on my tongue. I swallowed before

I'd fully chewed, nearly choking as I scooped up another overflowing forkful.

Kate stopped eating and glared across the table. "Easy, Melina. It's not healthy to *wolf* down your food like that."

"Uh. I didn't mean to." I hovered my fork over my plate as I snapped out of my feeding frenzy and glanced around the restaurant. At least no one else was staring at me. "I'm sorry."

Kate laughed then pointed her butter knife at me. "It's just a joke, rookie. Don't be so serious."

"Once that food kicks in, you'll be absolutely fine. Be happy we came here for breakfast and didn't leave you to go all feral and hunt down a squirrel," Astrid added.

"Oh my gosh, you're awful. We would never do that." Kate shook her head. "But can you even imagine? That would be hilarious."

"Do you remember the first time Melody turned? She was so hangry she sat down at someone else's table and ate half their breakfast when they were in the bathroom." Astrid chuckled and slapped her hand against the table. "Then when they came back she tried to convince them they were sitting at *her* table and just grabbed a fistful of the bacon and bolted. We had to chase her for five blocks before we caught her."

"I forgot about that." Kate tossed her head back and giggled. "To this day, she swears it was the best bacon she's ever had."

I fell back against the vinyl seat and laughed at the image of Melody devouring strips of bacon while she sprinted down Front Street. The tension in my limbs eased. Now that the first few bites of food began sharpening the fuzzy edges of my consciousness, everything seemed a little less dire. Sure, turning into a wolf was super messed up, but the rest of the squad got over it. Maybe I *was* just a little too serious?

"So how exactly does this all work? I mean, I don't remember saying any magic words or anything. And I definitely would've remembered being bitten by a wolf." Or at least I thought I would've remembered.

"No one really knows for sure," Kate said. "It's been going on for so many years, if anyone ever really knew, they are long gone by now. All we know is that it works and seems to come from the power of the pack. We decide who's in and who's out, and then by agreeing you basically just become one of us. The universe does the rest."

"Seems a little too simple, don't you think? Like, why wolves? Why not cats or deer or whatever? And how does changing give us wolf instincts? It just doesn't make sense."

The table fell silent except for a few heavy sighs, and I snuck a few more bites of my breakfast, hoping it would clear my head faster.

"Think of it like this." Astrid grabbed the salt and pepper shakers and slid them to the middle of the table. "The salt shaker is us. All our skills, strengths, weaknesses, and stuff. And these"—she held up the pepper shaker—"are wolves. If we want to have what makes them so strong, then we basically have to take on what they are."

She dumped a pile of salt on the table then added the pepper to the top and swirled the tip of her glittery fingernail through them to mix it all together.

"See? Now you have everything that makes us awesome and everything that makes wolves awesome, but we can't really separate them anymore. They become part of us. A new butt-kicking combination that can't be undone."

"Kind of like siphon magic," Sunni added.

Kate shook her head and glared at her. "What are you talking about?"

"Well, we basically siphon the power from the wolves through becoming them. Like, you know…" Sunni made little wave motions with her hands then rolled her eyes. "We just absorb their essence or something. I saw it in a movie once. It's totally a thing."

Kate's face twisted as if she'd just eaten a handful of sour candies. "Sure, whatever. But the rules are simple. As long as you're part of the squad, you change every night, and then you get total rock star powers during the day. It's really not that hard."

"Every night? Like forever?" I definitely didn't agree to this for the rest of my life. Even if I did, my parents would never let me out of the house every night. I could transform right in the middle of the kitchen and they'd probably just leash me to the refrigerator.

"No, silly. Only until you're done cheerleading. So, senior year, mid-May-ish, after we pick a new captain and set the team for next year. Just in time for prom. Can you imagine if you had to ditch your date and ruin your dress? That would be a total disaster." Kate laughed again, but no one joined her this time. "And besides, it's not that bad. The full moon is when you turn the earliest, about nine or so, but it's shorter and shorter after that. Most of us don't even change on new moons anymore."

I pushed my eggs around my plate with my fork and focused on the yellow yolk smearing across the center of the plate. This wasn't just joining a team anymore. This was a lifestyle choice. "What happens if I change my mind? If I want out?"

"Why would you want that? I'm sure you know what being a cheerleader in this town means. It's instant celebrity. It's invites to the best schools. It's going to the best parties and having the most popular friends. It's having everything you've ever wanted and more. Most girls would kill to be in your spot right now, but all we're asking is for you to give up a bit of sleep until you graduate. That's not even a sacrifice." Kate reached across the table and grabbed my hand. "Look at me, Melina. Even if those reasons aren't enough, don't tell me you didn't like it. I saw it in your eyes last night. That freedom to just totally run wild is addictive."

I clenched my fork tighter in my hand, the metal heating under my grip. Maybe I did. But that didn't really mean it was something I wanted, did it?

Kate smirked as she settled back against the booth seat. "See, I knew I liked you for a reason. You looked like someone who wanted to let loose now and again. But trust us, you're never going to want to give all this up. Your life is about to get better than your wildest dreams, and you'll have us to thank for it."

Sunni and Astrid exchanged uneasy glances.

I pulled my hand out of Kate's grip and held my arm over my stomach as it churned again—but this time it didn't feel like hunger.

12

"Remember, Starlight Pond. Eleven o'clock. Got it?" Kate leaned out the passenger window of the Escalade and adjusted the side mirror before smoothing a few flyaway strands back against her head.

I nodded and walked backward up the concrete path to my front door. "Got it. Eleven."

"And Melina, it'll be fine. Your life is going to get so much better."

A forced smile curled across my lips. "Of course."

The passenger window raised, finally putting a barrier between them and me. I waved after the car as Astrid squealed down the street, freeing me from their hold for the first time in about twenty hours. Twenty very long hours.

Neither Papa's SUV nor Mama's Corolla were in their normal spots in the driveway. At least the universe had granted me that minor miracle. I closed my eyes and breathed in the cool November air, holding it until my lungs ached in my sore chest. My jumbled thoughts arranged themselves in the silence, and the strangeness of everything started to fully take hold. Power and pain. Strength and weakness. Two sides of a very confusing coin. And I still hadn't fully decided how I felt about the whole thing.

I dragged my feet up the front walk and slipped my key into the lock. It turned too easily, and my shoulders fell. If my parents were out, that meant they left Marco in charge. I didn't have the energy to deal with his condescending, annoying questions, which I'd most definitely get. Especially if I looked anything like I felt.

Easing the door open, I crept in and gently pushed it shut again, keeping the knob turned to avoid the telltale click. I tiptoed across the kitchen and avoided the squeaky floorboard at the entrance to the hall. The door to my room inched closer and closer. My arms dropped limp at my sides as I imagined the amazingness of slipping into my comfy bed and napping for an eternity. Maybe when I woke up, all this wolf business would make more sense. Closing my eyes, I reached for the doorknob.

"Melly!" Tommy's excited voice squealed from down the hall. "Melly. Melly. Melly."

His little feet thumped toward me until he threw himself at my leg, his arms hanging on tight.

I ran my fingers through his curls, my dream of being undetected shattering on the floor. "Hey, buddy."

"Why, hello there, dear. We didn't even hear you come in. The two of us were far too busy building barns for his dinosaur ranch, isn't that right, Tommy?" Our elderly neighbor from the next block, Mrs. Danley, carefully shut the door to Tommy's room.

I exhaled a sigh of relief. If she was here, it meant Marco and the others were not. Another small win. "He sure loves dinosaurs."

"Rawr," Tommy said, finally letting go of my leg and stomping toward her with his hands crooked into claws. She rolled her sleeves up to her elbows. I bit the side of my cheek, trying not to laugh at the two white kittens embroidered in furry wool across her chest. Hopefully, when I got older, I would never own a sweater like that. She bent down on one knee, the motion slow and strained, then stuck up her own set of fake finger claws.

"Even the toughest dinosaurs are no match for a tickle monster." She caught Tommy's belly, and he squealed in delight as he surrendered.

Mrs. Danley straightened Tommy back on his feet. "All right now, why don't you go get those toys cleaned up. You wouldn't want any of your dinosaurs to get lost under your bed, would you?"

He shook his head and rushed off into the bedroom. Mrs. Danley pressed her hand against the wall and shifted her weight to try to get up. I rushed over and held out my hand, helping steady her until she was standing.

"Thank you," she said, a kind, warm smile stretching across her face, her hand still laced tightly with mine.

"No problem." I tried to slip my hand away, but she held firm and wavered on her feet as her eyes closed. I lunged forward as I gripped her other arm to hold her steady, my stomach hollowing. "Are you okay?"

She shook her head and blinked a few times, then released my hand. "Of course, nothing to worry about. This happens from time to time. Nothing of concern."

"Are you sure?" I asked.

"Absolutely," she replied without hesitation as she carefully scanned me over. Even her blind left eye seemed to focus too intently on me, and an odd chill pebbled goosebumps across my skin. Could she somehow tell that I'd changed? Or maybe I'd developed a case of paranoia since yesterday.

"That's a lovely bracelet." She grasped my arm, yanking it higher and tilting her good eye closer to my wrist. "Lavender moonstones, am I right? You rarely see those around here."

"I'm not really sure. It was a gift, so they could be."

"And such an intricate weave." She lowered my arm as her silver eyebrows knit together. "You said someone gave this to you?"

"Well, kind of. Everyone on the cheer team has one. That's why they're purple and gold, to match the school colors."

I pulled my arm from her soft grip and cradled it closer to my body, my fingertips running over the bracelet strands.

Mrs. Danley pursed her lips and looked at me closely, either studying my face or thinking extremely hard. For a woman blind in one eye, she never seemed to miss a thing. Almost as if she made up for her lack of eyesight with intuition.

"It's probably just cheap costume stuff that one of the girls found at a dollar store, or maybe someone just made them," I said. "I'll bet the stones aren't even real."

Her face relaxed as she took a haggard breath. "Very possible. Now if you're home to take care of the young dinosaur hunter, then I'd best be on my way. My supper won't quite make itself, now, will it? Besides, Mr. Danley gets irritable when he's hungry, and I'd rather he not make a mess of the kitchen."

I laughed. Yeah, definitely knew that feeling.

She scurried past me and headed straight for the front door. I followed behind, my arm still held tight to my chest, and helped her slide on her long navy coat. She pulled her hood up over her tousled gray hair, yanked on a tight pair of leather gloves, and eased open the door.

"Thanks for coming to watch Tommy. Mama really appreciates your helping her out like this. But are you sure you're okay to walk home by yourself?"

She waved a gloved hand at me. "Yes, I'm completely fine. And it's no trouble at all. Tommy's such a good boy. A bit of a handful sometimes, but with the heart of a little prince."

I nodded and pulled the door open wider for her.

She stepped forward, one foot inside and one out, then froze. She glanced back, the lines on her wrinkled face etching deeper as she locked her stare with mine. "Forgive an old lady for butting her nose in where it likely doesn't belong, but you're a nice girl. Please be cautious of the company you keep."

"Okay. Thanks?" I replied as my tired, cloudy brain struggled to process her words. "What do you mean?"

Mrs. Danley sighed and dipped her head, twining her fingers together. "Hopefully, you'll never need to find out."

The storm in her expression quickly passed, replaced by her happy-go-lucky grin. "Tell your mother I'll give her a call later this week about the bake sale at St. Augustine's."

Then, with a lighthearted skip, she shuffled her way to

the sidewalk and headed off down the street. Mrs. Danley was a sweet lady, but she said the strangest things sometimes. Hopefully, her mind wasn't slipping, especially if Mama still trusted her to watch over Tommy. But if I told anyone what happened to me last night, they'd probably think I wasn't entirely sane either.

I closed the door, clicking the dead bolt home, and leaned my forehead against the wooden panels as my stomach growled at me.

Seriously?

I'd already eaten half my body weight in eggs less than half an hour ago. How could I possibly be hungry again? Or maybe time had slipped by faster than I'd thought? I tugged my phone out of my pocket and confirmed the time. The bottom half of the screen filled with unread text bubbles from my friends asking about my big night.

As I thumbed through the group chat, I stumbled back into the kitchen and rummaged through the fridge. My mouth watered at the blend of food smells blasting in my face. Any other day, my nose would've scrunched up and I would've rushed to close the door, but today, things had definitely changed.

Balancing a container of hummus on a half-eaten plate of chicken and pasta, I grabbed a carton of milk and carefully arranged everything on the counter. Just a quick snack and then I'd throw on some cartoons for Tommy and take a nap on the couch before everyone came home.

As I poured myself a glass of milk, I caught myself swaying, my brain drifting in an overloaded fog. The chill of the milk tickled against my palm as I lifted the drink to my mouth.

Then the glass slipped.

I cringed, waiting for the smash. But it never came. My arm snapped out, reacting without me—on instinct or reflex or divine intervention—and caught the glass before it crashed, only two small drops of milk splashing onto the brown laminate. I stared at the cup in my hand.

What the heck?

I rubbed my hand along my arm. Nothing out of the ordinary, except for the tingly feeling inside. The electric current cycled through my bones. Low and slow. Just tiny sparks, waiting to ignite.

Gripping the edges of the counter, I took a deep breath and closed my eyes, letting everything sink in for the first time. Pictures and pieces of last night cut through my hazy mind, as crisp and clear as if they were happening now. The power rushing through my limbs as I raced through the forest. My legs twitched as they remembered and ached to run again. A strange longing—a freedom— suddenly bubbled to the surface and drowned out the fear I'd been wading in all day. The twisted truth.

Kate was right. I didn't completely hate it, even though I'd convinced myself I should. Believed I should. Because that was the normal reaction, right? And this whole thing was anything but normal. Except where had normal gotten me so far? Barely even noticed. Struggling to earn my spot among the Faraway High elite. But maybe the universe had finally smiled on me. None of the other girls on the squad seemed to complain about their wolfish fate, and some of them had been cheerleading for years. If it was really that bad, then they would've exposed the entire team by now. Right? I was probably just overthinking again. Kate said this was just temporary. A means to a fabulous end with a bright future on the other side. Plus, stepping out of the shadows for once might be exactly what I needed.

I flipped into the group chat.

> Me: Last night was the absolute best. I'm so excited to be part of the squad.

Almost immediately the responses came back.

> Jaida: That's awesome. Congrats!
>
> Hailey: I can't wait to hear all about it.
>
> Isaac: Want to introduce me to some of your cute new friends?
>
> Allyssa: Solid.

I stared at the screen for a few more seconds, holding my breath until Leo's response finally appeared on the screen.

> Leo: I'm happy for you.

Okay, good. At least no one was suspicious. It's not like I could tell them the real truth. They'd never believe me anyway.

Leaning against the counter, I slid the phone in my pocket and slammed back the entire glass of milk in three gulps before refilling the cup.

Best to keep my strength up.

Eleven o'clock couldn't come fast enough.

13

"Good morning, Lions. Wakey, wakey, my little champions." Kate's saccharine voice attacked my eardrums as I dragged open the locker-room door. She must've had at least three espressos this morning to be that chipper, or she simply derived energy from tormenting other people. Likely the latter.

I shielded my eyes from the blaring gym lights and collapsed onto the wooden bench next to Joy and Sheena. The last thing I remembered before dragging myself out of bed and through the frosty morning to school was the bright white moon calling me forward. Saturday night might have started out as a nightmare, but last night seemed more like a fantastical dream.

In the darkness, the world lay still, as if frozen in time, resetting itself from the day as our pack charged through the woods, claiming them as our own. My heightened senses appreciated every faint whisper on the breeze, beckoning us onward and fueling our run. The splinters of moonlight reflected off the branches, creating glittery shapes as if the trees had sprouted diamonds. This time, no fear coursed through my blood. Only freedom. A jewel-laden playground where I no longer felt like an outsider. I was one of them.

I rubbed my hands over my face and forced my spine straighter. If I could fake my way into believing I wasn't exhausted, maybe I could actually make it through the day.

"How do you all manage to do this every night and still practice before and after school almost every single day?"

Sheena tugged the knot on her left sneaker then shrugged. "You get used to it eventually."

"Here, drink this." Joy handed me a water bottle with a sludgy substance oozing around inside.

I sniffed the top and crinkled my nose at the pungent, loamy aroma. "Ew. Is this mud?"

"No, silly. It's a smoothie. Try some."

Reluctantly, I placed the bottle to my lips and took a small sip. The sludge hit my tongue, and I winced, but it tasted shockingly citrusy mixed with a bit of sweetness. "It's pretty good. What's in it?"

"It's my own special recipe. Night runs are awesome, but I'm totally drained in the morning. This stuff keeps me functioning the rest of the day." Joy leaned her head closer to mine and whispered, "The secret is a bit of ginseng to help keep me more alert."

"Good tip. I had a huge breakfast this morning, but I guess it wasn't enough."

I handed the bottle back to Joy, but she raised her palm, stopping me.

"Keep it. Everyone needs to figure out what works for them, but I'm happy to help. Besides, it looks like you need it a lot more than I do this morning." She tossed me a sympathetic smile as both girls rose from the bench and headed toward the far side of the gym.

"Uh, thanks?" I sat up straighter and smoothed my free hand over my hair. I didn't think I looked that bad. But compared to Joy and Sheena, I probably did look like a total wreck. I stared after Joy and watched her silky dark hair tied in her perky ponytail swing hypnotically as she walked away. Not a strand out of place or any awkward lumps as it pulled against her scalp, unlike the messy bun I'd piled haphazardly on the top of my head. She'd even already done a full face of makeup, which looked dewy and clean, a feat I did not have the energy for this morning. I took another gulp of the smoothie and closed my eyes as I savored every last drop. Clearly, I still had lessons to learn about this whole cheerleader life.

"Let's go. We don't have all morning." Kate clapped her hands with three loud strikes. Each one taunted my tired brain, but my body followed the command, and I jumped to my feet, racing to my space on the floor.

Everyone assembled in their assigned spots around me. Immaculate straight lines faced Kate at full attention. Not one toe out of formation.

I glanced over at Ainsley on my left, but she didn't seem to notice, her head facing forward like an obedient soldier.

"I want to run our competition routine before we work on anything else," Kate said as she paced in front of the group, scanning each of us with a laser-sharp focus. When her eyes caught mine, I thought I saw her expression soften, a gentle smile pulling at the edges of her mouth, but it disappeared so quickly that I could've imagined it. "I know playoffs are exciting, but if we are going to bring home another trophy, then we need to make sure that we are one hundred percent flawless. From this day forward, I want you living and breathing this routine. When you sleep, you dream of this routine. Every single minute of every single day needs to be focused on winning. Got it?"

We all stayed in place, a few of us silently nodding.

She turned on her heel, the sole of her shoe squeaking on the gym floor as she thrust her hands onto her hips. "I can't hear you!"

"Got it!" we responded in unison.

"That's better." The power twinkled in Kate's eyes as she slipped her phone out of the pocket of her shorts and the familiar track of our competition piece blared through the gym speakers.

I took a deep breath and fought the nervous shocks sparking under my skin. I'd practiced this routine a hundred times before, but not with the team. Never as part of the actual show. No matter how tired my body felt, I needed to nail this.

Kate cranked the volume, and the rhythm flowed through my limbs like high voltage, shocking all my cells back to life. She took her position at the front, head bowed to her chest, and everyone followed along. Her right foot tapped on the floor in time. Five, six, seven, eight, and go!

My arms thrust above my head in a high V then snapped into the next move—sharp and absolutely seamless. The stiffness in my limbs faded with each move, muscle memory taking over. Or maybe something else. Something new. Something untamed.

Each flip flew lighter and tighter than the last.

Each landing stuck without a single wobble in my knees.

Even the final back handspring, which I always dreaded, executed masterfully.

With renewed energy, we ran the routine a few more times, and on each run-through, I performed even better. By the time we switched to the sideline cheers, all my worry faded into the bass of the background mix. I could do this. I knew I could, but now so did everyone else.

"All right, that's enough for today," Kate shouted.

The music cut out, replaced by a chorus of heavy panting. I leaned over and grabbed my knees as I lost my breath. The intensity drained out of me, as if I'd pulled the plug in a bathtub.

"So how was that?" Kate's pristine white sneakers appeared in front of me as she thrust a purple hand towel with an embroidered gold lion in front of my face.

"Amazing." I blotted the sweat off my forehead and forced my breathing to slow as I raised myself back to standing. "It's like my entire body just knew what to do. Like instinct, you know?"

She nodded. "We told you. It's like your potential has been locked in a cage this whole time and now you're finally free. Powerful, isn't it?"

"Yeah, that's exactly how it feels." I held the towel back out to her.

"Keep it." She waved me off and patted my shoulder. "Well, you slayed it for a beginner. I knew I made the right decision letting you on the squad."

"Thanks, Kate. I'm really happy—"

Before I had finished, she'd already rushed off toward

Astrid and Sunni, but it didn't matter. Captain Kate told me I did a good job. She actually noticed and took the effort to tell me, in person, instead of sending one of her lackeys or ignoring it. I fought the goofy grin cresting across my face, but it was no use. I practically floated on those vibes the entire time I showered and dressed. The whole situation was still beyond messed up, but Kate actually noticed me.

I folded the lion towel and placed it gently in my cheer bag as a blur of blonde hair whooshed past me.

"Ainsley," I called as I zipped the bag shut.

She didn't hear me and kept moving.

"Hey, Ainsley!" I called after her again, as I slung my bag over my shoulder and rushed behind her toward the exit. "Wait up."

Except as she hit the doorway, instead of turning back, she sped up.

14

"Ainsley!" I shouted the second I hit the hallway.

She'd already cleared five locker banks, and in only two more seconds she would've disappeared. Maybe she should've joined the track team instead of cheerleading. That girl was fast. Since Saturday night, I'd barely found a moment to talk to her about what happened, and a stinging thought in the back of my brain had started to think that wasn't an accident. Even my texts to her sat unanswered on my phone.

"Could you please just talk to me?" I yelled, tossing my hands in the air.

She froze, her shoulders rising toward her ears and still facing away from me.

One second. Two seconds.

Her body deflated, and she whirled back around, slowly heading in my direction.

I met her halfway and spun the combination into my locker while I waited for her to inch her feet back to me.

She stared down at her fingers twisted around the strap of her cheer bag. "Hey."

"You can't avoid me forever, you know? I'm going to see you pretty much every single day from now until the state cheer championships. Did I do something wrong?"

Ainsley sighed and stopped fidgeting. "Of course not. I've been busy, that's all."

"Seriously?"

Her cheeks flushed as she bit down on her lip as if trying to keep herself from saying something she shouldn't.

"Ever since they offered me a spot on the squad, I've been trying to talk to you. That first night in the woods, you wouldn't even look at me. I was totally terrified, and you didn't even give me a heads-up about what was going to happen. I thought we were friends." I threw my bag into my locker and slammed the door shut with a loud bang.

"I am your friend, and I feel wretched for how everything went down. But I know what's it's like to have a friend betray you, so I kind of assumed you probably hated me now. Trust me, if I could've told you, I would've, but I couldn't." She reached her hand out toward my shoulder then changed her mind and dropped it by her side again. "I swear I would've. I even tried to warn you at the game when Sydney got sick, but I guess you didn't pick up on that."

I fell against the locker bank, my head smacking against the metal. "Right, could you have been more subtle about it? I mean, how is breaking some cheerleader girl code worse than warning someone about snapping nearly every bone in their body then chasing rabbits through the woods all night long? I would never hate you, but you are so lucky that everything worked out, or I would be crazy upset with you right now."

Crossing my arms, I turned my head away from her and stared down the hall. Students had started dragging themselves to their lockers before Monday morning classes. Exhausted zombies here to fill their brains instead of eating them. I snickered to myself then shuddered. Zombies didn't sound as fictional today as they had last week. Maybe there were other things out there I didn't know about?

Ainsley's cool fingertips settled on my burning cheek, and she turned my head back, forcing me to look at her. "I'm happy you're feeling better about all this, but it's not like I had anyone to tell me about it when it happened to me either. It sucks."

I hadn't really thought about anyone else going through the same thing. I kind of assumed they knew what they were getting into but kept it from me as some sort of cruel trick. Like I was some sort of game. But maybe not.

"However, if you're still mad about it," Ainsley said, "Kate and her entourage obviously didn't tell you everything. Did they?"

"Seems like a trend, doesn't it?" I jerked my head out of her grip. "What am I missing now?"

"The reason I couldn't tell you about the"—she looked over her shoulder as her wide, fearful eyes scanned the crowds filling in around us, then she leaned closer—"wolf magic, is because I literally can't. You can't either. It's part of the deal. Unless you're part of the pack, we can't tell you about it. Something just switches in our brains, and the words won't come out. Believe me, I tried to fight it to warn you the night of the game, but there was nothing I could do."

"That sounds ridiculous."

"So do cheerleader wolves, don't they?"

Fair point.

"If you don't believe me, try it for yourself." She backed up and swooped her arm through the air. "Go ahead. Tell anyone you want. Scream it at the top of your lungs. I'll bet you don't get a single word out."

"Fine." I rammed the sole of my sneaker against the locker and pushed myself back to standing upright. People flitted past us, but who exactly would I be able to tell? Walking up to someone and telling them that the cheerleaders had magical wolf powers would guarantee complete social destruction. Even Jaida and Hailey would look at me like I'd hit my head—if they didn't simply burst out laughing as if it was all some kind of joke.

A joke? That could work. I narrowed my eyes and searched for the right target.

In the distance, a familiar dark-haired figure in a purple-and-gold football jacket huddled over an open locker, shoving notebooks into a black backpack. I glanced back at Ainsley. Her lips twisted into a smirk as she watched me march forward across the hall.

I stood behind Alex for a moment, the clean smell of shampoo from his damp locks rolling off him and causing my resolve to waver as I shook out the last of my nerves and plastered on my best smile. After one last deep breath, I tapped him on the shoulder, and he twirled around, his eyes lighting up as they met mine.

"Well, hello, Melina Cardona. Faraway's newest and

probably most beautiful cheerleader." He dropped his backpack to his feet and swiped his left hand through his hair, letting just the right amount flop almost too perfectly across his brow. "How are you on this Monday morning?"

I bit the inside of my cheek and forced my eyes not to roll, although part of me—against my will—flamed from the compliment. "I'm all right, but I would be better if you'd do me a favor."

"Oh really? Only if I get something in return." A devious grin cut across his face as he leaned closer. His voice lowered. "Like maybe your number so I can text you sometime? All I could think about on the way home Friday night was that I should've asked you for it at Tony's."

The flames roared hotter in my cheeks. It had to be a line. Polished enough that he'd obviously used it many times, but even my knowing the trick didn't stop it from working. Besides, what harm could come from a text message? "I guess so."

"Nice." He clapped his hands and rubbed them together, down for the challenge. "Then what can I help with?"

I sighed and twisted my fingers together behind my back, channeling my most coy smile. He might be laying on all his charm, but I had a show to perform myself. And well, yeah, maybe I was flirting... just a little. "I'm sure you know that when you start on a new team, you some-times have to prove yourself. Kind of like showing how committed you are to them."

"Sure. I get it." Darkness flashed across his expression

as his posture stiffened. "But hopefully, they aren't doing anything too horrible."

I shook my head, and he relaxed.

"Not at all. I just have to tell someone a ridiculous story and make a bit of a fool out of myself, so know whatever I tell you is just a joke, okay?"

He nodded slowly. "Okay, but doesn't it go against the rules if you tell me it isn't true?"

"Uh… not if you don't tell anyone I told you."

He leaned in closer. "Like our little secret?"

"Sure, whatever." Why did he have to make this harder than it already was? "Anyway, I'm supposed to tell you that the entire cheerleading squad all"—*turn into wolves at night and that's why they keep winning championships*—"have a huge crush on you."

I slapped my hand over my mouth.

"What?" He laughed and stood up straighter, his chest puffing out just a little.

"That's not what I meant. I was going to say that the Faraway High Cheer Squad are"— *really a pack of wolves*—"totally obsessed with you."

My face burned hot enough to raze the entire school and probably most of the next county. "Ugh. I never meant to say that. I just…" I threw my hands over my eyes and shook my head. "Never mind."

Alex wrapped his big hands over mine and pried them away from my face. I winced in his grip, waiting for his mocking laughter, but it never came. Instead, he bent down and held my uneasy stare, his blue eyes cool and calm. "Don't worry. I've had to do some really stupid things for football over the years. I totally get it."

Except I'd bet they never made him confess something

like that to anyone. How was it possible I might've said something more humiliating than the actual truth?

"Thank you." I stared down at our hands still entwined between us, and another rush of heat coursed through me. My head clouded as the scent of him overwhelmed my senses. But not just his cologne or brand of soap. Something else, primal but inexplicably him, that I'd never sensed before.

He opened his grasp, leaving my burning hands resting in his palms. An invitation to retreat, but not a requirement. "No problem."

I took the opportunity to collect myself, dropping my arms to my sides and leaning back on my heels to give a bit more space between us. I clearly needed to have eaten a bigger breakfast.

"Well, I guess I'll see you around then." I awkwardly pointed down the hall, suddenly overly aware of how much the hallway had filled up around us. The bell would probably go off any minute. "Thanks again."

Without wasting a second, I rushed back toward my locker.

"Aren't you forgetting something?" he called after me.

I stopped and slowly turned back around. "Huh?"

Alex slipped his phone out of his pocket and held it out toward me.

"Oh, right," I said, taking it from him as I tried to steady my still-trembling fingers. Except it wasn't clear if the trembling was from the humiliation or from the way he placed his hand on the back of his neck and tilted his head down, barely hiding his hypnotic smile.

He pinched the top of the phone screen and yanked the device out of my hands. "But only if you want to?"

"It's okay. A deal is a deal." I tugged the phone back and flitted my fingers over the screen to enter my number.

"Any truth to the rumor, though? I'd love to know," he said.

"What rumor?"

"The one you just told me about the entire cheer-leading squad having a crush on me."

"Don't go getting an inflated head now, Alex. You know they put me up to that." Well… kind of.

"That's too bad. Can't say I wasn't a little pumped about it, even if it was only a select few. Or maybe just one." He lowered his head then stared up at me through his long, dark lashes, clearly knowing exactly what he was doing and not caring how obvious he came across.

But I didn't hate it either.

"Here." I fought the ridiculous smile forming on my lips and handed his phone back to him. "Not like I actually expect you to text me."

He tapped the phone against his chest before sliding it back into his pocket. "Oh, trust me, I will. I don't ask just anyone for their number, you know."

"Why don't I think that's one hundred percent true?"

He scooped his backpack off the floor and shrugged. "I guess you'll never know."

15

Class had already started as I slipped into the room and grabbed a desk at the back. My usual seat sat empty near the front, but I wasn't prepared to make a scene, tiptoeing through everyone to get closer as Mr. Markowitz droned on to the class. Besides, I'd already hit my limit for making a spectacle of myself for one day.

Fortunately, Alex hadn't made the whole situation as bad as he could have. He'd actually been sweet, but it's not like he'd honestly ever bother talking to me again. Or would he? Guys like him charmed everyone like it was their job. And he was definitely amazing at it. Almost a little too good. However, even if the whole conversation had been a pointless flirtation, it proved one thing—Ainsley wasn't lying about the curse restricting the squad from blabbing about it.

No matter what I tried to say, my tongue wasn't under my control. A force I couldn't even explain, let alone fight. Ainsley said she'd tried to warn me at the football game. How hard had she really tried, if I hadn't even noticed?

Although I had been distracted by Sydney and how sick she'd been. I shuddered, remembering what had happened. Was she even okay? I hadn't seen her in the halls this morning, and she usually stood out. It's not like we were besties or anything. She was actually kind of dismissive of me most days, but I would've thought someone would tell me how she was doing.

A tingly sensation wriggled up the back of my brain as my thoughts merged into a singular sinister theory. Did Sydney getting sick have anything to do with this whole wolf curse business? Maybe this was another side effect that no one bothered to tell me about. More secrets? Or just an oversight?

I should just ask. Ainsley might know, or would at least give me Sydney's number to ask her myself. My hands trembled as I slid my phone into my lap and flipped to the text screen.

"Phones away, Miss Cardona. Unless there's an actual emergency," Mr. Markowitz called from the front of the room. He'd stopped his lecture and leaned against his desk, glaring down at me, his thick caterpillar eyebrows raised. The prying stares from the rest of my classmates joined him.

"Uh…" I dropped my phone in my lap and bolted upright in my chair. "No, sir. It can wait."

"I thought so. Unless you'd rather I hold your phone up here until after class." He lingered in the silence as I slipped my phone into my pocket and shook my head. Contented, he eventually looked away and clapped his hands, holding them close to his chest. "Now that everyone is focused again, it's time for the main event. History quiz time."

A low groan rumbled through the room as my stomach hollowed, and I slouched forward onto my desktop. With everything that had happened this weekend, I'd totally forgotten about the test. I should've studied, but I hadn't even cracked my notes. But I'd always been decent at history. Maybe I could wing it.

He leaned back and scooped up a handful of green pages off his desk. "Now don't get too excited. Save some of that energy for the essay question."

Ugh. An essay question? At least if it were multiple choice, I might've stood a better chance.

"Okay, you will have thirty minutes, so plan your time accordingly and make sure to leave a few minutes to double-check your answers."

Mr. Markowitz dropped the paper on my desk with a stern expression, and my stomach twisted again. I scanned the sheet, and the words blurred together.

Explain the term "Manifest Destiny" and how it impacted the westward expansion of the United States.

Okay, think, Melina. We'd talked about this less than two weeks ago. Before everything in my life had changed. I poised my pencil on the page and began to scratch out the words.

Manifest Destiny was the belief that...

But did believing in anything make it real? Maybe the reason I couldn't talk about the curse was that I believed I couldn't because Ainsley said so, kind of like a self-fulfilling prophecy.

That had to be it. The whole wolf magic concept seemed far-fetched, but believing that it could control what I could do and say with my own body or that it could make Sydney sick was insane. When I was little and terrified of the monsters in my closet, Mama used to tell me that feeding fear made it stronger. Made it real. But remembering that I was in control took away its power. Were we all just fearmongered into keeping the squad's secret? Besides, what kind of magic would we even be dealing with to make the combination of all those things true? Not possible.

I tipped my head back and took a deep breath. I was losing it, or maybe just sleep deprived, and needed to get a grip on myself—fast.

No one else on the squad really seemed to be fussed about this curse or whatever it was, except maybe Ainsley, but she was pretty new to it as well.

No one else seemed concerned or raised any red flags about Sydney's illness.

No one else's life seemed drastically affected by the curse at all.

We'd all just put in our time. Pay the price. Then get our trophies and our scholarships and get out of Faraway and never even think about high school ever again.

My family couldn't afford to send five kids to college. They were already struggling with Miguel's tuition and unfortunately Marco would at least scrape by enough to qualify for a junior college, and then they had to consider my youngest brothers in the mix. Cheerleading would be my ticket to a life that didn't involve getting some job on Main Street and living in this boring little town forever.

I just needed to change my mindset. Think positively. Stop overthinking everything. Stop—

"Time's up." Mr. Markowitz's baritone voice cut through the haze. "Pens down and pass your tests forward."

What? There was no way it had already been half an hour. I glanced down at my test. Barely half the questions were answered, and I had zero idea what I'd written, so they were almost guaranteed to be wrong. I started writing again, desperate to get anything else on the page, but Bryson Davis turned around and snatched the test off my desk, causing me to make a dark pencil line down the bottom quarter of the paper.

"What are you doing?" I pushed up on my toes and grabbed at the test, but he quickly passed it forward to the desk in front of him.

"Mr. M said pencils down."

A dark-red wave flooded my vision as a surge of energy jolted through my limbs. I knotted my fist in the neck of his T-shirt and lunged forward. "But I wasn't done," I snarled in his ear.

He shot out of his seat, ripping his shirt from my grip. "Geez, Melina, what's your problem?"

The rest of the room stared at Bryson as I slouched back and let the rage flow out through my feet into the floor, replaced by an uneasy bone-deep chill.

The bell rang, and Bryson stormed out of the room while I sat paralyzed, staring at the wall until most of the class had left. Eventually, I calmed enough to drag myself from my chair out into the hallway. I rested my head against the wall and took a few cleansing breaths.

If being in control took away fear's power, what would happen if I lost control completely?

16

If anyone could figure out what they put in the chicken casserole surprise from the cafeteria, they should win a Nobel Prize. With the way the dish was pureed into mush, anything could have been the surprise, or maybe the surprise was that it wasn't really chicken. I shuddered. If I wasn't so famished, I'd skip lunch and just eat when I got home, but ever since Saturday night, my stomach growled almost constantly. I scrunched up my nose as I surveyed the casserole again then opted for some fries that would likely have me begging for something more substantial in an hour. But at least it was something. Even my new animal tendencies weren't desperate enough to risk the lunch special.

"Hey." The sound echoed in my ear as fingertips pressed against my hip.

Instinctively, I snapped my hand to my side and squeezed tight as I twisted away, wrenching the offending arm close to my chest. "What do you think you're doing?"

Leo's emerald eyes widened as he stared down at my

fingers clamped around his wrist. The tart taste of his panic sat on the tip of my tongue as his racing pulse echoed in my head. Each throb triggered something under my skin. Adrenaline surged through my blood with each quiver of his breath as the rest of the world blurred around us.

"Whoa, Lina. It's just me." He slid his hand over mine, his touch cozy and soft, as he wrested his fingers loose and freed himself from my grip.

I shook my head and stepped back, willing my breath to slow and forcing myself back into the moment. "Don't scare me like that."

"I definitely won't." He laughed uneasily as he flexed his fingers. The rest of the line behind us stared.

Just great. I'd made it awkward. I desperately needed to get these outbursts in check or I'd be spending the next pep rally in the office, or worse, suspended. "Sorry. I just kind of spaced out."

"No worries. I should've given you a warning." He slid behind me in line, but kept a careful distance between us. "Anyway, we were all looking for you this morning. You basically ghosted the group chat all weekend. Everyone's wondering where you've been."

"I've been super busy, plus we had early-morning practice today." I shuffled down the lunch line and inspected the bowls of fruit, debating way too hard between an apple and a banana before taking one of each, tossing them on my tray, then taking a huge bite of a second apple, unable to make it all the way to the checkout before diving in.

"Captain Kate must be working you pretty hard, huh?"

"Mmm, yeah. It's definitely a lot more than I'd thought it'd be." Understatement of the century.

He nodded but didn't press any further then circled around me and slid a twenty-dollar bill to the cashier.

"It's fine, I've got it." I dug into my bag looking for my cash, but he shook his head.

"Thanks. Next time is mine." I grabbed my tray, and we walked along the back wall toward our regular table. It wasn't the best spot, but it sat close to a window that overlooked the parking lot so we could see who came and went—and occasionally other scandalous things that the student body, or sometimes the faculty, thought they were stealthily hiding.

As the crowd thinned, Leo tipped his head closer to mine. "How's it going, really? You kind of seem, I don't know, different today."

"Everything's fine. Great, actually." I swallowed and looked away as if his stare could somehow see the truth, somehow pull the hidden parts out of my soul and lay them bare. "I'm just tired. A lot going on."

"Okay, but you can tell me if something is up, you know?"

I forced a smile. "Yeah, I know."

"Hey, Melina, come sit with us," Melody called from the cheerleader's table in the center of the room.

I froze. I'd only ever been invited to sit there once or twice, and it was usually when there was an out-of-state away game and most of the squad was gone with the football team for the day. Unfortunately, there just weren't enough chairs for everyone, especially for an alternate.

"Just go." Leo leaned into my shoulder and nudged me

in Melody's direction. "I'll cover for you with the crew. But don't forget about us, okay?"

"How could I ever forget about you guys? Even if I tried, Jaida would never let me go."

"None of us would." His tone shifted slightly, the lightness fading into something darker.

"Go, Lina." He nodded toward the cheer table. "They're waiting for you."

"Thanks." I swayed into him, brushing my arm against his, then pivoted toward the squad.

As I hurried away, I glanced back at Jaida and Hailey sitting at our table. It didn't look as if they noticed my escape. But they understood, right? If they joined a new team or something, I'd support them. Before I changed my mind, I sped up and slid into an empty chair next to Ainsley, knocking half my fries off my plate onto the cafeteria tray.

"Hey, thanks for inviting me."

"Of course," Ainsley said as she grabbed my hand and squeezed it. The tension from this morning was finally gone from her tone. "You're always welcome to sit with us. After all, you are on the squad now. Besides, the senior girls had a prom committee meeting at lunch today."

"Did the smoothie help?" Joy asked.

"A bit, but I'm still starving. Plus, I've kind of been on edge this morning." Or at least that was the tame way of saying that I practically growled at a classmate and scared the heck out of one of my best friends.

"Here." Ainsley dug into her schoolbag and slipped me a chocolate peanut butter granola bar. "These are my favorite. It'll help you get through the afternoon."

I zipped open my bag and dropped the snack inside.

"Thanks. I'm going to have to get all this figured out fast before I become a complete menace."

"We were just talking about the new sideline cheer we learned this morning," Melody said as she opened a small plastic container of salad dressing and artfully swirled it over the plate of vegetables in front of her. She closed the empty container again and licked the splash of ranch off the side of her thumb. "I think it might be missing something, but Piper thinks it's perfect the way it is. What do you think, Melina?"

"It's fine, I guess." I took another bite of my apple and waited for anyone else to chime in, but instead Melody arched her perfectly shaped left brow and shrugged.

My shoulders tensed as I replayed the routine in my head. "I mean, it might be a little boring."

Ainsley winced, and I thought I saw her discreetly shake her head, but I'd already opened my mouth.

"Like, if we added a bow and arrow during the bridge and ended with a full twisting back layout, it would have more visual appeal."

Joy smacked her palm against the table. "See, I knew it was missing something. Those are way better ideas."

"Not bad, new girl." Melody nodded as she daintily bit the edge of a cucumber slice.

A lull fell over the regular lunch chatter as a familiar scent tracked past me. A blur of purple and gold streaked past our table as the whole first string of the football team strode toward their reserved spot near the front of the cafeteria. I tried to focus on my lunch but failed. Alex had always made his presence known when he walked into a room, but before today it had been a lot easier to ignore the show.

They all assembled around the table, like knights gathering in the center of their rapt high school court. Alex swaggered to his seat at the far side of the table and effortlessly flipped his chair around, plunking down directly in my line of sight. As my gaze locked with his, a playful smile graced his lips. He pulled his phone out of the back pocket of his jeans, and his thumbs tapped away at the screen as he ignored the chatter surrounding him. He tucked the phone away again and nodded in my direction.

My phone buzzed on the tabletop. I placed my hand over the top of the screen and discreetly slid it into my lap.

> Alex: Are you following me? If you aren't careful, I might start thinking that the entire squad has a crush on me or something.

I slid my hand over my mouth, trying to conceal the giggle bubbling up from my chest.

> Me: Maybe. Or maybe you're the one following me? I was here first.

He pulled his phone out again and laughed at the screen. He glanced over at me once more, his head tipped down and his eyes sparkling across the distance as his fingers typed out another message.

> Alex: Busted.

> Alex: But I did promise that I'd text you.

Joy's eyes widened as I noticed her watching me. She

spun around in her seat and followed the obvious line of Alex's smile to my giddy and absolutely obvious reaction. She leaned across the table. "Um, what exactly is going on between you two?"

I put my phone on the table, screen down and my palm gently resting on top of it. "Nothing. He just helped me out with something I was working on."

"Uh-huh. Whatever you say." Her words dripped thick with sarcasm as she nodded. "That looked a lot more than friendly."

"It's nothing, Joy." I shrugged and twirled a fry in my ketchup, refusing to focus on the collection of stares around the table that had suddenly become interested in me.

"Have you told Kate about this yet?" Melody asked.

"No, why? There's really nothing to tell. Or is there some cheerleading rule that we need to get approval for which guys we go out with or something?"

Melody dropped her fork, and it clanged on the table. "You're dating Alex Chase."

"No, I'm not dating him." I shook my head and crossed my arms, hoping that if I scrunched up small enough I could disappear before I said something worse, but my mouth just kept going. "We're friends. Well, maybe. Like, I don't know if we're even friends. We've talked a couple of times. That's it. Why does it matter?"

Silence fell over the table as everyone exchanged worried looks.

Ainsley cleared her throat. "There isn't a rule about who you can or can't date, but there's kind of an unspoken one about who you definitely shouldn't."

"Yeah," Melody said. "And Alex is top of that list. He

and Kate have been on again and off again for almost three years. Every time they break up, one of them starts dating someone else, then miraculously they end up back together. How do you not know this?"

Of course I knew. Or at least I had an idea. High school relationships seemed to come and go so fast it was sometimes hard to keep track. Not like I had my own love life to be concerned with, but for some reason when Alex stared at me, all memories of him and Kate flew out of my head. Like some sort of magic spell. "Right, totally. But just so I'm clear, are they on or off right now?"

"Oh, definitely off. It's actually been about four months this time. Kate swears she's never going back to him and"—Melody looked around the lunchroom then leaned across the table, lowering her voice—"I heard from a guy who has a locker next to Alex in gym that he broke up with her this time, even though she tells everyone that it was her idea."

"I'd watch what you say, Melody. If that gets back to Kate, she'll have us all doing burpees in practice for days," Joy said.

"Maybe, but if what just happened here gets back to Kate"—Melody picked her fork off the table, stabbed a cherry tomato, then pointed it at me—"I'm sure she'll be in for much, much worse."

17

I fell through the front door with dinner already over. The dishes were cleared, and everyone had moved on with their lives without me—again. I had warned everyone that I would be late, as practices were ramping up for the state competition, but unfortunately, everyone else's plans couldn't wait. No surprise. But it would be nice if someone hung around to hear about my day for once.

The emptiness of the house pressed heavy on my tired shoulders as I collected a plate of leftovers and holed up in my room, trying and failing to concentrate on the math homework I should've finished in class.

Eventually, commotion drifted up the stairs as my family returned in shifts. Footsteps in the kitchen. Cupboards slamming shut. Conversations muffled and far away. I blinked as I lifted my head off the floor, the pattern of the carpet weave imprinted on my cheek and a blue sticky note stuck in my hair. I must've fallen asleep somewhere between the quadratic formula and the law of zero product property.

I slid my phone closer and tapped on the screen. The bright light hurt my eyes as I scanned the list of group chat messages. Looked like Jaida and Hailey wanted to meet up for a study date, which I totally would've wanted to join but clearly completely missed. I hovered my finger over the screen to respond, but the 9:37 at the top blared too bright to be ignored. I didn't have much time. If I responded, I'd probably get lured into a full chat session, which I kind of craved but knew I wouldn't be able to follow through on.

Instead, I slowly peeled myself off the floor and piled my books on my nightstand, fighting the half-asleep dizziness as I pulled up on my knees. Hopefully, I could squeeze in a few minutes between practice and first period to finish my homework. Or maybe someone on the squad could help me with the answers. A little help couldn't hurt, right? It's not like I was asking someone to write my midterm for me or something. Just until I figured out a better balance. I'd been a full member on the squad for almost two weeks and I still hadn't figured it out.

I stretched my arms over my head, enjoying the pull in my sides, then immediately flipped into packing mode. The faster we sped through November, the faster the temperature dropped, especially at night. I opened up my backpack and shoved in extra woolly socks, my Lions hoodie, and even a beanie. My wolf ran hot, but as soon as the fur fell away, I was always freezing. But it helped to keep me awake until I got home.

A soft knock rapped on the door. I kicked my backpack under my bed and slid back against my headboard, pulling my algebra notebook onto my lap.

The door eased open as Mama popped her head in. "Hey, are you still up?"

"Yeah, I'm just studying."

She pushed the door open wider and sidestepped into the room, a laundry basket balanced on her hip. "Look at you, my little scholar."

"Yep. That's me." I laughed to ease the tension in my chest. Lately, it seemed like I hadn't had much time to focus on anything class-related.

Her face beamed as she dropped the basket at the end of the bed and ruffled her fingers through my hair. I leaned my cheek into her touch, and my eyelids fluttered closed, the scent of her rolling off her skin and settling my racing brain.

"Is there anything you want to tell me, my girl?" she asked.

I snapped my eyes open again. "What?"

She grabbed a stack of folded gym clothes and rested it at my feet.

"I was doing your brothers' laundry and thought I'd tidy up the clothes you had on the floor. But I noticed that some of your things had rips in them or were completely stretched out." Her face sank as she placed her hands on her hips and stared through me.

I sat up straighter, searching for any explanation that might make sense but drawing a blank. "It's... I..."

"Why didn't you ask us if you needed new clothes? I know there are a lot of responsibilities in this family, but that doesn't mean your needs aren't important too. We might not be able to get you anything fancy, but you don't need to wear torn things."

"Uh, yeah. I mean, you and Papa work so hard, I didn't want to be a burden." I regretted the words the second they came out. She'd given me the out I needed instead of being locked into the truth, but looking at the disappointment crinkling around her eyes from what I'd said stung worse than a thousand sprained ankles.

"Don't ever think of yourself as a burden." Her arms fell down at her sides, her shoulders slumping forward.

Looking at her so small, almost defeated, ached in my chest, my lungs tightening against my ribs.

"I didn't mean—"

As if on cue, my bedroom door opened wider.

"Mama, story." Tommy toddled toward us, carrying a bright-blue board book with a cartoon elephant across the front.

Mama shook her head. "What are you doing out of bed?"

He held the book up over his head, his eyes wide.

She sighed and scooped Tommy into her arms, holding him close to her hip.

"I'm really sorry. We can chat about this tomorrow, and maybe this weekend we can go on a shopping trip, just us girls. What do you think?"

"Sure." I nodded as she slipped out into the hallway, knowing that although her offer was well-intended, something would likely come up and that trip would never really happen. Or if it did, it would end up getting cut short by one of my needy brothers. The pain in my chest subsided as I remembered the many times I'd been left on the wrong side of a broken promise. It wasn't her fault. I knew my parents tried, even if it didn't always feel awesome. But bringing it to her attention wouldn't change things. It would just make them uncomfortable for both of us.

As soon as the door clicked closed, I swung my legs over the side of the bed and grabbed my backpack. With one last glance over my shoulder, I flipped off the lamp and unlatched my bedroom window, the chill of late autumn rushing over my skin. The magic pulsing in my blood arose for the night, called by the moon and drawing me toward my pack. My phone buzzed, and my screen lit up the dark.

Kate: Starlight Pond. Fifteen minutes.

Time to run. As much as I struggled with the lack of sleep, the thought of unleashing the stress of the day and breaking free of my quaint normal life, if only just under the nocturnal sky, renewed me. Like an energy drink pumped straight to my soul. No rules. No expectations. And for the first time in forever, I finally felt I'd found somewhere I belonged.

18

───────

The week passed in a haze of cheerleading practice, class, more practice, midnight runs, and trying to sneak in any amount of sleep I could possibly steal. By the time the sky shone under the Friday night lights, I could barely even remember what life had been like before. As Kate had instructed, I'd eaten, slept, and breathed our routines, and although there were a few bright spots of text messages from Alex and my friends, I didn't really see anyone and rarely had a chance to respond.

But it had all been worth it.

Being in Kate's circle felt like nothing else. Like normal life but better. Jokes seemed funnier when everyone laughed with you. When I spoke, people paid attention. When I walked into a room, people noticed. I'd watched people like me walk around Faraway High before, but I'd never realized how exhilarating all the attention actually felt. Like a sugar rush I couldn't get enough of.

"Okay, who's ready to cheer the hardest they've ever cheered before?" Kate shouted as we lined up under the bleachers before the game.

"We are!" the squad shouted back and stood at attention.

Kate marched up and down the line, looking for any infractions. An untied shoelace. A crooked bow. Not enough face glitter. Any little thing could set her off when the pressure of game time loomed, but fortunately, she'd seemed in a particularly good mood all week.

"Piper, the folds on your socks aren't even. Joy, your mascara smudged onto your eyelids. Melody, stand up straighter."

Everyone responded, jumping at her critiques. She continued until she came up behind me at the back of the line. "Melina, loving the ponytail curls. You should do that every game."

"Thanks. I used the wrist flick technique you taught me," I replied, as my shoulders relaxed at knowing I'd passed inspection. But I should've. Kate did my makeup, and I took every scrap of advice she tossed my way to make sure I met her standards. And it seemed to have worked.

"And you're coming to Tony's after the game tonight, too, right?"

"Absolutely. I wouldn't miss it."

She nodded in approval then returned to her spot at the front of the line. "Okay, Lions, let's do this."

We all rushed out onto the field, but Kate hung back near the entrance, and I nearly slammed into her as I cleared the bleachers.

"Whoa, Kate, is everything okay?" I asked as I side-stepped her.

Her face soured. "There aren't any water bottles. How are we supposed to cheer without water bottles? I swear you were the best at setting up equipment. Why can't people think around here? Nina was supposed to be setting up for the game, but clearly she forgot them." Kate cast a withering stare over at Nina as she finished positioning the pom-poms on the side of the field.

"Don't worry about it. I'll go get them," I offered.

"You don't have to. It's not your job to set up all the time. Now that we don't have an alternate, everyone needs to learn how to do things properly, right Nina?" Her voice raised at the end, but Nina either didn't hear or ignored her. However, I thought I saw her shoulders tense as she turned away.

"Seriously, it's no big deal. I'll be back in, like, two minutes." I started running back toward the school before Kate could say no.

"You're the best, Melina!" Kate's voice called after me, but I didn't stop to turn around.

I ran as fast as I could across the soccer fields and whipped open the school doors, a blast of heat tingling against my freezing skin. Tonight was the coldest night of the year so far, and part of me kind of wished the team might lose this game so we wouldn't have to perform outside anymore until next year. Even though we finally got to wear our long sleeve bodysuits and tights under our uniform, it did nothing to help the permanent goose-bumps I'd have across my legs all game.

The halls were virtually empty, with the sound of a floor polisher in the distance, and only every second overhead light illuminated the way to the gym. I propped open the door and ran across the room to grab the two water bottle holders outside the locker room. I hoisted them up. Fortunately, Nina had at least filled them. Otherwise I would've taken way too long, and Kate would've freaked out. Suddenly, the timer lights cut out, and the gym fell into darkness. I shivered as I quickly rushed toward the door, relying on my extra wolfish sight to help maneuver without seeing, but I still swiveled my head, half expecting someone or something to jump out at any moment. The eerie quiet didn't help.

"Welcome to the Lions' den. We don't mess around," I sang out, trying to fill the silence and calm my nerves. "If you try to step on us, we'll tackle you to the ground."

I repeated the cheer over and over until I finally navigated my way to the gym door. Turning around, I backed out in the hallway. "Welcome to the Lions' den. We don't mess around."

"Ah!" a voice screamed as the door swung open into the hallway.

I screamed back and dropped the water bottles on the floor, a few popping out and rolling across the tile. My heart pounded, and I slammed my arm against my chest to calm it down.

"I'm so sorry," the voice said.

"No, it's my fault." I closed my eyes and let out a deep breath. "I should've opened the door more slowly. I just wasn't expecting anyone to be in here."

"Me neither. I forgot my chemistry notes, and there's a test on Monday."

I opened my eyes and looked down as Sydney crawled

on her knees and gathered up the water bottles, sliding them back into the holder.

"Hey, you're back." I raced across the hall and grabbed the last two bottles that had rolled too far to reach. "I didn't know you were at school again."

She glanced up at me, her brow furrowed. "You're a junior, right? Melanie something?"

"Melina." I slipped the bottles into the holder and held my hand out to help her up, even though she didn't deserve it. I'd catered to her every need when she was a cheerleader, and she didn't even know my name. "I was the alternate when you were on the cheer team, remember?"

"Not really. I don't remember much about cheerleading." She took my hand and pulled herself up. "Just that it was one of the greatest experiences of my life, but I'm kind of done with it now."

Okay, that wasn't exactly the answer I expected.

"How are you feeling?" I asked.

She took a few steps backward, her expression still as confused as ever. "I'm fine, why?"

"That's good. I'm glad you weren't too sick."

"Nope, I'm totally fine. Good luck at the game or whatever." She shrugged and stepped around me, heading toward the main doors.

I grabbed the water bottles and rushed after her. "Sydney, wait."

She paused but didn't turn around. "I really need to go."

"But I've been wanting to talk to you about that night."

"What night?" She peeked back at me over her shoulder with a frown.

"The night you got sick. I wanted to know if"—*you thought it was related to the wolf curse*—"the hospital gave you any pudding for dessert."

"Is this some kind of joke? 'Cause it's not funny. Please leave me alone." Sydney stormed ahead and pushed the main door open, the night breeze swirling in.

I rested the water bottles on the floor and stared at the closed door ahead of me. What just happened? Sydney remembered almost nothing about cheer, or her violent illness, and I couldn't ask her about it. Like when I tried to talk to Alex or anyone else not on the squad about wolf magic. The air around me thinned, and I struggled to breathe. What did it all mean?

My phone vibrated, and I pulled it out of the waistband of my cheer skirt.

Kate: Where are you? The game's starting.

I glanced up and down the empty hallway, my nerves still rattled, but I didn't have time to figure it out now. I had somewhere to be.

19

---

ive, four, three, two, one.

The whine of the final buzzer hung in the freezing cold air as Faraway High racked up another victory on their way to the semifinals. Another close game, with Alex and Griffin working a final touchdown in the last three minutes, and then we fortunately managed to tie up their offense to pull it out.

The crowd erupted in front of me in screams, cheers, and rounds of high fives from even the most stoic fans. These key wins brought the positive vibes, and I loved it. I performed better when the audience came along for the ride. And on frigid nights like this, I needed any heat I could generate. Even the wolf blood in my veins, which normally ran hotter than the average human's, wasn't enough to keep my body from feeling the sting.

"Go Lions!" I kicked my left leg high and shook my pom-poms over my head as the bleachers began to empty.

Kate appeared beside me and threw her arm over my shoulders. "Heck yeah. Go Lions."

I laughed as she danced to some song only she could hear and started tossing out her legs like she was in a showgirl kick line.

"Did you need a ride tonight?" she asked, finally ending her performance with a graceful bow. "I brought my car, if you don't mind squishing in the back with Sunni and Tessa."

"Really? That would be great! Thank you so much."

She peeled her arm off me and straightened her ponytail. "No problem. I've got to grab a few things inside, but meet me at the front of the school in, like, ten minutes."

"Sounds good."

"Oh, and you're going to have to show me that shimmy hip thing you were doing during the third quarter intermission. That energy is exactly what we need in a routine."

I nodded, trying to avoid vibrating with excitement. "Absolutely."

Kate winked and headed toward the exit.

"Looks like you and the captain are getting closer," a voice shouted behind me.

I whirled around. Ainsley stood near the far bench, bent over and loosening her shoelaces before slipping her feet into a pair of black ballet flats.

"Doesn't hurt to be tight with the person who makes the decisions," I said as I joined her.

Her lips pulled into a tight line.

"What's the big deal? She's being abnormally nice to me, sure, but why not ride the wave while I can, right?"

"I get it. But we both know how fickle Kate can be. I'm just worried about you."

"Thank you, but I'm not going to do anything to upset

her. It'll be fine." I nodded and grinned at her, but her gloomy mood didn't budge. "Be happy, Ainsley. We're going to the semifinals!" I grabbed her biceps and rocked her back and forth until a smile shook loose. "See, I knew you could do it. You're coming to Tony's, right?"

She nodded. "Of course. Where else would I go?"

Good point. Anyone who was anyone would be celebrating with the team tonight.

"Okay, I'm gonna go grab my stuff and head over." I pointed toward the opposite bench and started to move toward it. "See you there."

As the crowd cleared out, the night wind set in, whirling around the field and teasing up more goose bumps on my numb legs. Or maybe the adrenaline had finally started to wear off.

I chucked my pom-poms on the ground and tugged my cheer bag onto my shoulder, unzipping the main compartment to look for a granola bar to squash my already irritating hunger.

"So you get to cheer another day, huh?"

I looked up. "Hey, you."

Leo strode slowly toward me, maneuvering his way through the other girls as they collected their things and congratulated each other on the win. He wore the swanky peacoat again. Either he really wanted to step up his style game, or it was just that warm. On a night like this one, that would be a huge asset. "Looking all fancy again, I see."

He ignored me.

"You seemed like you were having a blast out there tonight. I'm glad this whole cheer thing is working out for you." His gaze jumped around at the chaos surrounding us. It was always a different perspective being down on the field instead of in the bleachers. It was one of my favorite feelings.

"Did you come to the game by yourself?" I asked as I pushed up onto my tiptoes and peeked around him. "Where are Jaida and Hailey?"

"Oh, they were here, but they already left to score our regular table at Twisted Top. I just wanted to see you first and invite you to come along. If you wanted to."

"Thanks, but I already made plans. Sorry." I scrunched up my face and shrank myself down. "Besides, I don't think I could handle ice cream right now. Maybe some hot chocolate, but definitely not the usual triple-scoop sundae."

"Right. You must be freezing." Leo unbuttoned his coat and shrugged it off. "Here, take my—"

Before he could finish, a wave of heat rushed over my body as something heavy and warm wrapped around my shoulders.

"I could see you shivering from the field." Alex stepped up beside me and flashed his trademark charming smile, his uniform still on and his hair soaked with sweat or maybe Gatorade. "Thought you needed my jacket more than I do."

"Thanks, but I'm good. But it was sweet of you to offer." I slipped the varsity jacket off and handed it back to him. "Honestly, I'm fine."

"If you're sure," Alex said as he gripped the jacket in both his hands and pulled it close to the number on his chest. "I'll see you later?"

"Yep, I'll be there."

He nodded and headed off to the locker room and,

hopefully, a much-needed shower. Boy sweat wasn't better when you had a heightened sense of smell.

Leo rocked back on his heels, the chill coloring his cheeks a deep crimson. "So, what was that about?"

"Oh, that." I glanced over my shoulder and watched Alex walk away. "It's nothing. We're friends, that's all."

"Sure, whatever you say."

"What?"

He shook his head and waved his hand toward the team bench. "It's just… you've been friends with him for—what? Five seconds? And *the* Alex Chase is coming over here and giving you his jacket without even asking. That seems like more than friends to me."

"Weren't you just about to give me your jacket?"

"Um, yeah, but…"

I stepped closer to him and poked my finger in the middle of his chest. "Leo Moretti, are you jealous?"

"Of course not." He scoffed and shook his head. "Why would I be jealous that you have new friends? That's amazing. You should have all the friends."

"All the friends, huh?" I tilted my head to the side and peered up at him.

He dropped his head down and locked his eyes on mine, opening them comically wider. "Yes, all the friends. I know what I said."

I wrapped my arms around his waist and gave him a quick squeeze. No one would ever replace Leo in my life. Not the way we knew each other. How he could read me like no one else could. But Alex was completely different —bold, charming, and impossible to ignore. He made me feel wanted. Like I mattered. And it was probably more than friendship, but I wasn't ready to admit that out loud in case I was wrong. "Did you want to come to Tony's with me instead? I'm pretty sure half the town will be there tonight."

Leo hugged me back then quickly let me go. "Thanks, but I think I'll text Isaac and see what he's up to. I've gotta spend time with my long list of friends too."

He laughed then stepped away, his hand wrapping around the back of his neck as he headed off toward the parking lot.

I picked up my pom-poms and plucked out the few blades of grass that had stuck to the foil, then I turned to go.

"And Lina," Leo's voice called from behind me.

I glanced back over my shoulder.

"I'm not really surprised," he said. "I don't know anyone who could meet you and not want to be your friend."

20

___

$\mathcal{B}$eams of moonlight shone through my window and started their nightly walk across my floor as I lay perfectly still under the covers, listening to the sounds of my home going to sleep. Mama put Tommy to bed a few hours ago, and from the rumbling snores in the distance, both she and Papa had retired as well. Which also meant that Matthew wasn't awake either.

I peeled back the comforter and slipped my feet to the floor as slowly and stealthily as possible. Marco's muffled voice wafted through the vents as he played some video game online with his buddies in the basement, and for once, I was actually thankful for the noise, as it covered every rustle of my backpack and random creak of the floorboards as I snuck across my room. I still hadn't determined if sneaking out never got easier because of the nagging guilt in the pit of my stomach or because my new animalistic abilities amplified the sound. Either way, my heart pounded like feet on the bleachers at a big game.

After sliding my desk chair beneath the window, I

climbed up and slid the glass to the right, letting in a gust of cool air. Heavy gray clouds draped the sky to the north, and the world lay impossibly still. Eerie even. I raised my nose to the sky and breathed in. Smelled like snow. But it didn't really matter. The strong electric current of my upcoming transformation already pulsed thick through my veins. It could be a blizzard out there, but I'd still need to go.

I swung my backpack over my shoulders and pulled my body through the open window into the darkness. With a huge leap, I jumped over the naked shrubs near the house and crunched onto the frost-covered grass, trying my best not to fall.

One more task before I'd be home free, though. I wiggled out two loose bricks from the retaining wall surrounding the garden and squeezed between the shrubs to stack them in the dirt beneath my window. The branches picked at my sweater as I climbed up and slid the glass back in place. As the latch clicked closed, my shoulders eased and a wave of relief rushed through me. I glanced at my phone. 10:45. I probably should've left earlier, but if I cut through a few back lanes, I'd still make it in time to meet the rest of the squad before I completely changed. A few white flakes fell onto the screen and melted into droplets. I wiped the phone with my sweater sleeve and slid it back into my pocket as I tilted my head back. Big, fluffy snowflakes drifted around me. I closed my eyes and breathed deep, letting it trickle through my body to calm the beast trying to push its way out of its fleshy cage. *Not yet. Soon.*

"Melina? What are you doing?"

I jerked my head up and stumbled forward, my feet

sliding off the bricks. A weightless sensation rose in my chest as I reached out to stop my fall, but my fingernails merely grazed the stucco. I yelped way too loud. A guilty confession echoing between the sleeping houses.

I clenched my jaw, waiting for the impact, but instead of crashing to the ground, my shoulder collided against a warm chest. Strong arms wrapped around my waist and held me tight until I managed to steady myself.

"Are you okay?" Leo's deep voice whispered near my ear.

I pulled myself out of his grip and straightened my stance. "Don't sneak up on people like that. You scared the heck out of me."

He cringed and stepped back, giving me more room. "I'm sorry. I didn't mean to. I just—"

The lights in the upstairs bedroom flicked on.

"Shhh. My parents." I thrust my left hand over Leo's mouth and gripped his coat with my right, pulling him toward the side of the house.

His forehead crinkled as if he was questioning my sanity. I nodded toward the lit window, and his green eyes widened as he leaned closer against the wall. I eased my palm off his mouth.

"Are you not—"

"Shhh," I hissed again.

"Sorry," he mouthed silently.

Time slowed. Every second my parents' light glowed in the darkness dragged out into eternity, each sound around me louder than ever before. The light breeze winding through the treetops and rustling the last few dead leaves on the street. My anxious breath wheezing past my lips. My pulse thumping at my temples. I counted the time in my head. *One one thousand... two one thousand... three one thousand... four one thousand.*

The light vanished.

I exhaled and rested my head against the wall. The snow fell harder now, and the flakes covered Leo's hair and shoulders. A few even caught on his eyelashes, but he didn't bother to brush them away. The savory smell of buttered popcorn lingered on his skin from his shift at the theatre, and I unconsciously swayed toward him as I fought my mouth from watering.

"What were you doing sneaking out of your window?" he asked, his voice barely more than a whisper between us.

"I was"—I glanced out at the empty tree-lined street and tried to clear my brain enough to think—"I was just going out for a walk."

"With a backpack?" He jutted his chin at my bag dangling off my shoulder then gave me a wide, tooth-filled grin, except the amusement didn't extend to his eyes. They darkened. Like a light shut off in them too.

"Yeah. I meant I was going over to Jaida's. I couldn't sleep, so I sent her a message, and she said to come over, and if I woke Tommy, I knew my parents would slaughter me, and since they were already asleep, I just figured this would be easier." I gazed up at my dark window, trying to keep his prying stare from extracting the truth. I didn't lie to Leo. Until recently, I didn't lie much to anyone at all. It always gave me a burning feeling deep in my stomach that I hated. But with Leo, it wasn't so much to avoid pain. It was because I never had any reason to lie to him. We shared our secrets. That's what we'd always done. But now I had a secret I couldn't share. Not only could I literally not get my tongue to say the words because of the curse, but I had no idea how I would explain it to him anyway. He'd never be okay with what I'd sacrificed to get what I wanted. He'd never understand. "I didn't want anyone to worry."

"Why didn't you just sneak out the back door and through the porch instead of climbing out the window? It would've been quieter."

"Sure. I mean, maybe." My tongue tripped over the logic. "Wait. What are you doing lurking outside my house in the middle of the night?"

Now it was his turn to squirm as a blush brushed the top of his cheeks, and I doubted it was just the late autumn chill. "I needed to talk to you."

"You could've just called."

"I know, but I wanted to talk in person. I was just figuring out what I was going to say when I saw you jumping out your window. Besides, I used to come by after my Sunday shifts all the time. I didn't think it would be problem."

"Yeah, you did. In the summer when we didn't have school the next day." I closed my eyes and sighed. It wasn't his fault. And I kind of missed sitting with him on lawn chairs in the backyard, talking late into the night. Like we were on our own little planet away from the rest of the world—just us and a million stars. But that seemed like lifetimes ago, so why start up again now? "Is something wrong, Leo?"

"No, it's just that I've been trying to talk to you for a while, and it kind of seems like you've been avoiding me. Maybe Jaida or Hailey said something, and well, after what happened at the football game, I just... I really needed to know."

I shook my head. "What are you babbling about? I haven't been avoiding you." I had. "I've just been really busy with school, and the squad, and all the new responsibilities." Massive understatement. "Just tell me what's going on."

He dropped his head down, refusing to meet my eyes and sprinkling snowflakes on my black sweater sleeve. He cleared his throat as his hand slid over mine and loosened the death grip I held on his coat. "This wasn't exactly how I pictured saying this, but I really like you, Lina."

The pad of his thumb tickled across my knuckles as his long fingers twined with mine. A pleasant tingle rippled up my arm, surging from every place his skin brushed my own.

"I mean, not just as a friend. More than that. And when you called me out for being jealous the other night, you were totally right, and I completely choked."

He pulled our hands down to our sides and narrowed the fraction of an inch still left between us. "I've been wanting to tell you since before the first playoff game. That's why everyone was suddenly busy afterward—to give me a chance to be alone with you."

"You told everyone?"

"I didn't have to. They figured it out on their own. I guess no matter how many spy movies I watch, I still haven't figured out how to keep important things top secret." He laughed and glanced up at the sky for a moment then dropped his forehead close to mine, the heat from his breath falling hot on my cheeks. "But I guess what I'm wondering is whether you could tell? And if you did or even if you didn't, do you maybe feel the same way?"

His fingers trembled in mine as his eyes searched my face for an answer, except his words kept swirling around in my head like fireflies buzzing around with no logical order. Leo liked me. Like *liked me*, liked me. My throat dried up, and I tried to swallow but couldn't. If everyone else noticed, why hadn't I? Or did I? The last few months played in clips through my brain, each one building on the other to tell a story I'd been too focused on other things to notice. The way he always stayed behind to spend time with just me. The little touches. The intense stares. If he'd been anyone else, I'd have been blowing up Jaida's phone trying to analyze what it all meant. But this was Leo. This was different. Except, was it really?

"You don't need to answer. I mean, you can if you want, but this wasn't how I planned on telling you. It's just that it's been killing me not being able to say something, then after last night, I thought maybe if you knew…" His eyes fluttered closed, and his chest deflated as he let out a long breath. He inhaled again then opened his eyes, a sharp focus flooding into his gaze. "What I'm trying to say is that you're the best friend I've ever had, and I never thought I'd want that to change, but lately I've been wanting to risk it if there was a chance you might want that too."

A heavy seriousness fell over Leo's face, his stare darkening to a deep evergreen as his heartbeat quickened, the steady thump echoing in the silence of the night. The scent of him flooded my senses. Something sweet with an edge of yearning. He leaned closer, the moonlight casting his shadow over my face as his voice dropped low. "I think you know I'd do anything for you."

His words rolled, slow and smooth, along my skin, leaving a trail of goose bumps in their path. Before me stood the Leo I'd always known, but also now somehow changed. This new version stirred up feelings I couldn't comprehend. I definitely didn't *not* feel something for him, but was it enough for what he was clearly asking? One thing I knew in my bones was that he would actually risk anything for me. I just hoped I'd never have to ask.

I stared up at him as I tried to pin down words to say, my fingers instinctively swiping back the hair that had fallen across his brow. He held his breath as my fingertips traced across his forehead.

Maybe I hadn't really seen what was right in front of me?

The air thickened, layers of unspoken emotions wrapping around us like warm blankets.

"Leo, I—"

A shooting pain stabbed into my side, ripping the words from my tongue. I tried to fight against it, but the familiar feeling spread through my limbs, too impatient to let me have this moment. It was too late. I'd run out of time.

My knees buckled, and I lurched forward, crashing into Leo's chest.

He wrapped his arm around my waist, steadying me on my feet. "Are you okay?"

No, definitely not okay.

"Uh. I have to go," I said as I pulled myself out of his grip and ran toward the street.

As I hit the sidewalk, I glanced over my shoulder at

Leo standing alone in the dark, empty yard. It had probably taken every ounce of courage he had to be honest, and I just walked away. A punishing heaviness pressed down on my chest and stole my breath as he hung his head, letting me go.

Everything human left in me ached to stay.

But the wolf inside couldn't wait.

21

I stumbled through the fresh snow. The itch of my imminent transformation scalded through my limbs and burned deep in my chest with an ache that might consume me whole if I didn't let myself succumb to the process. Gasping the night air to cool me down, I sprinted toward the back road that would eventually lead me out to the clearing where I needed to meet the squad. Except I'd never make it now. Not without changing first.

Impulsively, I swerved and doubled back to the dead end of Granite Drive and the small wooded park that lay hidden at the end. Mama used to take Marco and me there when we were little to splash in the kiddie pool, but it had long closed for the season. However, as I rounded the final corner, the old changing house appeared, dark and desolate, the perfect place to hide for a few minutes of solitude. I forced my legs to push harder as I weaved through the large swing set and past the spiral slide until I collapsed against the far side of the building. The worn wooden siding caught at my sweater as I tipped my head back and sank to the ground, letting the fire surge through me to rage wild and free.

As I fell forward on my knees, I quickly stripped off my outer clothes then shoved them in my backpack and tucked the whole lot beside the battered electrical box. It wasn't the best hiding spot, but it'd have to do for now. The cool breeze nipped at my flaming skin as I dropped onto my hands in the crisp white snow. I bit down on the inside of my cheek as the rest of the wolf took hold in waves, rippling up my spine and through my arms and legs, over and over again, until finally, the firestorm in my blood receded. I arched my back, stretching out the muscles that I'd clenched so tightly. My hands vanished from beneath my body, replaced with my silvery paws, poised to run. I exhaled a deep breath, the steam circling my wolf head as my ears perked up to the sounds of the night.

The world awoke as my animal eyesight took over. Shades in the sky multiplied to depths of grays and blues I hadn't known existed, the intricate points and branches of the snowflakes falling around me visible without a microscope. The hyperrealistic beauty of this sleeping town glittered at my furry feet.

I scanned the horizon before making my next move. If I stayed close to the tree line, I'd probably be able to catch up with the rest of the girls while still staying out of sight. It would be a much longer trek than taking the highway, but likely a lot safer. It wasn't exactly that late, and running into my neighbors—or worse, a frightened stranger—might make things challenging if they reported me to the police. However, I wouldn't mind running into Mr. Floyd's annoying Chihuahua in this body.

As I raced around the corner of the changing house, a figure moved in my periphery. My heart pounded as I skidded to a halt, nearly falling forward but saved by my remarkable wolfish balance.

The figure towered in the darkness, tall and still, its head tilted down. But I didn't need the starlight to recognize their posture or the familiar smell of them on the wind.

Leo.

Had he followed me or just ended up in this same park at the very wrong time?

He glanced up and froze, his eyes widening as he registered my presence. But instead of leaving, he moved closer. Slowly. Carefully. Closing the distance between us to mere feet, until he finally stopped and straightened his stance.

What did he think he was doing? Didn't he know it wasn't safe to confront a wolf?

I stepped forward and bared my sharp canines, hoping he'd run and get out of my way, but he stood still. Maybe he was trying to play dead or thought I'd be like a Tyrannosaurus rex and somehow not notice him if he didn't move. He had made me sit through a lot of dinosaur movies.

I inched closer, my paws denting the undisturbed snow.

He still didn't move.

A growl rose in my throat—low and primitive—commanding him to leave. To get as far away from me as possible. His body shook and the steam from his breath puffed heavier around his head, but he didn't give any ground.

Slowing my advance, I dropped the drama and held firm in my position. If intimidation didn't work, maybe he'd just eventually give up. I wouldn't hurt him. I'd never hurt him. I couldn't, beast or not.

Snowflakes drifted silently onto his shoulders and tangled in his hair as streaks of moonlight painted the ground between us.

Please leave.

He finally dared to step forward again and held out his palm, his arm trembling.

I could smell his fear. Stronger than I had in the cafeteria when I'd twisted his wrist and pulled him close to me, but he refused to back down.

Deep in my gut bloomed a powerful longing to lower my head and creep forward. To let him run his fingers through my fur. To let him see me.

My brain still hadn't processed his confession, but clearly it woke something up inside my soul. Something I'd maybe been pushing down for a while. But I couldn't think about that now. I was late to meet the squad. Besides, a vigorous run might be what I needed to get my head straight, and maybe even my heart.

But this stalemate wasn't helping. If he wasn't willing to stand down, I'd have to concede first.

I let out a huff as I turned and slowly padded off toward the woods.

"Wait," he called. "Please."

Without thinking, I paused at his command and dared to look back.

Leo tipped his head to the side and locked his stare

with mine. He held me there for a few moments, his chest rising and falling slower as he seemed to calm. Then an unexpected expression twisted across his face as he whispered into the darkness. "Melina? Is that you?"

22

The music pounded in my brain. Electronic drumbeats smashed against my skull as my limbs floated through the choreography from memory. Fortunately, the sideline cheers weren't much of a challenge, or I might've been in massive trouble. I tried to concentrate, but my head was a total mess. From everything that happened last night to the disappointed glare from Kate and the accompanying snarky side glances from everyone else as I snuck in seconds before practice this morning, my life felt upside down compared to the same time yesterday. Or maybe my anxious paranoia hit harder when I skipped breakfast?

Either way, I didn't make it to the meeting place before the rest of the squad took off for their run, and who knew what that might mean. I'd tried to catch up, but I couldn't track any of them. Plus, I'd had to head back early to reach the changing house before I transformed unless I wanted to be wandering around without my clothes in the snow.

Then when I finally made it home, I lay awake staring at the shadows on my ceiling as my mind focused on nothing but Leo. I tried to outrun him. Block out all my humanity and sink into my wolf brain that didn't care about getting caught or even worse, maybe, possibly catching feelings for her best friend. The only clarity I had as the morning sun blinded me through the crack in my curtains was that I had to pretend the whole thing never happened and make sure that no one else found out what Leo knew. If it were true that we'd all been cursed not to talk about the wolf magic, what would happen to someone outside the squad if they found out?

Kate clapped her hands as the song ended, piercing through my dark web of intrusive thoughts. "All right, that's enough for today. But just remember, the deeper we go in the playoffs, the less time we have to focus on our competition routine, so everyone should be practicing every spare second they have."

Spare second? I didn't seem to have any of those these days. But I was grateful that we were finally done with practice. If I ran, I might be able to get to Bean There and back for a breakfast sandwich before class started.

I bolted for the locker room while everyone loitered around the gym. Tossing my cheer bag on the floor, I collapsed on the bench and rested my eyes, my legs tired and my mouth salivating at the thought of the crispy bacon I'd soon have in my hand.

The door creaked open, but I didn't bother to look.

"Where were you last night?" Kate's commanding voice echoed in the empty dressing room as her shadow fell over me.

I snapped my eyes open and sat up straighter. "Uh… hi, Kate. I'm sorry… I just…"

The brain fog set in, and I forgot what words were. Fortunately, Kate's face softened, and she lowered her crossed arms to her sides.

"Is everything okay?" she said. "We waited until almost midnight for you. We were all really worried."

"You were?"

"Of course. We take care of each other." She splayed her hand over her chest near her throat, her glittery gold nail polish twinkling under the fluorescent lights. "Then when you slipped into practice late, I wanted to make sure you were all right."

"Um… yeah… I'm fine. Totally fine." I leaned forward and tugged on my laces, concentrating on every flit of my fingers as I slackened the knots and slipped my foot out, trying everything to push down the red flush creeping up my neck. I'd fully prepared for Angry Kate, but Concerned Kate came out of nowhere and actually made me feel worse. "Things just got a bit intense at my house last night with my parents and I couldn't get out as early as I'd hoped."

She sat down beside me and nudged her shoulder into mine. "That sucks. I'm sorry. Parents can be such a headache."

I nodded and slipped off my other shoe, shoving the pair into my bag. "Yeah. Exactly. Sometimes they hover too much."

Except mine really didn't. Maybe they should. I definitely couldn't be trusted these days.

Kate bounced back to her feet and straightened her athletic skirt. "Hopefully, next time will be easier."

"Absolutely. I'm sure it will be."

"Sounds good." She turned on her heel and marched back toward the door.

I exhaled, and the stray strands of hair around my face blew off to the side. Too close. If she'd known that Leo—

"However, it seems super odd that you didn't text anyone that you weren't coming." Kate walked back and placed her index finger underneath my chin, tipping my head up to meet her questioning gaze. "I mean, if you'd just let us know, I wouldn't even have to ask you about it today."

"Uh..." My brain spun in circles trying to come up with a plausible excuse, my nerves unsettled by this sudden case of Kate Fleming whiplash. "My parents took my phone away."

She slid the tip of her finger off the length of my chin, her sharp fingernail scratching against my skin before letting go.

"Must not have been that big of a deal since they already gave it back." She tapped the toe of her shoe against the front pocket of my gym bag, where my shiny purple phone case stuck out the top, incriminating me.

Heat rushed to my face again, but this time from panic over what exactly Kate knew. Because she definitely knew something. Or at least suspected it. "Yep. Nothing important."

Kate's eyes narrowed as she scanned me as if she had some sort of lie detector implanted in her brain. I held still, letting her scrutinize me but refusing to give any more away, at least any more that I could help. Eventually, she stopped and leaned back, pursing her lips, her arms crossed over her chest.

"Okay, if it's nothing, then that's good. But we don't keep secrets from each other on this squad, so I hope you aren't keeping anything from us."

"Nope. Never." I shook my head.

"Good." She nodded, seemingly satisfied. "Because I'd really hate to make an example of you to the rest of the squad. We don't like liars here."

"Makes sense." I swallowed and held my breath as she continued to stare through me.

Finally, her icy glare melted into a perfect smile as she held out her fist. "Go Lions."

"Go Lions." I knocked my fist against hers, suddenly feeling like I'd made a deal with the devil.

23

———

Sometimes a little protein is all you need.

After waiting in line at Bean There for what felt like hours, I scarfed down my breakfast and raced back to school. The halls had already emptied, and I snuck into my desk as Mr. Markowitz droned on about Congressional powers, but honestly, if anyone had had to deal with me before I'd put something in my stomach, it would have been a dangerous endeavor—for them.

However, it also helped calm my brain. Clearly, I'd been overthinking, obsessed with the idea of everything falling apart, when really, it wasn't all that bad. Kate might seem suspicious, but what exactly was there to fear? I got delayed. No big deal. It happened to people all the time. And the whole Leo thing. Who was going to believe that he thought his best friend was a wolf? He'd be laughed out of school faster than the guy who said he saw an angel in the parking lot after homecoming. It's not like he could prove it. I'd just need to be more careful around him in the future. All good.

I wrote the lines over and over in my notebook as I tried to manifest some good vibes.

Everything is going to be fine.

Everything is going to be fine.

Everything is going to be fine.

All my pent-up anxiety from last night and this morning bled out on the page in swirls of blue ink.

The bell rang. I capped the pen and took a deep breath.

Everything is going to be fine.

I scooped up my books and joined the flow of students rushing for the door. Of all classes, the speed of exit for History was definitely in the top three.

"Melina," Mr. Markowitz called from behind me.

I froze. I must not have been as stealthy as I thought when I slipped into class.

Biting down on the inside of my cheek, I plastered on a forced smile and turned around. "Yes, Mr. Markowitz?"

"Can I please see you before you go?" He raised his hand and waved, beckoning me toward his desk, then proceeded to sit down while keeping his sharp stare locked on me.

Bryson snickered as he passed, smashing his shoulder into mine. "Don't go psycho on him, too, okay?"

I let out a low growl, and his footsteps sped up.

Jerk.

As the last of the students exited, I made the slow march to the front of the room.

"Is there something I can help you with?" I asked, layering on my most innocent voice. The one I pulled on Papa to get me out of trouble for fighting with my brothers. However, from the stern way Mr. Markowitz's eyebrows knitted together, I doubted it would work this time.

"Had you arrived to class on time today, you would've noticed that I handed back everyone's quiz from last week, except yours." He opened up a cream file folder sitting on his desk and handed me the exam. A bright-red 37% glared up at me from the page.

My stomach hollowed as I stared at the numbers. I failed? I knew I hadn't felt super confident about some answers, but at least I had filled them all out this time, which had to count for something. But clearly not enough to pass.

"I don't know what's gotten into you lately. You used to be such a talented student, but over the past few weeks you've been barely paying attention in class, if you're not practically nodding off. When I call on you, you're not prepared on the necessary course material. Then today you walk in obscenely late, and now you're failing tests. I disregarded the first quiz that you failed abysmally because you said you were sick, but I can't keep letting you slide. Is there something going on that I should know about?"

I shook my head and picked up the test, scanning through the comments. As I read my answers, I barely even recognized the sentences. If I didn't even remember writing the quiz, it shouldn't be a surprise that I didn't perform well on it. But this wasn't me. I didn't fail. Ever.

"Melina, I'm serious." Mr. Markowitz waved his hand in front of my face, drawing my attention back to him and away from the paper in my trembling fingers. "Are you struggling with something? Problems at home? At school? I promise this is a safe space. You can tell me."

Actually, I couldn't. Not like he'd believe me anyway. I swallowed as my throat tightened, trying not to gasp as I struggled to breathe. "No. Everything's fine."

He leaned back in his chair and rested his palms behind his head, studying me a little too closely. Then the hard lines in his forehead eased as his visible disappointment seemed to give way to concern.

"Really, I'm okay."

He nodded, but his expression refused to fade. "Well, if you change your mind and need to talk, you know I'm here, or you can make an appointment with the school counsellor if you'd prefer someone you don't have to see every day of the week. But I really hope that whatever it is gets straightened out soon. You are better than this grade. I know it."

"Yes, sir. I'll do better." I rolled the quiz up in my hand and held it at my side, hiding the mocking grade. "Promise."

"Good. Because if you don't, I'll have to bring the problem to Principal Andersen, and that might mean suspension from extracurricular activities until you get your grades back up."

"What? That's not fair."

"What's not fair is you wasting my time and your potential. And don't think I haven't spoken to your other teachers. I'm not the only one who's noticed your marks slipping. At this rate, you'll be repeating this semester in summer school."

Summer school? Seriously? There was no way I'd allow myself to be hanging out here all summer break. "It won't happen again."

"Okay then. Glad to hear it. You may go." He waved

toward the door as if I'd forgotten where it was, but in that moment it was the only thing I could think about.

I rushed away as quickly as possible without breaking into a full-out run.

"And Melina," he called as I'd almost made my escape. "Make sure you have your parents sign your quiz and return it to me by the end of the day tomorrow."

ay too many people were in the library for lunchtime. Even I didn't go to the library in my free time, and I'd been on the honor roll for the past two years. Except maybe not this year. Fortunately, the row in the back corner of the stacks, the place where all the sunlight in the room went to die, sat empty as if waiting for me. I chucked my backpack across the floor and let it slide to the end of the aisle, slamming into the bookshelf and rattling the metal dividers.

Gripping the sides of my head, I dropped cross-legged onto the floor and stared up at the beige ceiling tiles. The last scrap of optimism I'd had when I left first period had completely vanished the second I walked into the cafeteria. I'd been so distracted by the prospect of summer school, I didn't think about the moment when my two worlds would collide. Or worse, crashed and burned into each other like speeding cars, on fire, playing chicken. Leo, Jaida, Isaac, and Hailey on one side of the room with my old seat still sitting empty, and the squad with Kate sucking all the attention like light into a black hole on the other. Whatever choice I made left me vulnerable to suspicion from the opposite side—and I really didn't like those odds. So I chose the third door, which meant hiding in the stacks until the bell rang. It should all blow over in a day or two anyway.

I sensed him before he approached. The sound of his footfalls on the carpet, the right side slightly louder than the left. His citrusy scent, like fresh grapefruit and limes layered on top of his own unique smell. The charge in the air as he closed the gap between us and his silhouette darkened over me.

"How did you even find me?" I asked without turning my head.

"You mean after you practically threw your cafeteria tray across the room and bolted when I saw you?" Leo stood facing me, the toes of our sneakers touching as he leaned above my head, his biceps flexing against the thin cotton of his gray T-shirt as he grabbed hold of an upper shelf to keep his balance. His sandy-blond hair flopped forward, and I fought the urge to reach up and swipe it back. But something seemed off today. He was missing his smile. Leo always smiled when he saw me, even just the slightest upturn of his lips, like his own silent hello. Something I realized I'd taken for granted until now.

"Well, I tried the normal places then realized that you probably didn't want to be found, so I needed to look in the least likely places you'd be, and that left here, the band room, or your house, but I knew you wouldn't bother with the last one because you'd have to face your mom and explain why you were skipping school, and there was no way you'd do that."

I hung my head. Of course he'd know. "I'm not skipping class, you know. It's lunchtime."

"But you thought about it to avoid running into me, didn't you?" He pushed off the shelf and eased down beside me on the floor, his hands wedged between his bent knees.

"Of course not. I've just had a rough morning and needed some quiet to think. This has nothing to do with you." I leaned closer and rested my head on his shoulder.

He didn't look up, simply stared at his thumbs as he crossed them and uncrossed them, his silence more unnerving than anything I thought he might say. Besides, he'd said so much last night he might not have anything left. Or maybe the dark circles under his eyes explained his hushed tongue. He looked even more exhausted than I felt.

I'd replayed last night on repeat so many times the memory might wear out soon. Every word he'd said, every longing look, and I still didn't know what to say. I'd let myself focus on the part where he stood in the snow and called out to my wolf, but was that just a distraction to avoid the harsh reality that Leo and I would never be the same again? My entire life had changed in one night, and I hadn't adjusted to that yet. I couldn't lose my best friend too. Not now. Except it might already be too late.

"Do you hate me because I ran off last night?" I said, finally breaking the silence. "I'm so sorry. I just wasn't expecting you, and I really had to go."

He sighed and closed his eyes tight, still refusing to look at me. "I could never hate you, Lina. But that doesn't mean I'm not mad. Why didn't you tell me you were in trouble?"

There it was. At least he'd confronted me in private instead of in front of our friends, or worse, the entire school. I'd still hung onto the hope that he'd think the whole thing was too crazy to be true, but at least I had a chance to shut it all down.

I sat up straight again and feigned ignorance. Maybe if I didn't react he could think he imagined the whole thing and drop it, saving us both the humiliation. "Who told you I failed my history quiz?"

"Please don't play games with me. It already hurts that you kept all this a secret, but I know what I saw. I'm not blind."

My throat tightened. "I don't know what you're talking about."

"Oh, really." He shifted to the side and pulled his cell phone out of his back pocket. His fingers jabbed at the brightly colored icons, then he held it up to me. "How do you explain this?"

A shaky video flashed across the screen. Though the quality was blurred by the darkness, the bluish moonlight illuminated the slide and swings at the park near my house. I clutched my arm across my stomach as the camera closed in on the thicket of trees and something moved in the bottom of the frame. It grew closer, larger, in the dim light. The light-gray fur rippled across its shoulders as it padded slowly through the fresh snow.

My hand shot up to my mouth as the wolf stopped and the camera focused on its yellow eyes piercing through the night. The stare ripped through me. I knew that look. An unfamiliar face, but the expression was mine. This was wolf me. What I really looked like from the outside.

The wolf moved silently toward the empty park pool

and behind the changing house. My body shook as the video of the building dragged on, knowing full well how this movie would end but still feeling the reality of it shatter over my head as I watched myself, my human self, walk out from behind the building with my backpack as I ran out of the frame toward my house.

Leo yanked the phone away and stuffed it in his pocket. "Now tell me you don't know what I'm talking about."

Warm saliva gathered in my mouth, and I swallowed hard to avoid throwing up all over the library carpet. Not only did Leo know, he had proof.

"Who have you shown this to?" I asked as I tried to keep my voice from shaking.

"Does it matter?"

"Of course it matters. You can't show anyone. Delete it. Please."

His face hardened. "Why, so you can protect your precious cheerleading squad?"

"What makes you think that any of this has to do with cheerleading?"

"Why wouldn't it? You've been completely sketchy since you started on the team. Plus, in case you forgot, I live down the street from both Charlotte and Melody. As soon as I saw you do"—he flailed his arm in the air like he was casting his own magic spell—"whatever it is you did, I couldn't sleep, so I sat on my front porch to clear my head. Both of them came home just before dawn too. I doubt that's just a coincidence."

I pushed myself off the floor and started to pace. The shelves seemed to close in around us, constricting tighter and tighter.

"Is this why you've been avoiding everyone lately? Because you've been trying to hide what's going on? You know you could've told me. I would've tried to help. You don't need to do this on your own."

"So what? You videotaped a wolf walking through the park and then me walking away. It means nothing. For all I know, you could've just edited that footage." I thrust my hands onto my hips and tried to hold strong in my deceitful conviction. We both knew it was real, but I had to make this disaster stop. "Maybe the better question is why you were following me. A little creepy, don't you think?"

His body stiffened, his jaw clenching hard as he turned his head away from me, absorbing my disrespect like a slap across the face. "Because I actually care about you."

My knees quivered. I'd gone too far. "I'm sorry, I didn't mean—"

"Didn't you?" He rolled his eyes and stood, backing up a few deliberate steps. "I know cheerleading is important to you, but keeping their secrets is going to bite you back one day. What's going to happen when they realize they don't need you anymore and you're already in too deep?"

"That's not going to happen."

He shook his head and started toward the exit. "Sure. We'll see."

I lunged forward and grabbed his hand, holding him in place. "It's not that I don't want to tell you what's going on. I can't. I literally can't, Leo."

"Whatever." He wriggled his hand from my grip. "And if you ever find time, call Jaida. She's been pretty upset at how you've been ditching her too. Especially since we both know you didn't really go to her house last night like you said you were."

"Hey, I didn't—"

Leo turned away and tossed his hand through the air. "Save the excuses, Lina. If you ever want to tell me what's going on, you know how to find me."

I stepped forward, a plea to stay on the tip of my tongue, but I swallowed it down. It wouldn't matter. I couldn't make this better unless I told him the whole story. He deserved that, but I couldn't give it to him.

As I watched him walk away, a tightness curled around my lungs, stealing my breath. I didn't want to lose him, so instead I chose to push him away. Except now that it was done, I wasn't sure that's what I really wanted.

My phone vibrated in my pocket.

Alex: Where's my lucky charm hiding?
Hoped to see you at lunch.

I stared at my screen, my finger hovering, trying to find the words to type back. Except there weren't any that matched his flirty tone. Not any that were true. Everything had suddenly gotten extremely complicated, and managing Leo proved to be more challenging than I'd thought. Not only did I have to make sure he kept the squad's secret, I couldn't forget his unexpected confession either. Snippets of last night had crept into my brain all morning. The harder I tried to push them down, the more they squished out the sides like a marshmallow in a s'more and snuck back to the surface, exposing things I didn't know how to process.

But it didn't matter anymore. After what I'd said and my disastrous attempt at gaslighting him, he'd probably take back every raw and delicate word he'd said to me, if given the chance. If he did, it would make things easier for both of us. He wouldn't have to risk getting dragged into all my drama, and I wouldn't have to risk telling him the truth.

25

A blast of warmth mixed with espresso and a hint of cinnamon tingled against my cold cheeks as I slipped into Bean There from the frost-covered sidewalk. My mouth watered as I gazed at the bakery display and all the delicious fall-themed treats in various combinations of pumpkin, caramel, and mulled cider. Coffee shops in autumn knew exactly how to hit their market. Seven-dollar lattes wrapped in cozy flannel blanket vibes—and I was a sucker for it every single year.

I was about to join the line when I heard someone call my name over the indie folk music wafting from the in-ceiling speakers. Jaida sat tucked in our usual corner, two paper cups already laid out on the table in front of her. She raised a hand and waved me over.

Leo still hadn't spoken to me since Monday morning, and I didn't blame him, but his warning about Jaida stuck in my head. I'd already made such a mess of things I didn't need to risk losing more friends. Even if I couldn't tell her everything, I needed to try to mend our broken relationship, or I'd lose her forever too.

"Hey," I said, as I slid into the chair beside her. This was supposed to be my apology to her, but in true Jaida style, she'd arrived early and already taken care of everything. Not only did she have my drink order, she had a carefully placed napkin for when I inevitably spilled a few drops on the table and a stir stick so I could mix the whipped cream into the mocha to make it creamier. If only I'd been as thoughtful toward her over the last few weeks, I might not have a lump in my throat when trying to talk to one of my best friends.

I rummaged through my backpack for my wallet. "How much do I owe you?"

"Don't worry about it. Consider it a belated 'congratulations for getting your big break' gift," she said, waving me off. "We haven't talked much since then, or I would've told you sooner."

"Thanks. But you really didn't have to." I stirred my drink, hypnotized as the whipped cream folded into the hot liquid, letting her words sting in my chest. She didn't sound angry, but it didn't change the ache of hearing her say it out loud. I'd been a bad friend.

"So…" She leaned back in her chair and crossed her legs, her own cup dangling precariously from her hand. "Did you invite me here just to stare at each other, or did you want to tell me all about your exciting new life? Give me all the details. What's been going on?"

"Nothing too exciting. Mostly practice, games, and homework." I replaced my cup lid and took a sip, letting the peppermint tingle on my tongue before swallowing. "I'm sure you have way better stories to tell."

She nodded then drank from her own cup as the silence grew between us, thick and stifling. She scanned me, likely looking for cracks in my story. But I'd been lying so much lately, I might've actually been getting good at it. Except Jaida wasn't just anyone. Her stare could X-ray your soul. I waited for her to say something—anything—but she kept on staring. My leg tapped as my cheeks started to flush. I gripped my thigh under the table, trying to force it to stop, but my nerves had other plans. Leave it to Jaida to wield the stillness like a razor-sharp weapon. The crook of her eyebrow insinuated that she knew more than I'd told her. The tiny methodical sips of her coffee. Even the hypnotic way she traced her index finger in a figure eight along the wooden tabletop was crafted in a way to make me spill my guts. If this girl didn't end up in the FBI, she'd for sure have a lucrative life of crime ahead of her. Normally, she'd have me confessing to things I hadn't even done, but for once the tongue-tie curse came to my rescue.

I swallowed hard and shrugged. "Honestly, my life's been pretty boring lately."

Her demeanor finally broke as she leaned across the table. "Don't lie to me. You suck at it. I don't know what's been up with you, but between you totally ghosting everyone and whatever happened to Leo—"

I dropped my paper cup onto the table, a bit of mocha sloshing out the top. "Wait, is Leo okay?"

"Who knows? He's got something serious going on, and he won't tell me about it either. It's like I'm losing both of you, and I don't even know what I did wrong because neither of you will tell me anything."

Well, at least he hadn't leaked everything to Jaida—or

at least not yet. Plus, it hadn't gotten back to me or the squad about the video, so maybe he actually did keep it to himself like I'd asked. No wonder he was losing it in front of everyone else. Leo didn't usually keep secrets very well. Keeping mine probably ate him up inside, and everyone else was paying the price. All of their misery was my fault.

"I'm so sorry. Really." I reached across the table and wrapped my cool fingers around her hand. "Kate and the squad keep me a lot busier than I expected. It's not as if I'm trying to avoid you, but I really do miss you."

I squeezed her hand tighter, hoping my one lie would be cancelled out by telling one truth. I missed her and the others so much, but not being able to say what I was thinking made it too difficult, and as I suspected, Jaida saw right through my attempts to dissuade her anyway.

"Are you sure that's all it is? Because it feels like you're keeping something from me." Her hand trembled in mine. "Or maybe you friend dumped me and were too nice to say it." Her eyes flickered for a second, her confidence slipping.

"I'd never do that to you." At least not on purpose. "Maybe after the state championships things will slow down and we can get back to how things used to be." Or at least I hoped so. "But we don't need to talk all about me." In fact, it was way easier if we didn't. "What have you been up to? The group chat has been a ghost town these days."

"We haven't really used it much. No one wanted to bother you since you hardly respond anymore, so we kind of abandoned it."

"Oh, I'm sorry. I didn't realize everyone was quiet because of me."

"Don't take it like that. We were trying to help you out, not make you sad. Honest." She gave me a big smile, but it wasn't enough to coax one from me, even though I did try.

"Plus, I almost forgot. Hailey's mom is taking us to Des Moines for her birthday next month. We're going shopping, then to the spa, and then we're staying in some fancy suite for the night." Jaida's face lit up, and she waved her hand in front of me with excitement. "I know she'd love it if you'd come. It'd be like old times."

My stomach churned. Of course I wanted to. Getting out of Faraway sounded like the perfect mini vacation. The three of us hadn't had a sleepover in months, and Jaida's basement wasn't exactly some swanky hotel. Plus, it would be so amazing just to talk all night long like we used to. But it wouldn't work. There was no way I'd be able to sneak off undetected for half the night.

I hung my head and stared at the chipped violet polish on my fingernails. "I can't. I really want to, but it's just that…"

"It's fine." Jaida filled my awkward silence, her tone edged with disappointment and a pinch of irritation. "She doubted you'd be able to make it anyway. It would've just been nice if you could, you know?"

"Yeah. Maybe next time."

A brick wall in a purple-and-gold varsity jacket appeared beside our table. Alex grabbed the chair next to me, swung it backward, then flopped down, his thick arms crossing over the top as he leaned toward the table. "How's my lucky charm?"

Jaida choked on her latte and nearly spit it out.

"Oh hey, I'm Alex." He stuck his hand out to Jaida.

"I'm pretty sure everyone in town knows who you are." She glanced over at me then cautiously took his hand and shook it. "I'm Jaida. Melina's oldest friend."

"Well, then I guess I better be on my best behavior."

"As you always should be," Jaida added.

He laughed and tipped back in his chair. "She doesn't mess around. I like her."

"Yeah, she's pretty great." I gave her a wink.

"So what are you two gabbing about?" he said, leaning into the conversation.

I looked over at Jaida, and her eyes widened. Whether it was Alex's charm, as he totally had that effect on people, or just the interruption, I wasn't sure. "Um, hey, so I'm excited to see you, but maybe I can text you later instead? I'm kind of in the middle of something here."

"Oh, yeah, totally. That's cool." Alex bobbed his head and released his grip on the chair. "I figured when you told me you'd be here that you wanted me to come. My mistake."

"It's not that I didn't want you to come, it's just that"— I grimaced—"I never get to see Jaida anymore, and I hoped to spend some time with—"

"Hey, Melina, Alex, what's going on?" Piper and Astrid shuffled up to the table, the tips of their noses red from the cold. "Mind if we sit here?"

"Actually, I was just gonna bail," Alex said, pointing toward the other side of the cafe.

"Oh no," Astrid said, as she made a faux pouty face. "I saw Griffin and a few of the other guys coming. They'll be disappointed you're leaving."

Alex glanced over at me again, probably checking if I'd changed my mind.

"You can all sit. I think I'm just going to go." Jaida slid out of her chair and stepped away from the table, her hands tightly gripping the bag strap over her shoulder. "I'll see you around, Melina."

"Wait." I jumped up from my chair and started after her. "You don't have to leave."

"Yeah, I'm pretty sure I do." She shimmied through the crowd and headed toward the door, and I followed close behind.

When we were finally out of earshot, I tapped her on the shoulder until she turned around. "I didn't know everyone was coming. Honest. Please don't be upset."

"I'm not." She sighed and grabbed both my hands in hers, her skin clammy against mine. "You've just moved on, as much as I don't want to admit it."

"No, I haven't. Really. It's just that…" I glanced over my shoulder at the table then back at Jaida. I didn't want to choose. I couldn't. Or maybe I already had and couldn't admit the truth to myself either.

"Let's not make this a whole thing. You've gotten what you always wanted, and that's great. So go. Be you." Jaida's hand slipped from mine as she turned toward the door, the sting of tears pricking in my eyes as her essence deflated around her. Like she'd made herself smaller as she drifted out of my life.

"Don't go," I whispered as I watched her walk away.

She paused at the door and gripped the handle. One second, two seconds, then she looked back with a glassy stare and a slow nod before sliding out of the cafe and disappearing into the street.

Her goodbye hit like a gut punch, stealing my breath and making the room spin. I limped back to the table and took a seat as I tried to shake off my second friend breakup of the week. Fortunately, no one seemed to notice my mood as Piper recounted the same story about her meeting with Texas Tech that I'd already heard four times and Astrid obsessed over applying a perfect layer of Dior lip gloss. Instead, I stared at my cup, swirling it around and around trying to make myself feel better. At least if she wasn't around I wouldn't have to feel guilty about hiding things from her.

"There you are." Alex nudged his shoulder into mine, knocking me out of my head. "Where did your friend go? She didn't take off because of us, did she?"

"Um…" I glanced toward the entrance, half expecting Jaida to come charging back through, but the door stayed closed. I shook my head and locked onto Alex's dreamy eyes. "No, no, it's fine. She just had somewhere else to be."

"Cool. Cool." He stood up and flipped his chair back the other way then sat down again. "Hey, I'm going to go get one of those pumpkin ice cream swirly things. Want one?"

He gazed at me like an excited little kid and I laughed. "No, thanks, I'm good."

"All right. But first"—he leaned closer and held his phone above us at a ridiculous angle, our two heads squished together on the screen—"show me that gorgeous smile."

26

"Alex Chase? Are you serious?"

I'd barely opened the front door before Marco thrust his phone screen less than an inch from my face. My eyes crossed trying to make out the fuzzy image as I tripped over the threshold into the house and closed the door behind me.

"What are you babbling about?" I snatched the phone from his grip and immediately recognized my own face grinning like a fool back at me. The photo from Bean There. Me in the corner with Alex's arm wrapped around my shoulders and him looking as ridiculously handsome as always, holding the camera out as far as he could to get us both in the shot, the shop's neon sign glowing on the back wall above our heads. We actually looked great together.

I scrolled down and read the caption, my cheeks tingling as they warmed from the cold. Three coffee cup emojis followed by "This cutie's smile perks up my day more than 1000 espressos." Ha! I could almost picture him saying the words, trying to make me laugh with that cheesy line. But this time it wasn't just for me. A nervous twitch fluttered in my stomach as I flipped through the pages and pages of comments that had already accumulated under the photo, which he'd only posted—I whipped back to the top of the photo—ten minutes ago. Had everyone in the entire state already seen this?

Marco ripped the phone out of my hands and shook his head at the photo one last time before the screen went black. "Please don't tell me you two are a thing now?"

I struck my best power pose as I attempted to wither him with my stare. "Maybe we are."

Except we probably weren't. Were we? It's not like we'd really gone on a date or anything, but now with this picture, who knew what everyone would think. Did I even want to be a thing with Alex? Maybe. The scent of him as he leaned in close still lingered on my skin, still intoxicating my senses and making it hard to think. Being around him always made my thoughts cloudy, in the best way, like living in some sort of amazing dream I didn't want to wake up from. I never thought someone like him would be so sweet and enchanting, and even more surprising, into someone like me.

Then the flutter in my stomach intensified at the thought of all the comments on Alex's post. Or was I imagining him as some white knight to force my own fairy tale to manifest into reality? Maybe I was just this month's clickbait.

Marco jerked forward, pretending to gag and making a disgusting retching sound to match. "But Alex Chase, he's so, so..."

"What? Popular, handsome, and charming? Three

things you definitely aren't." I put my hands on my hips, digging my fingertips deep into my flesh to keep from fully lashing out at him like we were still little kids.

"Melina, that's not very nice," Mama called from the kitchen.

"If he's that wonderful, then what the heck is he doing with you?" Marco shot back.

"Marco, enough." Mama rushed over to the front hall and waved a stained wooden spoon in the air. "Both of you need to stop this endless bickering. You'll need each other one day, and then you'll regret how awful you've acted."

"Doubt it," Marco mumbled under his breath as he turned back to his phone and shuffled out of the kitchen.

I took a deep breath and slid off my coat, my hand lingering on the hook a few seconds longer than it needed to. Alex had posted a picture of us, together, publicly. He'd put that out in the world, and I had no idea what it meant. If anything. I could text him, but what would I even say? *Did you just soft-launch us as a couple, or am I completely delusional?* I'm sure that wouldn't sound ridiculous at all. Plus, what would I say if he said yes?

"Melina, can I see you for a minute, please?" Mama's voice cut through my overthinking, and I shook my head before heading into the kitchen.

The spicy smell of peppers tickled my nose, and I swallowed hard to keep from salivating all over the floor. Even after the latte and a pumpkin scone, I was clearly still hungry. No surprise.

Mama puttered near the stove, slicing vegetables like one of the pro chefs on those food competition shows. Leaning across from her, I snuck a handful of diced carrots from the cutting board and popped a few in my mouth.

"What's up?" I asked between chews.

Her face hardened as she glared up at me, likely wishing I wouldn't talk with my mouth full, like she'd always asked. Except she didn't just roll her eyes and shrug it off. Instead she doubled down as her lips pursed tight. "Why don't you tell me?"

Uh-oh.

I swallowed, the bits of carrots cutting down my throat as I tried to figure out what she meant. Hearing that line conjured dread like a death sentence in our house. It could mean anything from robbing a bank to simply forgetting to put away my laundry. Except lately there were a lot of things I'd been keeping from her that would deserve the harsh shapes her clenched jaw was making against her cheeks.

I focused on the clock on the wall behind her and tried to keep my voice calm. "I'm not sure what you mean."

"What is this?" Mama reached into the drawer beside her and slapped my history quiz onto the counter, the flaming-red 37% almost glowing against the white sheet.

My face flushed, likely as crimson as my failing grade. I snatched up the pages and clutched them tightly in my fist. "What were you doing going through my room?"

"Excuse me?" Her eyes widened, and she dropped the knife down on the counter, a few pieces of onion rolling onto the floor. "Last time I checked, your name wasn't on the mortgage."

Okay, offense was not the best way to play this, so maybe more of a defensive approach. After all, it's not like I could hide it now. "I don't even know why this is such a big deal. It's just one quiz. I can totally make this up before the end of the semester."

She looked at me intently, her cautious eyes moving over me slowly, as if I were a complete stranger standing in her kitchen. "It might only be one quiz, but your teacher sure seemed concerned when he left me a message about this today. He said he's seeing a negative trend with your participation and effort in class. That doesn't sound like you. You're always so diligent when it comes to academics."

"Am I not allowed to make a mistake? Besides, maybe there's more to life than just studying and getting good grades." I winced as the words flew out of my mouth, fully knowing that they wouldn't be received well, and to be honest, I didn't mean them either.

As expected, Mama's mouth dropped open and fury lit her stare. "I don't know what has gotten into you, but it stops now. Whether it's this boy Marco is talking about, or some teenage rebellious stage, or whatever. It's done. Do you understand?"

"But, I…" I let the words go unsaid. The argument brewing on the tip of my tongue wouldn't matter and would only make things worse. Instead, I hung my head. "Yes, Mama."

"Good." She nodded and returned to chopping. "I've already signed the quiz, but I don't want to hear anything like this again."

"Okay. No problem." I slunk away from the counter and turned down the hall.

"Also," her stern voice called, and I froze, "you're grounded for the next two weeks. If it's not school-related, it's not happening, and you'll be on dishwasher duty until the end of the month."

"Yes, Mama." I reluctantly agreed and raced off to my room, closing the door behind me, careful not to accidentally slam it and invite more trouble.

I slumped down onto the floor beside my bed and banged my head against the mattress. She had every right to be mad about the grade, but honestly, she could've cut me some slack. Grounding didn't really matter much as no one really paid attention to when I came and went unless I brought it to their attention, and lately all I had was school, cheerleading, and then sneaking out at night, which they didn't know about anyway. But I always kept my head down and stayed out of the way, unlike my brothers, who just sucked all the energy from this family. Being perfect was the minimum standard for me, but not for everyone else. However, at least it was just the quiz. If my parents actually knew what I'd really been up to lately, they'd completely freak out.

My phone vibrated in my pocket, and I fished it out. With one glance at the screen, my chest tightened, the air in the room becoming thick and suffocating.

Leo.

The last time we'd talked, I'd hurt him and let him walk away. It'd been self-preservation, but I'd kept myself too busy to have time to feel regret over it. Had Jaida talked to him since our coffee date disaster? Maybe she convinced him to reach out.

With shaking fingers, I unlocked the phone.

Leo: You might not care, but Faraway
High cheerleaders have a way of
disappearing when they leave town after
high school. Just thought you might want
to know.

What did that even mean? Disappearing? Like how? I planned on disappearing out of this nothing town after graduation, too, but there seemed to be a more cryptic tone to his message. Or was he just being dramatic? Or did he not know how to talk to me now either?

Me: Uh… thanks.

Leo: Sure. Nice picture btw. You look
happy.

My phone suddenly weighed five thousand pounds as I considered how to answer. Obviously, he'd seen the post. Not that I should be surprised. But somewhere in the back of my brain, I kind of wished he hadn't. But why? It's not like I'd made him any promises. If anything, I'd avoided him since he confessed how he felt. Except as I imagined him seeing that photo, I ached at the thought of him hurting. He didn't deserve that.

I slunk down to the floor and spread out across my carpet, my phone resting on my stomach as I chose not to respond. Or maybe just chickened out. The setting sun streaked pink light across my ceiling. It wasn't even dark, and the itch in my limbs had already started. The restless-ness grew into a full-out need to escape. To run and shed the day from my soul. Or maybe my wolf brain could do me a favor and sort out the things my human one couldn't process?

THE STARS HUNG LOWER than usual as I navigated through the dark woods, as if they wanted to sneak down and whisper secrets about everything they'd seen, to relieve themselves of the burden of knowing too much. I shivered, thinking about what probably happened in this little town that I didn't even know about, especially now that I'd become part of a town mystery myself, but sometimes secrets were best kept quiet. A lesson I was learning real fast these days.

As the noises outside my door fell off to sleep, my body ached to run, escaping out my window and into the night as if by instinct more than design. By the time I hit the back roads, I usually ran into the other girls on their way to the meetup spot by Starlight Pond, but tonight only the silent, looming shadows kept me company. Of course, on the one night I desperately needed chatter to keep me out of my own thoughts, I couldn't find any.

I pushed my way through the low brush as the shroud of trees overhead thinned, opening up to the familiar clearing. Except instead of the usual high pre-run energy, the air sat suffocatingly still.

"Hello?" I called, but no one answered. "Kate, Sunni, Ainsley? Anybody?"

Still nothing.

I slipped my phone from my pocket and checked my messages. Nothing from anyone about a change in plans. So odd.

As I took a seat on an old fallen log, I flipped into the group chat and scrolled through to see if I'd missed something. But nothing. Melody and Astrid didn't say anything at Bean There earlier today either. Finally, I typed.

Me: Hey, I'm at Starlight. Where is everybody?

I waited. Three dots appeared and disappeared and reappeared several times as I stared at my screen waiting for a response, but it never came. I texted some of the girls individually, but no one responded to those either. The night started to seep into my bones, and I pulled my coat closer around my body as the unsettling sense that I was truly alone out in the woods crept in. Where was everybody?

A long howl echoed through the night, and I shuddered, searching the trees for the squad, but only darkness stared back.

Forget this.

I started back toward the woods as the burn of my transformation flooded through my body. Too late. I didn't have any more time to wait. After shoving my clothes into my backpack, I braced myself for the rush in my blood as the wolf took over. The strength, the power, and the freedom overwhelmed my human self and brought the sense of relief I'd been craving all day.

But even under the spell of my primitive, animalistic high, I still couldn't shake the vibe that something was definitely wrong.

27

I crept into practice fully expecting everyone to be staring. Missing runs with the team two days in one week probably would not go over well with anyone, especially not Captain Kate. She'd already been super suspicious when I missed the first one. However, even after all the messages I'd sent last night, not one person responded to me. They couldn't really hold it against me if I wasn't told where the meetup was, right?

"Good morning," I chirped as I dropped onto the bench and pulled my sneakers out of my cheer bag.

"Oh, hey. How's it going?" Melody asked as she finished tying her own laces.

I leaned closer to her and dropped to a whisper. "Did they change the meetup spot or something? I showed up last night, and no one was there. Plus, no one answered my messages in the group chat."

"Uh…" Her face blanched as her eyes flickered away from me. "That's so weird, right?"

"Exactly. So what happened?"

Kate's sharp claps cut in on our conversation. "Okay, everyone line up. Single row on the attack line. Let's go."

Melody shot up from the bench and rushed toward the group already assembling on the floor. I quickly finished lacing up my shoes and slid in next to Ainsley.

I nudged her with my elbow. "Hey."

She kept her stare straight and didn't respond as Kate marched past us and looped back to the center of the gym.

"Before we get started, Melina, could you please step forward for a second?" Kate crooked her finger and beckoned me toward her. I glanced down the line of my teammates but met vacant stares and a confused shrug from Ainsley.

I walked forward and stood on the center circle Kate pointed at, my shoulders pulled back and my stance as straight as I could make it.

Kate paced around me, her arms crossed while she tapped her index finger against her chin, her eyes scanning me. A bloom of heat rose in my chest as the pressure of her scrutiny intensified, but it was her eerie silence that caused my knees to shake.

Eventually, she stopped in front of me, with a wide smile breaking across her face. She reached up and straightened my ponytail then smoothed the hair down the back of my head. "My scrappy little Melina, I heard a rumor that you think my sideline routines are a bit boring. So I thought we could start by you showing us your moves instead."

"Uh… it's okay." My cheeks burned as I tried to glance over at the row of cheerleaders, the reality that one of them sold me out setting in. But who? Plus, it wasn't like I was the only one who said anything about the cheers. The majority of the squad complained about them constantly. Why weren't they up here with me? "I'm sure you don't really need to hear my ideas."

I headed back toward my place in line, but Kate sidestepped into my path and placed her perfectly manicured index fingers against my collarbone.

"I'm pretty sure I didn't ask you to show me. I told you to." She backed up, giving me space while keeping her stare locked tight on my face, then pulled her phone out of her back pocket. "So let's see it."

She tapped her phone screen, and the pounding beat of our cheer mix echoed through the gym. I closed my eyes and took a deep breath, trying to center myself before the first movement, but my pulse raced too fast for any sense of calm.

I started the first motion, focusing all my energy on perfection. There would be no room for error, especially with everyone watching me. The back handspring executed flawlessly. A toe-touch tighter than I'd ever done it. Finally, I let the muscle memory of the routine take over and entered the state of flow I needed to pull this off, adding my own spin on the moves. Kate's face hardened, and her condescending smile faded as my confidence grew with each step. I might actually pass this test.

"Stop!" Kate yelled as the music paused.

My arms hung awkwardly in midair as my heavy gasps cut through the silence.

"Your freestyle on that move is too suggestive. Violates National Cheerleading Association guidelines. Try again." She backed up the track to the beginning and hit play again.

Okay. I dropped my arms to my sides and reset, the

fire in my face burning even hotter. I counted under my breath and started the first step combination. The music halted again, and I stumbled over my own feet, barely regaining my balance before falling on my face.

"Sloppy arm work. This isn't junior high novice cheer anymore. We expect precision. Start over."

I reset again, but before the music came on, I broke position and stepped forward. "Are you punishing me because I missed the last two night runs? Because I was there early last night and no one else showed up."

Kate marched back in front of me. "Do you think I really care about that?"

I did, actually. Since she'd confronted me about missing the Sunday run, I'd been tip-toeing around to make sure I didn't upset her, but obviously I'd failed. Except if missing the run wasn't a big deal, and she obviously didn't want my choreography advice, then what was her problem?

I leaned closer to Kate and whispered, "Is this because of the photo Alex posted yesterday?"

A loud gasp echoed through the gym as my discreet accusation clearly came off louder than anticipated, or everyone's ultra-sensitive wolf hearing was extra in tune with the drama unfolding between us. Kate's eyes widened for a moment as her head tilted back, recoiling as if my question had hit a vulnerable spot, but she quickly slid her tough exterior back into place and glared. She eased up on her toes, giving her another inch of height as she towered over me. I stepped back, regretting not just taking her punishment and humiliation, as anything else would likely be worse. Kate's power probably extended much farther than any of us knew. Much farther than I could fight.

Her lips pressed tight together as the skin around her neck flushed a dark crimson. An ominous hiss from my pom-poms rustling in my quivering hands pushed my pulse to an unhealthy pace. My tongue stuck to the roof of my mouth as I struggled to find anything to defuse the incoming reign of terror.

"I'm... I'm really so—"

Kate stuck her hand over my mouth, muffling my lame apology.

I closed my eyes and turned my face away as every muscle in my body clenched tighter than the elastic on my game-day ponytail.

"You really think I care about your pathetic little crush on Alex Chase?" Kate pulled her hand from my face and laughed.

I eased my eyes open and stood up straighter as Kate backed away from me and started to pace in front of the rest of the squad. Her laugh got louder and louder until the other girls joined in—equally loud but far more clipped and uneasy.

I let out a deep sigh and held my hand over my heart as I worked to catch my breath. "I'm so glad you're not upset, Kate. But I didn't mean—"

An ear-splitting squeak cut through the laughter as Kate turned on her sneakered heel and stared back at me, the lightness fading from her expression again. "Trust me, I'm still upset."

Uh-oh.

Kate started pacing. "I'm upset because you're so desperate to be like me you cozied up to one of my castoffs, and next week when he's bored with you and moves on—and believe me, he will—I'm going to have to deal with you crying your heart out because you actually thought he liked you when we're trying to get prepared for a championship."

"Ouch," I heard Astrid whisper behind me. I glanced over my shoulder at her entertained smirk while everyone else stared at their shoes like Kate was ripping into them instead of me. Maybe they'd been in this place before.

Kate continued. "I'm upset because after all the things I do for this squad, some rookie thinks they can walk in after—what? Two actual games? And tell me to change my choreography."

"I didn't tell you to change anything, I only thought—"

"Enough, Melina." Kate raised her hand over her head and pursed her lips tight. "I've heard enough of your thoughts for one practice."

I lowered my head and concentrated on the colored lines crisscrossing the gym floor. "I'm sorry," I mumbled into my chest.

"After all the things I've done for you. I gave you a chance to be around the squad when you didn't make the cut. I let you take Sydney's place when she's a way better cheerleader than you will ever be. And I let you in on our biggest secret because I thought you were one of us. But I guess I was wrong."

"Then I'll quit." The words burned the tip of my tongue as they passed my lips.

Kate's pristine white sneakers appeared on the floor in front of me as the sweet smell of her perfume clouded my head. She pushed her knuckles under my chin, lifting my head up to meet her stare. "You can't just quit. That's not how this works. You're part of this pack until we choose to replace you, and I don't have the time or patience for that with a competition coming up. So I suggest you fall back in line and try to salvage the rest of your cheer career, or we can make this very, very difficult for you." She pulled her hand away and placed it on her hip as she jutted it out and posed in all her queen-bee glory. "Do you have anything else you'd like to say, or can we get back to more important business?"

I shook my head.

"Perfect. Now, everyone get into formation for our stunting routine, and if I don't see one hundred and ten percent from each and every one of you, we're going to keep going over it until I do, even if it takes all day." She clapped her hands above her head, and the somber group of cheerleaders scattered into positions on the floor. I shuffled my way over to the edge of the formation beside Ainsley, and she dared to flash me a sympathetic smile before facing front, her poms held tight at her hips.

"Oh, Melina," Kate called from the front of the group, her syrupy tone sweet enough to cause cavities. "You're going to sit out for this practice. Seems like you have a lot to learn about what a winning routine looks like, so maybe take some notes or something so you're ready to go next time."

I glanced around, but no one bothered to look at me, let alone say something in my defense. Even Ainsley refused to meet my pleading gaze.

"Quickly now. You've already wasted too much of our valuable time," Kate added as I dropped my head and trudged past everyone toward the row of benches lined up near the locker room.

I slumped onto the seat against the wall as the happy, smiling faces of the squad ran through the same standard routine we'd always done. I did the robotic motions in my head and tried to force down the scowl I wanted so desperately to wear. But what was the point? Kate was right. I was hers to command now. I was trapped.

28

For most of the morning, I tried to forget about Kate humiliating me in front of the entire squad. I didn't, of course, but I did try. I even sat in the front row in history, knowing I couldn't drift off into my overthinking doom spiral without getting called out in front of the class. Plus, maybe it would create a little goodwill for my next quiz.

Eventually, the clock ticked noon, and I couldn't hide in class any longer, but I wasn't even sure where to go. The library had been a bust last time. Plus, I couldn't just hide until Kate graduated, even if I kind of wanted to. Instead, I dropped my things in my locker and joined the crowd heading to the cafeteria. For the first time in a while, I actually didn't feel much like eating, so I grabbed an apple and headed for the cheerleading table.

As I approached, my shoulders relaxed when I realized Kate wasn't there today, or at least not yet. Except the traitor who told her I complained about the routines might still be lurking among the crowd, so I still needed to be careful.

"Hey," I said, as I grabbed an empty chair from the next table and scooted it between Ainsley and Joy.

The chatter at the table stopped as I sat down, and it wasn't like I didn't expect it. But if I wanted things to be any easier, I needed to confront this head-on. Kate had made that clear. I wouldn't be able to escape until she and the squad decided they were willing to let me go, so I might as well make the best of it.

"You don't have to stop talking because of me. It's not like I'd tell anyone or anything." I leaned back in my chair and took a big bite of my apple as the stunned stares took on a tinge of guilt.

"If it helps, I didn't say anything to Kate, and I don't know who did," Ainsley whispered once the initial shock wore off and the rest of the group resumed their yapping.

"Thanks, but why didn't you text me back last night? It would've been nice to know that I was being sacrificed to the pack alpha this morning."

She sighed and dropped her fork on her tray. "I'm really sorry. I didn't know she was going to do that to you. All she said was to skip the meetup and not tell you where we were or she'd bench us for the big game on Saturday."

"So, cheering in the game was more important. Cool." I took another big bite, my poor apple getting all my channeled rage.

Ainsley rolled her eyes. "You know it wouldn't just be the game. Kate would do to me what she did to you or worse. If you want to survive here, I'd suggest you play along and fly under the radar. If you haven't noticed, Kate doesn't like competition, at least not any competition directed at her, so just stay out of her sight and her business and you'll be fine."

Stay out of sight. That was something I was good at. I'd slipped through life unseen, and I honestly thought being a cheerleader wasn't just going to be my way out of Faraway, but also maybe I'd be something in this little town before I left it in my dust.

Except maybe there might be one person who still wanted to see me.

I slipped my phone into my lap as discreetly as I could, but everyone had already forgotten about my dramatic entrance. I guess flying under the radar was a true talent I possessed.

> Me: Are you going to Bean There after school? Did you want to?

I glanced over at the football table and quickly caught a glimpse of Alex in his regular spot in the middle of the action. Today his navy T-shirt cut expertly across his biceps, and I imagined how up close the color must make his blue eyes pop. Maybe he was a bit of a distraction, but it was one I could definitely use right now. He picked up his phone off the table. Almost on cue, he looked up, and I tilted my head away to avoid looking too obvious, but he didn't seem to see me as he placed the phone back down and continued his conversation. I stared at my phone and waited for a response, but it never came.

> Me: I'll get you one of those pumpkin swirly things. My treat.

I hit send, second-guessing whether I should've added an emoji or exclamation mark or something flirtier, but it didn't seem to matter. Like the last time, he glanced down at the phone then promptly ignored it.

What?

My stomach hollowed. Maybe there was something wrong with my phone? I scrolled through all my other apps, but they seemed to be working fine, then checked Alex's thread again. The messages now showed as read, but still no response.

My head instinctively swiveled back to the football table to gauge his reaction, except Alex was already gone.

"I gotta go," I announced as I grabbed my bag and bolted out of my seat, heading straight for the door.

"HEY," I said as I dropped my shoulder into the locker bank with a crash.

Alex glanced at me around his open locker as his backpack slid from his hand onto the floor. "Oh, hey."

I'd actually given up looking for him. I'd checked the gym, the football field, and the courtyard, and even buzzed past the main office, just in case, but he hadn't made it easy to be found. Then, as I'd resolved to just try texting him again later, he appeared, head down in his locker in the fortunately nearly deserted hallway. But not for long. Lunch would be over in less than ten minutes.

"I don't know if you got my messages," I said, careful to mask any hint of suspicion in my voice, "but I was wondering if you wanted to go to Bean There with me after football. There's no cheerleading practice tonight, but I could catch up on some homework until you're ready or just meet you there."

He closed the locker door and sighed. "Sounds like fun, but I probably shouldn't."

"Shouldn't?" I stood up straight, and he stepped back, maintaining the distance between us.

"Well…" He brushed his fingers through his hair and shifted his stare from my face to my shoulder. "This weekend is kind of a big game. Semifinals and all. I should probably head home early. Get some rest, you know?"

"Oh. That's fine. I get it. No problem."

He scanned up and down the hall then leaned closer, the intoxicating scent of him overwhelming my senses like an enchanting spell, his warm palm resting on the side of my neck. He ran his thumb slowly across my chin, shooting sparks beneath my skin like tiny bottle rockets on the Fourth of July. "You know I wouldn't miss a chance to see you unless it was important. But cheerleading season will be over soon, and then we'll have tons of time to hang out."

His bright eyes pleaded, but something still seemed off.

I swallowed and reluctantly shifted my face out of his grasp. "What did she say to you?"

"What?" he mumbled as he glanced behind him then rested his gaze on his feet. "Nobody said anything. I just need to focus if I'm going to get that scholarship to Oklahoma I've been working so hard for."

"Oh, really." I placed my hand on his arm, and he twitched beneath my touch. "Then why were you concerned about cheerleading season being over? Football has two more games at most. Cheerleading goes all the way until the state championships. If this were about your focus, then cheer season wouldn't matter. Unless you were concerned that a certain cheer captain might be a problem."

He didn't need to answer. The flush of red creeping up his neck and tingeing the tops of his ears told me everything I needed to know.

"Are you back together?"

"No." He jerked his head away. "Of course not. It's just that…"

I knew it. That picture Alex posted had rattled her more than she let on.

"Just what? Kate's opinion means more to you than your own? That's really comforting."

"You don't understand. Kate and me, we've got a lot of history, and it's probably better for everyone if we take a time-out for a while."

"Are you being serious right now?"

I tilted my head back, and it banged against the locker. I closed my eyes, trying my absolute hardest not to cry. He was the only person I'd thought I had left in my corner, and he'd still been compromised. If this were chess, Kate would have me in checkmate. Or worse, she'd basically have tossed the entire board off the table, sending all my pieces flying across the room.

"I'm sorry. But hopefully this will be better for you too."

The zipper jingled as he scooped his backpack off the tile, and a soft breeze whispered across my flaming cheeks as he marched past me, the essence of him fading on the air as he headed farther down the hall. Farther away from me.

I had to admit; the girl was thorough. When Kate held a grudge, she left nothing on her warpath untouched. I wasn't sure exactly which of my supposed sins had won her wrath, but now my only chance was to figure out how to fix it. She'd humiliated me in front of the team, and who knew what she'd said to crush whatever might've been happening with Alex. If I hadn't already messed up my grades and blown up the relationships with my old friends, they probably would've been next on her hit list. Who knew, she might even toss Jaida a well-crafted rumor, just in case.

Unfortunately, my only choice would be to play her game. Follow every rule to the absolute letter. Just like Ainsley suggested, I needed to blend in and get myself off her radar before she went completely nuclear.

Voices erupted around me as the hall filled. The afternoon bell was probably set to go off any minute. I peeled myself off the lockers and dragged my feet down the hall before the next period started.

Sunni and Astrid passed, and I raised a feeble wave. Astrid gave me a pitying half smile, then when she thought I'd looked away, she whispered something to Sunni that made her jaw drop. I inhaled deeply and trudged forward, lacking the energy to bother confronting them. It wouldn't matter anyway. Kate was untouchable and five steps ahead of me. I could probably march into Mrs. Lochlann's office and show her Leo's video and she'd do absolutely nothing.

I opened my locker and stuck my head inside, savoring the darkness. Maybe I could crawl in there and disappear into another dimension that didn't have cheerleading, or classes, or Kate Flemings. The comforting thought rattled in my brain as I collected my notebook and pens until it shook loose the memory of Leo's text. Cheerleaders disappearing after graduation or something like that. I whipped out my phone and opened the texting screen. There might be one person I hadn't completely alienated yet who could help.

> Me: Hey. I need some help from someone with your special set of skills. Unless you hate me too.

29

The school basement might have been where daylight went to die.

Even after I flipped the switch on the wall, the lonely light bulb that flickered over my head barely broke through the unending dark, while the other two fixtures leading down the stairs stayed conveniently unlit. *Perfect. Why couldn't one thing come easy for me this week?* I steadied myself against the wall as I took each careful step deeper into who knew what. My breath hitched every time the metal steps clanged under my sneakers.

On the plus side, if I ever needed a place to hide a body, I'd definitely found it.

"Hello?" I called out as I finally reached the basement floor.

Only the hum of the furnace answered back.

"Hello?" I tried again as I groped for another switch on the wall but failed to find one.

Was I too late? Today I'd been so focused on staying out of Kate's orbit as much as possible that I'd taken the long way through the freshmen hallway to get here. At practice that morning, I'd kept my mouth shut, stuck to the routine, and cheered harder than I'd ever done in my entire life to avoid getting caught on the wrong side of her rage. It seemed to have worked, as she chose to be annoyed at Charlotte being a half step off instead of berating me, although she flashed the occasional dirty look my way. If I delivered an impeccable performance at the pep rally today, I might even work my way up to being simply ignored, which was something I could definitely work with.

As I tiptoed deeper into the basement, the weak beams of light from the entrance bulb faded, and I held my hands out in front of me to avoid running into something as I moved farther and farther away from the stairs. The musty, stale air thickened and tickled my nose as I inched my way along until I couldn't stop myself and sneezed.

"Looking for someone?" a voice called from behind me.

My heart stopped. I whirled around and scanned the darkness but saw no one.

"Heads up," the voice called again.

A black mass flew from the top of a large cabinet and crash-landed in front of me with a loud smack.

I screamed and shuffled backward, smashing my calves into something hard and metal.

"Whoa, Melina. Chill, girl."

"You almost scared the soul out of me." I clasped my hand over my chest as my heart pounded hard like a techno bass drop against my ribs. "What are you doing lurking around in the dark down here?"

Allyssa bent her knees and popped up to standing, the

glowing screen of a laptop dangling from her hand lighting up the room with an eerie blueness.

"It's quiet, everyone leaves me alone, and it's underneath the server room so the Wi-Fi signal is super strong, especially if you can get up high." She stuck her hand out beside her and flicked a switch on the wall, illuminating the piles of dusty torn boxes and broken desk chairs scattered around us. Made sense why she kept the lights off.

She yanked her red headphones off her ears and rested them around her neck.

"Those are cute," I said, pointing at the glitter cat ears attached to the band.

"Yeah, I guess." She shrugged and closed her laptop, tucking it under her arm and showing off the large "Reality Needs a Reset Button" sticker across the front. "They're some new noise-cancelling pair, but they aren't that great. I heard you clomping down the stairs pretty easily."

I crossed my arms and glanced down at my feet. I didn't clomp. Did I? "I didn't even know there was a basement until you texted me to meet you here."

"It's not exactly on the campus tour, which is perfect for me. But I thought Captain Kate would've sent you down here to the storage room at least a few times by now."

"Nope. Cheer shares a storage room with the baseball team on the main floor behind the locker rooms. We don't have anything down here."

Allyssa scrunched up her nose and scowled. "Huh. Weirdness. I see one of your Ponytail Posse down here at least a couple of times a week."

"Do you even go to class, or do you just hang out in the dungeon all day?"

"Hey, it's my dungeon, and I love it." She narrowed her stare at me then glanced around the cluttered room as her lips twisted into a devious smirk. "But I guess it could use a little decor work. A few throw pillows could do the trick. Or maybe a beanbag chair?"

"Ha. Just add a big fuzzy throw rug, and you'll never want to go home."

"Yeah, right." She laughed. "Principal Andersen would completely freak out if he found me living down here."

"He absolutely would." I twined my fingers behind my back and rocked forward on my toes. "So… did you have any luck getting that information for me?"

"Of course. Easy peasy." She crouched on the floor and unzipped her army green messenger bag then shoved in her laptop and removed a beige file folder. "Here."

My hand shook as I took it and flipped to the pages inside. A printed list of names and graduation years, along with addresses and contact information of about sixty or more Faraway High cheerleaders.

"Is this for some alumni event or something? Doubt you'll have a lot of luck contacting people, though. Not one of them made it to their thirties." She wrinkled her nose and closed the flap on her bag. "So messed up, huh?"

The constant sting of uneasiness in my stomach intensified to a full-out ache. Not one survived to thirty? Was that going to be me? If Leo was right, maybe it would be. I didn't want to die.

"You okay, Melina?" Allyssa dropped her bag, the buttons pinned to the front clacking on the concrete floor, then she jumped to her feet and grabbed my wrist. "You look like you just saw a Level 80 Helltooth."

I shook my head, my pulse still pounding at my temples. "A what?"

"Video game monster. Super strong. Very scary." She sandwiched my hand in her clammy palms, her stacks of silver rings digging into my flesh. "Plus, you're practically freezing."

I slipped my hand away and crossed my arms, my fingers tightly gripping the file of dead girls' names. "Must be cold down here, that's all."

"But it's actually the boiler room..." She nodded and snatched up her bag from the floor. Her smoky eyes narrowed as she waited for me to respond, but I forced a tight-lipped smile.

"Yeah, that must be it. Totally feels cooler than normal down here today," she said, her scrunched face still looking unconvinced.

"Thank you for this." I held up the folder and fought to keep my arm from shaking.

"No problem." She nodded and moved to the side to let me pass. "But what was all that stuff in your message about me hating you?"

"I guess you haven't talked to Jaida and Leo lately. They're all kinds of mad that I've ghosted everyone for cheerleading."

She shrugged. "I ghost people all the time. No big. I wouldn't hate you for that."

At least that was one person I didn't need to worry about.

"Oh, I almost forgot." I dug my hand into my pocket

and flipped a gift card between my fingers. "Payment for services."

"Sweet." She snatched the card out of my hand and tapped it against her fist. "Ooh. Bean There. Nice. Love their White Mocha Red Eyes. They're great for all-nighters."

"Well, thanks for helping me out. It would've taken me weeks to put all this information together."

"No worries. Anytime." She slipped the card into the side pocket of her black cargos and eased her headphones back over her ears.

I tucked the folder close to my chest and headed toward the stairs. The pain in my stomach twisted its claws deeper into my side. I grabbed hold of the railing and dragged myself up the first step.

"Hey, Melina," Allyssa called.

I forced myself up straighter. "Yeah?"

She poked her head down from her perch, her wide grin and cat ears like a character from a kid's book. "It's all good if you don't want to tell me what's going on, but whatever it is, I can tell it's heavy. Tell someone before it kills you, okay?"

I nodded. "I'll try."

"Good." She nodded, too, and her head disappeared into the dark.

My head fell back as I gulped a huge breath and let it out slowly before hauling myself up the stairs.

If I could tell someone, I would. I'd give anything for that.

30

$\mathcal{E}$verything was flawless.

The pom-poms were arranged on the gym floor in perfectly straight lines. Water bottles sat filled to the ideal temperature of sixty-one degrees—not warm, but not too cold either. I'd even managed to hang the Lions banner behind the performance area all by myself and added purple and gold streamers to complete the school-spirit aesthetic. Kate should be pleased. Not that she deserved it. But if I was bound to her and the squad until they chose to be done with me, then this would hopefully be a step toward a less painful existence. Besides, it was like Jaida had said.

I asked for this.

I wanted this life.

Now I had to make the best of the situation until I could figure out what to do or until I understood what I was up against. I hadn't had the guts to look at the file Allyssa gave me all day, but the thought of it in my bag plagued my thoughts as I faked the image of the perfect cheerleader. Part of me hoped Leo's warning was simply a dramatic overreach, yet another part still feared it wasn't. No matter how mad he might be—which he clearly was because he'd stopped answering my texts—I doubted he'd mess with me like that.

"Wow, this looks amazing." Ainsley appeared in the doorway of the gym, her arms full of purple signs with "Go Lions" written across them in gold sparkle paint. "You even decorated the megaphone. So cute."

"Here, let me help you." I rushed over and grabbed a chunk of the signs, steadying the remaining pile for her so they didn't spill all over the floor. "I thought about what you said, and if I'm going to make things easier on myself, I'm going to have to play nice with Kate. If she has nothing to be upset about, then she can't take it out on me."

"A wise choice. Hopefully, this will all be behind you soon. I hate watching all this happen to you and knowing there isn't anything I can do." She laid the signs on the front rows of the bleachers then smoothed back the tiny stray hairs at her temples.

I stacked my pile on top of hers. "Me too."

"And of course you had to be super adorable in your uniform today." She forced a smile, but it faded a little too quickly.

"All part of the 'save myself' plan. Might've blown off all of last period to get each one of my ponytail curls perfect." Plus, the temptation to look brutally hot in front of Alex provided a bit of motivation as well. Obviously, I couldn't talk to him without derailing my redemption with Kate, but I could, hopefully, make him regret not standing up for me. It's not like he was bound by some magical curse like I was—or at least I didn't think so.

Ainsley didn't laugh or even roll her eyes.

"Are you okay?" I asked as I followed her shifty stare back to the closed gym door. "Expecting someone?"

She sighed and flopped down on the bleachers then rubbed her hands over her face, slightly smearing her pink lipstick. "I'm not really sure how to tell you this."

A heavy weight tightened around my chest. "What?"

"Kate sent me to tell you that she doesn't want you cheering at the pep rally."

My fists clenched at my sides. "Tell me you're joking."

She shook her head, the pained uneasiness in her downcast gaze confirming her words.

"Why? She's already taken everything that she can from me. Why did she need to do this?" I paced in front of Ainsley, but she didn't speak, just wrung her hands in her lap, twining and untwining her fingers, refusing to look at my face.

The gym door squeaked open, and the familiar chatter of the rest of the squad echoed around me, only stoking the anger bubbling in my blood. No matter what I did, it wouldn't be enough for them. I'd thought I belonged here. Like I'd finally found something that was mine, and it had all crumbled down around me. I'd lost my friends and my reputation to chase a fairy tale. I'd lost my so-called prince to an evil queen. I'd even lost my last bit of freedom, and possibly my life, to an unexplainable curse. I honestly didn't have anything left to lose.

The high-pitched whine of Kate's voice grated against my eardrums as I stormed across the floor and pushed my way into the center of the group.

"If you're going to bench me today, then just tell me yourself. Don't make Ainsley do your bidding."

Kate rolled her eyes and put her hands on her hips. "Is that any way to talk to your captain? This is exactly why I don't want you around the squad right now. You have an attitude problem."

"What? This is ridiculous. The only reason I have an attitude is because you've been treating me like total garbage. Humiliating me in front of the squad, silencing me in the group chat, even telling Alex to stay away from me, and now telling me I can't cheer. You shouldn't be shocked that I'm upset."

She planted her feet and stared me down as the rest of the squad backed away to give us space—or maybe to avoid any possible fallout coming their way.

"I told you the second you joined—which I made happen, by the way—that everything has to be for the squad, and your behavior lately isn't exactly benefiting the team. Sometimes as captain, I have to make hard decisions, but unless you're a true leader like me"—she splayed her hand across her chest as she batted her false eyelashes to her adoring followers—"I doubt you'd understand that."

I bit down on the side of my cheek to keep myself from screaming and giving her more ammunition for her constant barrage of cheap shots.

"Enough. What do I need to do to make you stop punishing me?"

"Well, I thought the pep rally would be the end of your penance, but after your outburst here, maybe you need to take the entire weekend off to think about your recent behavior and hope that I find it in my heart to forgive you and let you back in rotation." She flipped her hair over her shoulder as she jutted out her left hip. A total power move. Classic mean girl. "Or if you want to see how real cheerleaders act, you can come to the game and watch from the stands with everyone else."

"You're pulling me from the semifinal game? Seriously, Kate? If you hate me that much, replace me already."

"And let you off that easy? Not a chance. You made a commitment, and I'm going to make sure you uphold it. But apparently you need a reminder that I'm the alpha around here and not the other way around." She stepped closer, the toes of her sneakers pressed against mine as she used the few inches' advantage she had to tower over me. Her red lips curled into a snarl. "I suggest you stand down, rookie."

Her jaw clenched, and for a moment her eyes flickered a deep amber. Her other self. The animal inside that could tear me apart if she saw fit.

"Now run along before you cause an even bigger scene." She flitted her hand in the air, dismissing me.

I breathed deep then let it all the way back out. So many objections sat on my tongue, but I knew voicing them wouldn't make any difference except maybe to make me feel better. And they really wouldn't even do that in the end. Fighting with Kate would never work while she dangled me in front of the squad like a mouse by its tail, waiting to be swallowed whole. A message sent to keep everyone else from even considering going against her. Instead, I glared back as my final act of defiance and turned, heading for the exit.

"Oh, and don't bother with any of the late-night meetups either," Kate called after me. "Maybe some more lone-wolf time will remind you what it is to be part of a pack."

As I hit the hallway, waves of students flooded toward me, heading to the pep rally, and I fought upstream against them. I kept my head down as I pushed forward, banging into chests and elbows, garnering dirty looks from almost everyone. Tears prickled in the corners of my eyes, but I refused to let them fall. At least not in front of the entire school.

Hollow emptiness grew inside me, aching in my stomach, as everything from the last few days replayed through my brain. I needed to get out of there, and fast.

I pushed my legs to move faster.

To escape.

A smooth brush of skin slid unexpectedly against my palm as fingers twined in mine, my arm tugging back behind me. I spun around and glanced up at soft emerald eyes holding me in place amidst the chaos of the crowd.

"Are you okay?" Leo mouthed, his silent words cutting through the noise of everyone around us as if we moved in slow motion while everyone whipped past in double time. I hadn't seen him all week. Either me avoiding him, or him avoiding me, or maybe a little of both. The adrenaline rush coursing through me calmed, replaced by a familiar ease as my feet shuffled toward him. I wasn't okay. Far from it. But I didn't deserve his concern, and I definitely didn't want his pity.

I squeezed his hand and then tugged mine away. "I'm fine."

His stare lingered for a few more seconds before he turned and continued on.

The hole in my gut widened, and I placed my palm

over my stomach as I battled the last few feet out of the mob and disappeared through the bathroom door.

I gripped the edges of the porcelain sink, catching my breath as I stared at my reflection. The girl in the mirror looked different now. Not like the day at the Red Dog Diner when I'd been on the verge of something new but couldn't see it. Under the polished prettier exterior, I could now see the broken parts. The pieces of my soul I'd sold and would give anything to get back. I yanked the purple-and-gold bow from my hair, a few dark strands catching in the elastic band and ripping from my scalp, destroying my last defense as my tears finally fell. I squeezed my hand and slipped the cheer bracelet off my wrist then grabbed a scratchy paper towel to wipe away the gold glitter on my cheeks. All I'd ever wanted since my first day at Faraway High was to be a Lions cheerleader, but clearly that was a big mistake.

Red marks streaked across my skin as I scrubbed my face and let the tears fall. I gasped and sobbed and shook, letting every sharp emotion pour out of me until none remained. After washing my face, I stared at the girl in the mirror once more and vowed never to be in this position again.

If the squad wasn't going to let me go, I was going to find my own way out.

31

I swore I heard the marching band as I sat next to my window.

We lived close enough to the school that it was possible. Or maybe my fear of missing out on the semifinal game was just driving me completely mad. Even after everything I'd been through, my heart still ached to be there in front of the roaring crowd. Craved it like chocolate. Except I couldn't bring myself to be there and watch Kate's smug face as I sat in the stands. Plus, I had work to do.

Fortunately, everyone in the house had left for the day, so I wouldn't have to answer any questions about why I was hiding in my room when I should be on the field. Mama, Papa, and the younger boys were out of town at one of Matthew's tournaments, and Marco had to work an eight-hour shift. He'd probably hear from one of his lowlife friends that I wasn't cheering then grill me for the gossip, but I'd deal with my nosy brother problem later.

I chucked the beige folder from Allyssa onto the floor and spread out all the pages across my desk. Someone on this extensive list of names had to know how to escape the squad. I just had to find them. The names written in bold red underline shouted an ominous warning, and I shuddered every time I read the word "deceased" beside the words, "stroke," "aneurysm," or "cardiac arrest" where their address and phone number should be. Maybe no one ever truly escaped at all.

After forcing a deep breath, I dialed the first number on the list. Mallory Abbott graduated a couple of years ago and ended up on the Ohio State cheer team. I used to go watch her when I was in junior high. She had the best high kick I'd ever seen. However, knowing that maybe it wasn't all natural talent cast a shadow over those memories. As the phone rang—once, twice, three times—I curled up in my desk chair, my knees tucked against my chest, part of me hoping that maybe she wouldn't answer.

Seconds before I would have clicked the end button, a cheery voice sang on the other end of the line. "Hello."

"Uh, hi." I sat up straight and tried to regain my focus. "I'm calling from the Faraway High cheer squad. Is this Mallory?"

I already knew the answer. I recognized the musical lilt of her voice after just one word.

"Yep, that's me. But I'm not really interested in donating. Maybe try me in a few years. Thanks for calling though." Her voice quieted as she pulled the phone from her face.

"Wait, I'm not looking for money," I blurted before she could hang up. "I'm… I'm working on a project for the yearbook. A cheerleaders past and present kind of thing."

"Oh, okay. That sounds fun. What did you need from me?"

"Not much. But if you can answer a few questions about your time here on the cheer squad, it would be a huge help."

"No problem. Shoot."

I pulled a pink sticky note off my stack of papers and read my first question.

"Can you tell me about your experience on the Faraway High squad? Any special memories that stand out for you?"

"Hmmm. Let me think." I heard her rustling in the background. Maybe she was walking around or lying down on her bed. I pictured her living in one of the big college dorms. A place of her own. Meeting new people. Experiencing new things. My pulse quickened as I visualized myself there instead of in my boring childhood bedroom.

"Nothing really comes to mind." Her response cut through my fantasizing and grounded me back in reality. "I mean, I remember having a total blast, but it's all kind of a blur. It was just so long ago, you know?"

It really wasn't that long ago. Plus, Mallory made the squad as a sophomore. Three years on the team and she didn't remember anything? Or maybe she was trying to blow me off?

"I'm sure you must remember winning State? Or anything about your teammates?"

"Yeah." Her light singsong vibe faded. "I guess so. But nothing really comes to mind."

So strange. I absolutely expected her to go off about

winning State. In her second year, they had the highest score in over twenty-five years.

"You don't remember any details? Didn't you have any late-night meetups with the team?" I paused, hoping for her to jump in with some sort of reaction, but her silence responded for her. I took a deep breath. "You know. When you"—*turned into a wolf*—"played truth or dare?"

I couldn't say it. My real words stung at the back of my throat. The same tongue-tied feeling like when I tried to confess to Alex the day after I first turned. At least this time, I didn't completely humiliate myself.

"Nope. Doesn't ring a bell," Mallory said, seemingly unfazed by my leading questions. "I'm sorry, I can't be much help for your—what was it?—yearbook thingy."

"I guess not. But thanks anyway. Go Lions."

"For sure. Go Lions." She giggled then hung up, leaving me with annoying silence and far too many questions.

If every cheerleader for the past several decades fell under the wolf curse when they joined, why couldn't I talk to them about it? Did they just graduate and someone met them behind the gym for a brain wipe or something? Either way, if I couldn't talk to her about the curse, it meant Mallory wasn't part of the pack anymore. Just like Sydney. She didn't remember anything when I tried to talk to her at the football game either. I'd just assumed it was because she was replaced, but maybe it didn't matter how you left. You still lost your memory of everything.

I stared at the phone in my hand. Maybe I should call Sydney and try to talk to her again? Except she'd probably gone to the game like everyone else. Instead, I scanned the list and called the next name that was still living. There had to be someone out there who could help me, right?

"No worries. Thanks anyway. Go Lions," I said as I buried my face in my palm, trying to scrub off my disappointment.

"Go Lions," the voice on the other end echoed before hanging up.

I placed the phone on my desk and crossed off the last name on the list. Belinda Zaire. Graduated four years ago. Claims cheerleading was the best time of her life. Remembers absolutely nothing.

After hours of pointless phone calls, I'd still ended up in the same place as the first call with Mallory. No ways to escape. No explanation of why no one on the list was older than twenty-seven. And no way to ask the questions I really needed answered because being blunt wasn't allowed in the wolf curse playbook. Basically, I had two choices: convince Kate to let me go, or tough it out like everyone else. Neither option solved the mysteries that kept rolling around in my brain.

I propped my elbow on my desk, rested my head on my hand, then scanned the names again. What was I missing? There had to be something. A connection between the names that was just out of my grasp. I stared so hard the pages faded in and out of focus, the rest of the room blurring into a watery pool of color in my periphery. My nose itched, and I brushed my hand over my face. A red dot splashed onto my notes, making a spiky splotch against the stark-white paper.

What?

Another drop fell and stained the list.

I held my hand in front of me. A trail of crimson streaked across my fingers.

Fantastic.

Pinching the bridge of my nose, I leaned my head forward as another drop escaped and splashed the pages again. Perfect. I was probably getting sick from all this stress. As I stretched toward my nightstand, a wave of dizziness crashed over me. With a trembling hand, I snatched a fistful of tissues as I eased myself to the floor. I slammed my other hand on the carpet and tried to ground myself as my furniture started to spin. What was happening?

My stomach gurgled, and I winced as a sharp pain jabbed near my left kidney. I cried out, but there wasn't anyone home to hear me. The pain spidered across my back and dug deeper into my side until black spots appeared in my vision.

I grabbed onto the edge of my bed and dragged myself to a standing—or at least a partially upright—position then staggered down the hall, leaning against the wall to keep from falling. Finally, I reached the bathroom, bursting through the door and dropping to my knees. The ache in my gut intensified as I gripped the tub, begging for the pain to subside. Golden sunshine streamed through the tiny bathroom window, bathing the room in a warm glow and heating my already sweaty face. It was too early for the moon and my nightly wolf out. Besides, this didn't feel the same. I'd learned to anticipate the discomfort of my change, but even my first change hadn't felt like this, like my organs liquefying from the inside.

The torment pulsed through me, over and over, until it all pooled in my stomach and I retched, no longer able to contain all the agony in my body. I collapsed on the floor, the cool tile against my forehead relieving a bit of the burn on my skin. But the pain didn't stop. It slowed for a moment but rebounded for a round two, and I doubted I'd win that fight.

I closed my eyes and tried to focus on what to do next. But my brain was too raw. Broken. For the first time in weeks, I'd barely eaten, so it couldn't be food poisoning. Or maybe it could. Who knew? Or maybe I'd caught a virus at school. But I hadn't heard of too many people out sick. Only Sydney.

My throat tightened, stealing my breath.

Sydney had been a mess just like this. Her terrified face flashed in my brain. Images of her folded over on the ground, hanging on to the side of a garbage can as her body betrayed her, like mine just did to me. Right after she'd torn through me and Ainsley because she lost her bracelet.

It couldn't be?

On shaking limbs, I hauled myself back down the hall, barely crawling on all fours and swaying back and forth as my balance waned. For once, I'd have given anything for my wolf body, or any one that wasn't made for walking upright. After finally making it back to my room, I reached my hand over the side of my bed and ripped my backpack to the floor as my trembling fingers struggled to unzip the front pocket. Pens, highlighters, and sticky notes spilled out over my beige carpet in a messy pile. I sifted through the stack but couldn't find it. My heart pounded faster as adrenaline hit my bloodstream. Where was it? I dug my hand through the front pocket and found nothing, then I pulled open the main zipper and dumped the entire contents onto my floor and tore through my school supplies until the polished purple stones shone in my dim bedroom light. My hands shook as I untangled the bracelet from the coil of my algebra notebook and slid it onto my wrist. Immediately, my racing pulse slowed.

I lay on my carpet with my legs pulled up to my chest and breathed slowly, concentrating on the air moving in and out of my lungs. Hopefully, taking the pain with it.

One deep breath. Two breaths. Three.

The stabbing pain in my abdomen started to subside. I stretched my legs out and rolled onto my back, staring at the white-speckled ceiling.

Four breaths. Five. Six.

The world came back into focus, and the brain fog lifted. Except things didn't really seem to make much more sense. I'd taken off my bracelet, and I'd gotten sick. Sydney had lost her bracelet and suffered the same strange illness.

I held my arm above my head and stared at the lavender stones. Shiny rocks couldn't do this much damage, could they?

Maybe Sydney and me getting sick was only an unlucky coincidence.

Or... I swallowed against the lump building in my throat as the truth of that night clicked into place. Someone took Sydney's bracelet knowing it would make her unable to cheer. Kate made sure I took my bracelet when I accepted the spot on the team. What if I was wearing Sydney's bracelet? I'd heard Kate say she wanted Sydney gone the day before the game.

What if the curse wasn't tied to the squad itself but to the bracelets?

If so, two things were certain—Sydney figured out the power of the bracelets and Kate silenced her for it.

32

A line of red blazed across the sky, giving the rooftops of our sleepy little neighborhood an eerie gleam as I ran down the sidewalk and cut through the park to Buttercup Crescent. My stomach still churned with a bit of the aftereffects of whatever supernatural sickness had taken hold of me, but I pushed through the uneasiness, knowing I was running out of options and time. If someone had sabotaged Sydney, and that someone had been Kate, the chance that she'd come for me next heightened by the hour. I definitely wasn't on her list of besties at the moment.

The front window of the little house glowed with a mix of warm lamplight and the flickering electric-blue of a television. I pictured Mr. and Mrs. Danley in matching armchairs watching some British baking show or maybe some sort of cozy mystery together, and it almost made me feel guilty for barging in on their evening. After all, I wasn't even sure I'd come to the right place, but Mrs. Danley seemed to be the only lead I had left.

I meandered up the crooked flagstone path to the arched wooden door and knocked. The low roar of the television stopped, and feet shuffled closer until Mrs. Danley greeted me with her typical kind old lady smile.

"Why, Miss Melina, what brings you out on a chilly autumn evening like this? Shouldn't you be with all your friends celebrating the big win?"

Big win? The football team must've won the semifinals. I glanced quickly at my phone as my spirits sank. No one bothered to tell me. But honestly, at this point, who would?

"Actually, I'm here because I need to talk to you about something." I leaned my head closer, the comforting scent of warm apple cider hitting my nose. "It's kind of important."

Her eyes widened, and she glanced behind her. "James," she called then turned back to me. "This sounds like a situation that requires tea. Lots of tea."

Mr. Danley appeared behind her. "Yes, my love."

Her cheeks blushed, and the reaction teased a grin across his lips. Old people could be so cute sometimes. I hoped someone looked at me like that when I was her age. I shuddered. If I lived that long.

She rested her wrinkled hand on Mr. Danley's shoulder. "Could you please start a pot of tea for us? Decaf, please. I don't want to be up entertaining the shadows in the middle of the night."

He nodded and disappeared down the hall, a yellowish light cutting across the dark hallway.

"All right, dear. Come in. Come in." She stepped back, giving me room to enter, then leaned out, scanning down both sides of the street before closing and locking the door behind us. Without a word, she jerked her head toward the back of the house and led the way to a cluttered four-season room that overlooked her backyard.

I placed my palm on the cool glass of the floor-to-ceiling window and stared out into the thin blanket of snow covering her now-empty garden.

"All right, what exactly do you think I can help you with?" Mrs. Danley asked as she eased up beside me.

I took a deep breath and focused on trying to keep my tone light. This whole idea might've been as pointless as my afternoon of alumni calls, but she didn't need to know that. "I need to know more about lavender moonstones. You seemed like you knew a lot about crystals the last time I saw you, or at least more than anyone else I know."

"I know a wee bit." She shuffled over to a packed bookshelf and ran her index finger along the rows of colored spines. I tilted my head and squinted, trying to read the long titles etched along the sides, but most were written in words I couldn't decipher, and some seemed practically ancient.

Mrs. Danley turned, her face twisted as she scanned me, then pulled a sapphire volume from its shelf and quickly flipped through the pages. "Malachite. Moldavite. Ah, here they are. Moonstones. Generally good for intuition and balance, helps with controlling emotions, and is tied to feminine energy. Is used to aid with many feminine issues."

She plunked the book on the table, open in front of me, and tapped at the description she had just read aloud. I took a seat on a fussy padded chair and scanned the page, taking in all the information, but it still didn't help answer the questions in my head.

"So, nothing about whether they are good or evil or anything like that?" I asked, reading the passage over again for anything I might have missed.

"Heavens no. Crystals are just pretty rocks. They don't actually hold any power. As much as they may help with certain elements or situations, they don't possess their own energy, so they can't really be either." She gently closed the cover and held the volume close to her chest. "But anything I've just shown you, you could have searched up on the internet. Why don't you tell me why you're really here? I'll bet it isn't for a geology lesson."

I dropped my head to my chest and concentrated on my fingers as I twined them together in my lap. My brain listed off all the questions I wanted to ask, but I couldn't quite pin down the right one for this situation, especially since the ones I really wanted to say wouldn't come out if I tried anyway due to the curse.

"When you were over watching Tommy, it seemed like you were warning me about the moonstones, and I wanted to know what you meant." I clenched my hands into fists and leaned across the tiny table, my gaze sweeping through the darkness outside the windows as if a thousand yellow eyes were watching my every move. Maybe they were. I dropped my voice to a whisper. "Not many people know this, but there are some strange things happening in this town."

Mrs. Danley's face soured as she perched in her cushioned chair across from me and rubbed her thumb and forefinger over her chin. The temperature in the little room spiked. Maybe I'd said too much. I opened my mouth to apologize or retract or something, but before I had a chance, her good eye twinkled in the dim light, and she let out a soft chuckle.

"My sweet child, you have no idea. But I was never concerned about the moonstones. I just like shiny things."

I slunk back in the seat as my shoulders dropped. I'd built up so much hope that I'd finally have answers, and again I'd hit a dead end.

"What I was worried about was the weave of your bracelet. I had a peculiar feeling come over me when I was near it, but I couldn't be sure at such a quick glance and didn't want to alarm you if it was nothing. It's been years since I'd seen one like that anyway."

The weave? What did that even mean?

"I can show it to you again if you'd like?" I held my wrist out to her, and her soft hands gripped my fingers, a brief sense of calm trickling up my arm from her touch.

"Would you mind taking it off?" she asked.

My arm trembled, and a phantom jolt of pain jabbed at my stomach as a flash of my writhing body lying on the bathroom floor appeared in my mind. But it took nearly all day for it to affect me last time. A few seconds couldn't hurt. Could it? With shaking fingers, I untied the strands and held it out for her, keeping a tight grip on the end, just in case.

"Hmm, it definitely could be." She smoothed her fingers over the bracelet then flipped it, poking her fingernails into the strands and pulling it closer to her face. "I could be wrong, but it definitely looks like what I feared. A witch's knot."

"A what?"

"It's a special type of knot used in spell work. However I haven't seen one in person before. So either someone stumbled across this pattern and was ignorant as to what it meant, or someone is trying to work some big magic." She let go of the bracelet and closed the book on the table, crossing her hands politely on top.

"You mean there could be a witch out to get me?" My voice came out too harsh and too loud, my cheeks flushing at the sound of it echoing in the small room. I watched the windows again, half expecting someone to be staring back, but no one was.

"Perhaps or perhaps not. A witch would surely be capable of something like this, but it wouldn't be the first time someone inexperienced attempted to craft a spell for their own gain. The history books are full of them."

Mrs. Danley flipped her hand in the air dismissively, as if we'd been gossiping about Mrs. Shuttleworth and her messy yard from down the block, but her stillness took the edge off the heavy feeling building up in my chest.

"But how does the witch's knot work?"

She paused and tapped her index finger across her lips. "It's kind of hard to explain. Have you ever tossed a coin into a fountain and made a wish?"

I nodded.

"It's similar to that. Basically, it's the setting of an intention and channeling that energy into an object to carry out that intention. If it was an amateur who tied the knots or if they didn't set any sort of spell or intention with them, there's nothing to worry about."

"And if they knew what they were doing?"

"If the caster was a true witch or at least someone with innate power, there's no telling what could be possible, but it's highly unlikely that's the case. Born witches are far rarer than movies lead us to believe."

"But there is a chance?"

She paused and tilted her head toward the roof. "Well, I guess nothing is out of the realm of possibility, is it?"

She wasn't wrong. A few weeks ago, I would've laughed at a conversation like this, but now I couldn't deny that there existed another layer to the world I didn't know about. I'd always focused on getting out of this little town to move on to bigger things, but I'd never stopped long enough to see what was happening in front of me. Except getting caught in a witch's curse was definitely not on my dream to-do list.

"So, let's say that a witch created a bracelet like this and used it to cast a spell. Does that mean someone could cut the bracelet and it would break whatever curse they were under?"

"Now you're starting to worry me, dear." She placed her hand on mine again and held tight. "Is someone trying to harm you, and what is this talk of curses? Those are a very different beast than regular spells."

Beast was definitely right. Except I couldn't talk about that. "I'm fine. It's just a hypothetical question."

She stared at me, maybe trying to draw out more of the story, but I refused to give. Eventually, she eased her grip on my hand and leaned back in her chair. "It wouldn't be that simple. Cutting the strings won't change the energy already in motion in the universe. You'd still need to reverse the spell. Which, of course, requires finding out exactly what spell was cast in the first place."

"Makes sense." I nodded as my heart sank. Of course it wouldn't be an easy solution. I pulled my hands into my lap and ran the bracelet through my fingers. I could've said no when Kate offered it to me, and this never would've happened.

But I wanted it.

Dreamed of it.

As I held the bracelet over my wrist, I shivered, torn between the pain not wearing it had caused and what choosing to put it back on could do. However, not wearing it would definitely raise bigger flags, and the height of the moon was coming faster and faster without any plan forming in my head. I knew nothing about spells and witches.

"How do you know about all this stuff?" I asked.

A wide smile broke across her lips as she waved her hand behind her. "As you can see, I'm very well read. Plus, I've lived in this town my entire life. I've definitely seen a thing or two."

"All right," a deep voice bellowed.

My fingers slipped, dropping the bracelet to the floor as Mr. Danley appeared in the doorway with a large tray full of dainty floral teacups and plates with an ornate steaming teapot in the center.

He inched closer as he took each step carefully so as not to upend the tray, the cups rattling in his unsteady hands. "Three cups of red raspberry tea, and I managed to find a box of chocolate biscuits in the back of the pantry."

"Let me help." I jumped up from my seat and scooped up the bracelet in one smooth motion before grabbing the tray from Mr. Danley and setting it down on the tabletop.

"Very kind of you," he said as he took a seat next to Mrs. Danley and reached over to squeeze her hand. "Would you like sugar and cream?"

Something fluttered outside the window. A movement

so quick, I barely caught it. I leapt toward the glass and scrutinized every menacing tree, looking for something or someone. I didn't quite know. The more I looked, the more the night drew me to it. The darkness gripped tight on my soul and squeezed. If the bracelets were created by a witch for a magic spell, was Kate that witch? I'd always thought her power came from her confidence and her popularity, but maybe there was more to it. What exactly could she do? My body tensed as a strange sensation prickled along my skin. Could she be watching me right now?

"Are you okay, dear?" Mrs. Danley called from behind me, except her voice sounded distant and hollow.

I shook my head and snapped back into the present. "Um, no, no. Everything's fine."

Gripping my forehead, I stumbled back to the tiny table.

"Would you like sugar, Melina?" Mr. Danley asked as he poured a steaming cup of red tea into my cup.

The walls closed in tighter around me. My breath hitched in my throat. "Thanks, but I think I need to go."

He frowned and glanced at Mrs. Danley. "Are you sure? There's no rush."

"Yes. I have to be somewhere. Thank you both." I made a series of awkward bows as I stumbled toward the front of the house and the main door. I'd probably broken an entire chapter's worth of etiquette rules by running away from them, but I needed to get out of that room. In there I was trapped. An animal in a cage. The dark surrounding me as the enormity of the curse crushed down on my shoulders.

Outside, I gulped a gluttonous breath, but I still felt cornered. At least out here, I could run if I needed to.

A silver sliver of moonlight peeked through the clouds and cut across the frosty sidewalk. My bones itched as my pending transformation loomed. I tied the bracelet loosely, letting it hang lower and farther from my skin than before, at least until I knew what kind of harm these pieces of string were capable of. But if Kate was really a witch, what would she do to me when she realized I knew?

Panic overtook my brain, and I spun in circles, trying to figure out what to do. Where to go. If I went home spooked like this, Mama would never let me out of her sight to sneak out later. All the cheerleaders would be out celebrating. Jaida and the others wouldn't understand, if they agreed to see me at all. Plus, I'd probably freeze if I just wandered around aimlessly until I put on my fur coat. I let out a gigantic sigh, the steam from my breath curling around my head as I realized my only real option. I knew who I needed to see, except I didn't want to go there. I'd already caused enough damage for one relationship to handle.

But I had no one else left.

33

<hr>

I stood on the doormat watching the stars glitter in the sky, the waning crescent rising higher in the east. The familiar itch started in the soles of my feet and rippled through my veins. There wasn't much time.

My hand shook as I knocked, begging that Leo's mom was working the night shift today or maybe that he wouldn't even be home. I waited for a minute. Two minutes. Three.

No answer.

Figured. The cold air stung my eyes, and I held my arms tight to my chest.

I'd run all the way here from the Danleys', trying to put the pieces of the puzzle together. Kate was clearly a witch. She'd cursed me and the rest of the squad, but it didn't make sense how she could've cursed the years of cheerleaders before us. Or maybe it was all a lie? Maybe this hadn't been happening for years? Or maybe there were other witches, passing down the spell from one generation to another? Was it some sort of witch legacy?

But with every question came five more and no answers to any of them. The weight of this new truth hung heavy on my shoulders, pushing me down. Who was I kidding? I couldn't fight a witch.

The fear turned to despair, which turned into an empty black hole inside my chest, sucking all the hope I had left into it. I rubbed my eyes with my frozen fingers but couldn't keep the tears from falling any longer.

As I turned to leave, the porch light flicked on. The front door creaked as it opened behind me.

"Melina, what are you doing here?"

I halted and wiped the tears from my cheeks before turning back around. Leo had the door open just wide enough for his annoyed stare to peek out. I leaned closer and fought the waver in my voice. "I needed to see you."

He paused for a moment, as if weighing his options, then let out a surrendering sigh as he swung the door open wider.

"I thought you made it clear that you didn't want to talk to me anymore." He rubbed his hands over his face then rested his elbow on the doorframe, blocking the entrance. I'd always been welcome here, but now he obviously wanted to keep me out. The rejection cut deep, but it was my fault. I'd hurt him, and it made complete sense that he didn't trust me anymore. But I had no one left to trust.

"I'm really sorry about that. I know I left things pretty messed up—"

"Messed up?" His body tensed as his lips curled with disgust. "You basically called me a liar then accused me of stalking you, then even when I tried to talk to you, you just blew me off."

I held my breath. He was right. I had said that. Every last word. "I know, and I'm so sorry about all of it. I was scared, and I didn't know what to say."

"And that is what you decided to go with? Real nice." He grabbed the side of the door and started to close it.

"Wait, please." I jumped forward and pushed my hand against the door panel. "I know you're mad. You should be. I was completely awful. And I feel terrible that I did that to you."

He gave up on slamming the door but still kept his distance. "As you should."

"And I know I owe you so much more than an apology, but I am eternally sorry for what I did. Especially because you were right about everything, and now my world is completely falling apart, and I should've listened to you. But I didn't. Now I don't know what to do."

The heaviness pressed down on my lungs as the tears flooded my eyes again.

"And I was at her house… and she said… and I just ran…" I gasped, tripping over the words to explain what had happened over the past few days and the bombshell I'd uncovered at the Danleys'. Whether it was my own brain moving too fast for my mouth to catch up or simply a side effect of the curse tying my tongue, I couldn't tell.

Leo's eyes widened as the nonsense kept spewing at his feet. As I struggled to string together a cohesive thought, his resolve softened, and he lowered his arm from the doorframe and backed up. "Hey, calm down. Just breathe, then tell me what's going on."

"I didn't know where else to go." I stumbled over the threshold into the house and crumpled against him, my face buried in his chest. "I'm in big trouble."

He rested his chin on the top of my head as his arms relaxed and reluctantly wrapped around my back. "It's going to be okay, Lina. Just tell me what's wrong."

Calmness settled over me, battling against my panic, as I fell into the soft rhythmic rise and fall of his breathing. I closed my eyes, the scent of him grounding me, holding me together as every part of my being tried to shatter.

"I don't know if I can, but I will try. I owe you the truth."

34

There's something about daylight that takes the sting out of the sharpest bite.

After bawling my eyes out at Leo's, I wolfed out alone in the woods and literally tried to run away from my problems. Except they still followed me, no matter how fast or far I ran. By morning, my mind and body were absolutely wrecked. Every nerve ending raw. Every brain cell cooked.

I crawled into my bed, begging the universe that when I woke up, everything would be a bad dream. Then when I finally awoke just before noon with the sun beaming across my face, my wish hadn't come true, but reality didn't seem quite as extreme either. Although it was definitely still pretty bad.

Except now I had someone on my side.

Maybe.

The porch boards creaked beneath my feet as I knocked on Leo's door for the second time in the last twenty-four hours. But this time, I hadn't shown up uninvited.

"Hey," he said as he opened the door. And this time, he stepped back to let me in.

Dark circles rimmed his eyes, and his hair stuck out at odd angles on the sides, as if he'd just rolled out of bed. My stomach churned knowing I'd been the reason for his terrible sleep. He still didn't know all the details, but at least last night I'd managed to get the point across that things were way worse than he'd even thought and escalating fast.

"I brought donuts." I forced a smile and shoved a pink cardboard box into his hands. "All your favorites. Chocolate glazed. Frosted maple. Boston cream. And there's one vanilla sprinkle in there for me."

"Thanks, but you didn't have to."

"Yeah, I did. I owe you a lot more than donuts, but I didn't want to be late."

He closed the door and started down the hall toward his bedroom. Music streamed from the kitchen at the opposite end of the hall, along with the aroma of cinnamon and bacon. My mouth watered. Leo's mom must've made breakfast for him before I arrived. Normally, I would've rushed off to say hello, but today seemed different, as if I needed to ask permission in a house that used to feel more like home than my own.

I scooped up his navy-blue comforter from the floor and smoothed it back on the bed before taking a seat on the edge. Not much had changed since the last time I'd been here. The same movie posters hung on the walls, except for maybe a new black-and-white B-horror one on the closet door that didn't seem familiar. Leo glanced over at me and shuffled over to the desk, pulling out his wheeled chair and rolling it across the room before sitting.

He leaned forward, his elbows on his knees, and clasped his hands together in front of him. "Feeling any better this morning?"

"Yeah, I think so," I said.

"Good."

He nodded and spun the thin silver ring on his pinkie finger, focusing too intently on anything but me. Not that I could blame him.

"Leo, I wanted to—"

"Maybe we should—"

Our words crashed over each other, and I laughed. He finally dared to look up, his lips twitching as he fought a smile. "Sorry, you go."

Instead of talking, I crossed the room and knelt down on the carpet in front of him, taking his hands in mine. He lifted his head slightly, meeting my gaze. His bright eyes had dimmed since the last time we'd spoken.

My throat thickened. "I need to apologize."

"It's fine. You don't—" He shook his head and pulled away.

I tightened my grip on his hands. "Yes, I do. I meant it last night when I said I was sorry, and I still mean it today."

He sighed and unclenched his jaw.

"You've only ever been good to me, and I've been awful to you. You didn't deserve it, and I was completely out of line." My voice broke, and I swallowed hard. "But I want you to know that I didn't mean it. Any of it. Everything I know is imploding right now, and just being here with you, knowing that you're still in my life, is enough to keep me going. I will do anything I need to do to prove that until you forgive me."

Leo slipped his hands away and tucked his thumb under my chin, holding my face. "I missed you, you know that?"

My vision went watery, but he brushed the back of his hand under each of my eyes, wiping my impending tears away.

"No more crying, okay? Last night almost broke me."

I chuckled and sat back on my heels, wiping my face again. "Okay."

"But none of this matters if we can't figure out what's going on. So you need to tell me everything you know and don't leave out anything."

"That's the problem. Part of all this"—I waved my hands in a circle—"is that I can't talk about it. Like, literally can't."

"Can you write it down?" He pushed out of his chair and rummaged through the top drawer of his desk, producing a black marker and a pad of paper.

"I don't know. Where do you want to start?"

"How about what the rules are to this whole wolf thing? Any other bizarre things you can or can't do?"

The tongue-tied piece was odd, but bleeding out on my bathroom floor seemed like a much bigger deal. I rested the pad on my leg and wrote everything I could think of and handed it to Leo.

"Um, what do 'bubble gum stuck on a vintage couch' and 'a penguin shopping for a tuxedo' have to do with any of this?" He frowned. "If you want my help, you need to take this seriously."

"I am. That's not what I wrote."

He passed the pad back to me, and I read my scrawls. He wasn't wrong.

"Ugh." I threw the pad across the room, and it smashed into the wall then splashed on the floor. "This is so frustrating. I'm so tired of this stupid game."

"Wait, a stupid game. That might be it." He held out his hand. "Come with me. I have an idea."

We raced through the hallway, my feet slipping on the slick tiles as Leo whipped open the basement door and rushed down the steps. Dropping my hand at the bottom of the stairs, he rushed forward and scanned a stack of cardboard boxes in the corner.

"What are you looking for?" I asked.

"My mom is using my sister's room as an office while she's off at college and put all the stuff in Sophie's closet down here." He rearranged the top two rows of boxes and slid one out into the center of the room. He pulled back the flaps, dug into the middle, and pulled out a long, flat box.

"What's that?"

He cleared a spot then plunked down cross-legged on the floor. "It's a spirit board. If you can't say or write things out, maybe you can spell them."

I sat down beside him as he pulled out the alphabet board and a pie-shaped planchette and arranged them between us.

"Let's try again. Do all the girls on the cheerleading squad turn into wolves?"

I rested my fingertips on the planchette and concentrated on forcing it to point to the bold "Yes" written in the middle of the board.

Except it wouldn't budge.

"Great, another fail."

"Maybe you're trying too hard. Take a breath and try again."

I sat back and closed my eyes as I fought the frustration crackling in my veins. I exhaled and stared back down at the board.

Leo leaned closer. "Forget the board. Look at me."

I glanced up and focused on the small scar in his eyebrow from the time he fell skating at the park when we were ten. His skin brushed mine as he positioned his fingertips on the planchette next to mine.

"Now, answer the question."

I breathed again as the planchette started to move.

"It's working," I said as our hands floated across the board.

"See, I knew you could do it." He smiled, and my stare slipped from his scar to his lips. "And apparently, yes, all the girls on the squad turn into wolves."

"Thank you." I thrust myself across the board and pulled him into a massive hug.

He fell back on his knees then wrapped his arms around my back once he regained his balance. A sense of calm rushed through me as my head fell into the crook of his neck and he pulled me closer.

"Relax," he said as he finally released me. "We've still got a long way to go. I need to know everything."

THE RAYS of sunlight retreated all the way across the basement floor before Leo finally stopped asking questions. Somewhere in the third hour, he'd run back upstairs and grabbed a pad of paper to write down all my answers, as well as snagging us the box of donuts and a few glasses of lemonade.

He lay on the floor, with an old rolled-up sleeping bag for a pillow, and looked over the pages and pages of notes he'd written. "So, if I understand everything, if we want to stop this wolf curse, we need to find a way to reverse the spell that cast it in the first place. How are we supposed to do that?"

"Well, if I'm right about who cast it, then I say we start there. Search her locker, her car, even her house. Wherever she might be able to hide something." I paced as I tried to devise a plan then popped up to sit on top of the washing machine. "I have no idea what we're looking for, but we've got to start somewhere."

"That's not a bad idea. Plus, maybe I can head to the library tomorrow and see if there is anything in there about the history of Faraway and the cheer squad or even just research witchcraft and see what comes up."

A metal pinging cut through the basement. I sat up straighter then pulled my phone out of my pocket as the vibration rattled against the washer. I navigated into the text screen and scoffed.

Leo sat up and clicked the lid of his marker on and off against his leg.

"It's Joy. She says that Kate has decided I've suffered enough and sent me the meetup place for tonight." I slid my phone back into my pocket. "There's no way I'm going."

"Except you have to. If you don't show, everyone is

going to know something is up. Besides, it will be easier to find out more about Kate if you spend time with her."

"Ugh, you're right. I hate when you're right." I slid off the washing machine and stretched my arms over my head.

"No, you don't." He chuckled.

"But I should probably go. It's getting late, and no surprise, I'm hungry."

"I'll walk you out." He pulled himself up.

"It's okay, I've got it." I grabbed onto the railing and walked up the first couple of steps, then turned back around, nearly knocking Leo over as he followed behind me. I grabbed onto his arm to keep him from falling, his soft t-shirt lacing between my fingers as he tensed under my touch. He steadied himself, then stared up at me, his breath shallow and uneven. His vibrant green eyes darkened, just like the night outside my house before he'd been pulled into all my drama. The night he told me how he felt and I didn't answer.

I let go of his shirt and laid my palm flat on his chest. "Thanks again. I couldn't have done this without you, and—"

He shook his head and sidestepped around me, ascending the rest of the stairs and holding the door open at the top. "Thank me later. Right now, let's work on getting your life back."

35

I used to envy her.

Kate Fleming, the reigning queen of Faraway High. From the second I saw her freshman year, I wanted to be around her. The prettiest, the most athletic, and the most popular girl I'd ever seen. I wanted to be like her. I wanted to be seen and to have all the special treatment that came with being in her atmosphere. She had everything I'd ever wanted and more.

But it was all an illusion, and now that I'd seen the truth, I couldn't unsee the lies. Having my dream life didn't matter if my life was going to be cut short.

"Okay, everyone." Kate paused the music on her phone and clapped her hands. "Time to rotate stations."

I lowered my kettlebell to the floor and shook out my sore biceps. I still hadn't fully recovered from my sudden sickness over the weekend, and the last hour of training had made me lightheaded, but I needed to keep up appearances. Plus, the entire squad suffered along with me, except for Kate, of course, who didn't have to perform any of the exercises she'd subjected us to. Astrid and Sunni also seemed to be conveniently missing this morning as well. I closed my eyes and centered myself then plastered on a smile and headed toward my next circuit stop.

Ainsley waved as I approached the crunch station. "Hey, Melina."

"Hey," I replied as I plopped down on the floor next to her. "Does your body feel as broken as mine does?"

She laughed. "Yeah, pretty much. I'm guessing you want me to go first?"

"That would be amazing. Thank you."

Ainsley slid onto her back, and I gripped her feet as she positioned herself for her first set of sit-ups. She started to move but stopped, instead glancing up and smiling. "I'm really glad you're back. I missed you."

"Aw, I missed you too." And it was true. Out of everyone on the squad, she was the only one who actually seemed like they might still be my friend. Except I knew getting too close to me would have dire consequences for her, and if there was anything I'd learned from cheerleading, it was self-preservation.

"So what did you do with a whole weekend off? I'm not surprised you weren't at the game. I don't think I would've gone either, if I were in your spot."

"Yeah. I didn't feel right being there. Kind of hung out around my house and did some research for a project I'm working on."

She nodded. "Keeping busy. Very smart. What's the project for?"

"Um…"

Ainsley's big doe eyes followed me with genuine interest. Maybe I should tell her. She'd been around the squad longer than I had, so she might know something about Kate that I'd missed. But I had basically zero proof. She'd probably think I was insane. Like Leo said, I couldn't risk raising suspicion yet.

"Chemistry," I finally blurted out. "Huge midterm project. Worth half my grade."

"Cool. I kind of hate chemistry. So many formulas to remember."

"Right? Such a pain."

I rolled my head from side to side, stretching out the stiffness in my neck and shoulders as Ainsley started on her first set.

"Why did Kate choose to make us do conditioning on a Monday morning? Isn't that a new low, even for her?" I asked.

"I guess you didn't hear." Ainsley huffed as she curled her body up close to me. "Joy fell out of step on Friday."

Okay, that wasn't the worst thing. It happened, and we'd all done it at least once.

But Ainsley kept going, spitting out the words between breaths as she raised and lowered herself from the ground. "During the halftime routine.

"Knocked Piper over.

"Almost took out the entire back row.

"The whole stadium laughed."

"Seriously? That's so bad. She must've felt awful."

She nodded, choosing not to keep talking, her face darkening to a shade of maroon as she pushed through her last few crunches.

"Fifty!" she shouted and then rested on the gym floor. "Your turn, partner."

I sank to the glossy hardwood and bent my knees, Ainsley's hands pinching my toes. As I eased myself up, I tried to keep proper form while scouring the room for Joy. I found her in the corner powering through a set of burpees, the hard expression on her face focused and intense. She probably felt awful after what happened and especially if everyone else assumed that this morning's practice plan was all because of her. In fact, I didn't remember seeing her at the new meeting point in Mercy Woods last night. I'd been focused on Kate, trying to uncover some unknown clue I hadn't seen before, but as I counted the wolves in my mind, I came up short. Maybe she'd been put in exile like I had?

"Is that why Kate's been leaving me alone today? She's got a new toy to play with? Or has she finally become bored with me?"

Ainsley nodded ever so slightly, her eyes wide and screaming. "Don't speak too soon."

I froze mid-crunch as a shadow cast over us. As I lowered myself back down to the floor, my nose caught the familiar scent of magnolia perfume, and I stopped breathing.

Kate loomed above me, her ponytail falling forward as if it was trying to reach down and attack.

"Good morning," I squeaked as I lay perfectly still.

She scanned me like a laser then glanced up at Ainsley. Her irritated glare softened a fraction as she stood upright again and dropped her hands to her hips. "You two can clean up all the gear after practice. Yes?"

It wasn't really a question, but it gave the illusion that we might actually be able to refuse. Another one of Kate's many magic tricks.

"No problem," I replied from my spot on the floor.

"Perfect." She turned on her toes, her sneaker soles on the gym floor squealing right beside my ear.

"All right, everyone." Kate clapped her hands over her head as she circled back to the front of the squad. "That's it for today. Good work this morning."

Ainsley let go of my feet, and I rolled up to a sitting position as everyone else quickly raced for the showers.

"Guess we better get to work," she said, tapping her hand on my leg as she got to her feet.

WITH OUR ARMS FULL, we exited the gym and popped out into the hallway, moving toward the storage room. I kept my head down as we approached Alex's locker, trying to avoid any possible eye contact if he was already at school.

He was. And he wasn't alone.

Kate stood in front of him, a little too close, her hand resting on his arm. Probably on purpose, knowing we'd be parading past and she could dangle him in front of me, just out of reach.

I slowed to walk in line with Ainsley and whispered, "Are they back together now?"

"What? Who?" Ainsley swiveled her head around until she saw them. "Oh. Kate and Alex. They talked a bit after the game on Saturday, but I don't think so."

I pulled my arms tighter to my body, trying to shrink myself invisible. They must've heard her, because as if on cue, Alex looked over and caught me looking back. He didn't deserve it, but my pulse still raced when I gazed into his piercing eyes, and I hated myself for it.

Kate wrapped her hands around the back of his neck and pulled his attention back to her like a siren leading her sailor to his untimely death. She leaned toward him, and I forced myself to look away.

"Or maybe I'm wrong," Ainsley said, still staring. "I'm sorry, Melina, that really sucks."

"I doubt she even likes him." I sped up, putting as much distance as I could between us and them, then rounded the corner and stopped outside the equipment room. I took a deep breath and exhaled, trying to push my feelings out with the air. Even if we were never anything real, it still hurt. Fortunately, a little less than yesterday and the day before that. I didn't need someone who wouldn't stick up for me. I already had enough traitors in my life.

Eventually, Ainsley caught up and unlocked the door, either oblivious to my reaction to the new happy couple or kind enough to ignore it and let me wallow in peace.

The cluttered room smelled like gym mats and sweat, especially on the baseball side. I tiptoed around the batting nets and equipment bags then chucked my two bags against the far wall.

"This room could really use some organization," Ainsley said as she navigated the path behind me, nearly falling into a pile of old catcher's gear.

I pinched my nose. "And an air freshener."

She laughed and dropped her bags next to mine.

I shimmied around her and started my way back toward the door, avoiding any other tripping hazards. "What about the other equipment room in the basement? Is it as messy as this one?"

She scrunched up her face. "We don't have an equipment room in the basement, or at least I don't think so. The only things down there are old desks and probably a rat or two."

I shuddered. I hadn't seen any rats down there, but my skin still itched like their tiny rat feet were crawling all over me. "Ugh. Now I'm going to have that image in my head all day."

"You're welcome." Ainsley laughed as she passed by me and tapped her hand on my shoulder. "Stay out of the basement, and you'll be fine."

"Right." I nodded and followed her out the door as she locked up then headed back toward the gym. Once she'd cleared the corner, I slipped my phone out of the pocket of my yoga pants. Allyssa might be a bit eccentric, but she wasn't a liar and had the eyes of a sniper. Probably all her computer game practice. So if she thought she saw a cheerleader down there, she definitely did. As I opened the text screen, I glanced up and down the hall. No one seemed to notice me or care what I was up to.

> Me: Meet me by the art classroom at lunchtime. I think I found something.

36

"Hello?" I called into the darkness as I patted my hand against the wall then flicked on the light switch. A dull glow pooled at the bottom of the stairs, but no one answered. "Allyssa? You down here?"

Silence.

"C'mon." I beckoned Leo to follow as I raced down the metal steps.

"Are you going to explain where we're going, or are you planning to feed me to some basement monster for information?"

"Well, I can't exactly trade my cafeteria lunch for information. I doubt even a monster with five arms and an insatiable appetite could stomach the tuna lunch special." I cleared the last step and rushed deeper into the dark. Ominous shapes twisted large in front of me, and I held my breath until my fingers grazed the switch Allyssa had used last time. I flipped it on, and the dim lights buzzed overhead as the shadows retreated to the corners of the cluttered room.

"See, no monsters," I said as I maneuvered around the boxes and old chairs farther into the mess. "Or at least, I don't think so." Apparently, just rats. The creepy, crawly feeling rushed over my skin again, but I powered onward and around the corner until a door appeared on the far end of the room. Strangely, it wasn't blocked by boxes or other debris like everything else.

Leo caught up and stopped behind me. "What's in there?"

"That's what we're here to find out." I took the last few steps to the door and crouched down in front of it. "Allyssa told me this was a cheerleading storage room, but I've been dealing with the equipment most of the year and hadn't heard of it. Ainsley hasn't either. So we're either going to find a clue to this whole thing or a bunch of old cheerleading uniforms."

"Sounds suspicious. Do you have a key?"

"Nope, but I do have this." I dug into my backpack and pulled out a small set of picks I'd found among my dad's tools in the back of our shed. I'd run home between classes in the morning and would probably get a call home for being late to English, but hopefully, it would be worth the risk.

I opened the little black box, pulled out a particularly pointy-looking pick, and jammed it in the lock. I jiggled it around, trying to find the right spot to pop it open, but nothing seemed to work. It'd looked so simple when I'd covertly searched lock picking online when I was supposed to be paying attention in class. Why couldn't this be easy?

"Here." Leo stepped closer and held out his hand.

"It's fine. I'll get it," I said, twisting the pick as I applied pressure like I'd seen in the videos.

"I don't doubt you will, but if we graduate before you get that open, you might be out of time."

I leaned back on my heels and stared at the lock again. "Ha ha, you're hilarious."

He wrapped his hand around mine and poked the pick back in the lock. He wiggled it back and forth a few times then jabbed it hard into the center. The mechanisms in the lock released with a soft click, and I turned the knob, the door easing open until it hit my knees.

I glanced up at Leo. "How did you figure out how to do this?"

He shrugged then took the pick from my hand and tucked it back in the case. "I've seen so many heist movies, how could I not know how to do this?" He extended his hand toward me. "Plus, my sister used to hold my game controllers hostage in her room when I wouldn't load the dishwasher for her, so I figured it out."

"Very vigilante of you." I slid my hand into his, and he tugged me back onto my feet.

"More like survival."

I stepped back and groped for the light switch on the inner wall then let out a sharp gasp.

"What is it?" Leo grabbed the side of the door and opened it fully.

"It's nothing." I walked in as my stomach hollowed. "Just a storage room."

The fixture above our heads hummed, as I spun in a circle letting the full weight of my disappointment sink in. A rack of old cheerleading uniforms. A wall of shelves along the back with a line of cheap trophies along the top, the gold finish already long faded. I ran my finger along the tops of the boxes lining the rest of the shelving unit and a thick fuzz of dust coated my finger.

"There's nothing in here but a pile of untouched junk." I coughed as I disturbed another one of the boxes in the corner. Inside were bits of old plastic pom-poms that crumbled as I tried to touch them. I wiped my hands on my thighs and cringed. "This was a total fail."

"Maybe we can still find something?" Leo gave me a wide smile, but his narrowed stare gave away his lack of real optimism.

He rummaged through a few old cheer bags as I plunked down on a rickety wooden chair near the door.

"I really thought I'd found something." I crossed my arms and slouched as I kicked a clothing rack beside me. The hard metal base hit back and my toe ached. Ugh. I couldn't even get mad without making things worse.

Leo glanced over as I clutched my foot and tried unsuccessfully not to laugh. "Take it easy, Lina. I know this isn't what you were hoping for, but there are still other things to try. Since everyone will be at the football game Friday night, I can see if I can get into Kate's house. Plus, we still haven't checked her locker or cracked into her phone yet. There might be something there."

"Thanks." I sighed and dragged myself out of the chair. "But it's my mess. I can find a way into her house. I've already put you in enough trouble by asking for your help. Why don't we go to Bean There and try to figure out what to do next?"

"Sure. But did you see these?" Leo had circled around to the back of the room and pointed at the side wall covered in photos and ribbons. "They're all cheerleading championship ribbons, and they go back for years. Here's one from 1967." He pointed to a green ribbon near the ceiling.

I walked over beside him and scanned the wall. 2001. 1984. 1972.

"This one is from 1953," I said as I searched the newspaper clippings taped in between.

Leo stepped back and stared, his hand holding his chin as he studied each of the pieces. "It's kind of cool, but also giving off a crazy obsessed vibe, right?"

"Not just one. All the crazy obsessed vibes." I placed my hands on my hips, taking in the entire collage. If this was someone's vision board, they definitely had a single-minded focus. "But someone is definitely maintaining it."

I bent down and grabbed the bottom of a newspaper photo. A grainy black-and-white picture of Kate stared at me from the *Faraway Times* sports page as a shiver rippled down my spine, her eyes seeming to look right through me even in print. *Where are you hiding your secrets, Kate?* I tried not to look at her face directly as I read part of the article on the bottom. I peeled the clipping from the wall and held it up to Leo. "This one is from the homecoming game in September."

"Hmm, okay." He scanned the photo over then passed it back to me and pointed at the wall. "But what's that?"

A dark groove ran up the wooden paneling on the wall where Kate's clipping had been attached.

I shrugged. "I don't know, but it looks like it keeps going. Maybe there's something behind there?"

Leo patted his hands along the wall and moved some ribbons back to reveal more of the line starting from the floor to about three quarters up the wall.

I ran my fingers along the groove, but it was too narrow to get a grasp on it. I tossed my backpack on the floor and dug through the front pocket until I found my wallet and my student card.

Leo moved on to the shelves, opening and closing boxes behind me. "Do you think anyone else knows there is all this stuff down here?"

"I doubt it. Plus, it doesn't make sense. I'm pretty sure most of the girls have no idea this room even exists, but Allyssa said someone from the squad is in here at least once a week. What are they doing down here? Just hanging out with the dust bunnies and updating their scrapbook?"

I slid the card into the slot and ran it down the groove, looking for a suitable spot to pry it open. Hopefully, my card wouldn't snap. Nothing like leaving something behind with my name written on it. I tried once, and my card bent.

"So are you even sure it's Kate coming in here?" Leo asked.

I slid the card farther down and then heard a click as the wall popped out an inch at the groove, revealing a hidden doorway.

"I don't know for sure, but—" I gripped the side of the panel and yanked it back. "Whoa. Look at this."

The space behind the wall reeked of musty earth and dust, with a heavy top note of cheap incense. Barely wider than a bathroom stall, but longer and with all light disappearing toward the back.

Leo leaned over my shoulder, staring into the void. "What do you think it is?"

"Not sure, but I guess we're going to find out." I swallowed and took a deep breath as I switched my phone to flashlight mode and dared to walk forward into the dark. The temperature plummeted as my shoulders brushed the close-set stone walls continuing toward the back. The stale air whispered in an ancient tongue, as if this room had been forgotten in time or maybe just carefully hidden. A tomb memorializing years past. I reached for Leo's hand and his firm grip kept my knees from shaking.

As we approached the end, a wide wooden shelf spread out in front of us. Three half-spent candles dripped red and black wax across the surface and leaked into the channels of symbols etched deep into the top.

I ran my finger over one of the symbols, the lines and curves like nothing I'd ever seen. A curious tingle rushed across my skin as I moved my fingertip over the next one. Almost electric. The same symbols were artlessly painted over the back wall, extending to the ceiling, where bundles of what looked like dried animal bones hung suspended by golden strings. I held my arm up to the bones and winced. The thread matched the ones in my cheer bracelet.

"What is that thing? An altar?" Leo asked as pushed his head closer to mine. His eyes caught the same view of the gold threads, and his expression blanched. "Oh."

I squeezed his hand tighter. A leather-bound book sat in the back corner of the altar, hidden in the shadows. It had the same vibes as the ones on the shelf at the Danleys', except for the well-worn spots on the spine and edges of the cover. I carefully laid it on top of the wax symbols then gently flipped through the thin and yellowed pages. Shaky handwriting filled the lines, mostly in English but some in a language I'd never seen before.

"Hey, go back." Leo reached around me and turned a few pages to the front of the book and pointed to a crude sketch in the margin. "That looks like your bracelet."

The pattern on the page exactly matched the knots on the bracelet, and the round black pen smudges in the middle must've represented the moonstones. Beside it, a drawing of a wolf and a cycle of the moon. I quickly read the first few lines.

"This must be it. This has to have the spell in it."

He turned his head toward me and forced a wary smile. "That's good, right?"

"I think so." Except now I wasn't so sure. Now that I'd found something proving that there was an actual someone behind the curse, it forced me to have to deal with it and who knew if this magic was dangerous or even deadly. I swallowed against my dry throat. I might make everything even worse.

My ears perked as the faint ring of the school bell sounded in the distance, and reality flooded back along with the nervous itch of potentially getting caught. "We should probably take this and get out of here."

I slammed the book shut and tucked it under my arm as I ushered Leo back into the main room, the goose-bumps on my arms retreating as we stepped back into the light. Leo fit the door-shaped panel back into place, while I stashed the book in my backpack then helped him put the ribbons flat against the wall again to hide the opening. I replaced the photo of Kate on the wall and turned away as her printed eyes still seemed to follow my every move.

I made one last scan over the room, making sure everything still looked untouched then flicked off the lights as we slipped back out into the basement, locking the door behind us.

As the door clicked closed, I let out a huge breath and I swung my arm behind my back, confirming that my backpack—and the book—hadn't suddenly vanished when we left the room.

My body trembled as I shook off the spooky energy of the hidden chamber and followed behind Leo through the maze of unwanted things. "Let's meet up after school to—"

"Shhhh!" Leo spun around and placed his index finger over his lips as the clang of the metal steps echoed through the basement.

I froze. I had to think of an excuse. If anyone saw us and it got back to Kate that I was snooping around down here, then...

My thoughts disappeared as Leo's hand wrapped around my bicep and yanked me behind a massive stack of gym mats in the corner. He pressed himself against the wall, his arms linking around my back and pulling me close.

If it was Allyssa on the stairs, she'd soon climb up to her gaming perch and she wouldn't even care when we walked right past her. Except the footsteps didn't stop at her normal spot, they continued, getting closer and closer with every single second.

My heart hammered against my ribs. Too loud. I slipped my arm across my chest to muffle the sound, but it still pulsed hard in my ears.

The steps grew louder. Almost beside us now. Leo's grip tightened as I rested my head on his chest, his chin buried in my hair. His legs trembled beneath us.

The door to the secret storage room creaked open.

Leo leaned close to my ear and whispered, "Who do you think it is?"

I shook my head and placed my hand over his mouth. His soft lips tickled against my palm, so I pressed harder to make them stop. My face flushed as fear mixed with the disarming awareness of being so close to him. Only a few days ago, I didn't think Leo would ever talk to me again, and now we were smushed together, all racing heartbeats and heavy breaths, hiding out from a potential witch with unknown powers.

Seconds drifted into minutes, which felt like hours, as we waited in the corner with no hope of escape. A few times I dared to peek out from behind the mats, but piles of boxes and the furnace obstructed a clear path between our hideout and the storage room door. Who was in there, and what were they doing for so long? Had they figured out we were there? And most importantly, did they know we had their book?

I counted to one hundred in my head, over and over, until finally the storage room door shut and the footsteps started again. I flinched as they neared our hiding spot, but Leo tightened his grip, keeping me from exploding and giving up our location.

The overhead lights shut off.

Footsteps clanged slowly up the metal stairs.

The basement door creaked open and closed with a loud bang.

I kept my hand clamped over Leo's mouth and leaned farther around the edge of the mats toward the staircase. No silhouettes lurked on the top step waiting to jump back out at us for a surprise attack. But no evidence of who it might've been down here either.

"I think we're safe," I whispered as I lowered my hand, my arm still pressed against his chest.

His shoulders relaxed as he exhaled all the tension out. I breathed in the smell of him. His fear and something else. Something strong and sweet. It swam through my veins, waking my senses more than a mint chocolate latte with three espresso shots and stirring up emotions I'd been trying to ignore. Messy, inconvenient feelings that confused me, but suddenly seemed extremely clear.

He rested his forehead against mine, the tip of his nose brushing my own.

"Then we should probably go," he said, his breath tickling against my cheeks as his arms stayed wrapped around my back.

"Yeah, we should." I slid my hand to the back of his neck and tipped my chin higher, as the world seemed to slow around us.

Our lips hovered close, near touching, but not.

I stopped breathing as his heart pounded, the quick *thump, thump, thumping* drowning out my thoughts and all the reasons I probably shouldn't kiss my best friend.

Not here.

Not now.

But then it was too late.

Our lips fell together, slow and cautious, as if asking the question I'd been avoiding. But this time, I responded as I inched up on my tiptoes and tangled my fingers in his hair. He gasped against my mouth, then rested his hand against my cheek, pulling me deeper into the kiss. I lost myself in the way we fit together perfectly. The soft rhythm of his lips, as they instinctively knew how to kiss me—the ideal pressure and tempo—as if he'd studied exactly how to treat me right. Although I never doubted that he absolutely would.

Then suddenly, Leo stilled and his lips pulled away.

He turned his head to the side, his arm at my waist loosening. "I'm sorry. I shouldn't have."

"No, it's okay." I tipped his face toward mine and held his stare. "It's totally fine."

"But it's not." He slipped out of the corner and headed toward the basement steps.

"Wait, Leo. What's going on? I know things have been awkward between us lately, but I thought you liked me and now you're pushing me away. I'm really sorry if I hurt you before, but you know I didn't mean it."

He stopped but didn't turn around. "Do you honestly think I don't want to kiss you?"

"Right now, kind of, yeah." My voice wavered as I put my hands on my hips, trying to channel confidence I didn't have.

"Well, you're wrong. I do want to kiss you, I just don't want… well… this." He turned around and flailed his arms, nearly knocking over a stack of old textbooks behind him. "You're upset and you're scared, and I don't want to be the impulsive hookup in a sketchy basement to make you feel better. Plus, I don't want kissing me to be something you'll regret later."

"Why would I regret it?"

"Maybe because you're dating the captain of the football team? Everyone's seen that post of you two."

I rubbed my hands over my face. "No, I'm not. Alex and I are definitely not happening."

"Because of Kate?"

I didn't know what to say. Yes, it was because of Kate, but it wasn't just what she did.

"So if Kate stops being a problem, then that changes things." He bowed his head to his chest. "It's fine. I get it. I've been trying for so long to show you how I feel, and you never saw it, but I know how this goes. Alex is the hero of this story, and I'm just an extra or, at best, one of your sidekicks. He's the one who gets the girl, and I've been delusional thinking that somehow it would end differently this time. But it's okay. That's just not the way it's supposed to be. We're just friends, and I need to deal with that."

Except what if we weren't anymore? That kiss didn't feel like friends. For either of us. How could he not see that?

He continued. "I'm not saying this to upset you. I just don't want to keep torturing myself, because it will only hurt worse when you eventually choose him."

The basement door creaked open, letting in a sliver of light as Allyssa's thick boots appeared on the top stair. Leo's eyes widened, and he rushed toward the exit.

"But what happens if I choose you instead? What then?" I called after him.

He turned around, the naked light bulb at the bottom of the stairs illuminating his defeated expression. "Then, if we get you out of this and you decide you still want to kiss me— not Alex Chase or the next guy who finally sees you the way I do—I promise I won't stop you. But it'll be your choice."

Allyssa descended the last stair and her head jerked

back as she looked us both over. "Oh hey, Leo, Melina. What are you doing down here?"

"I'm just leaving." Leo grabbed the railing and bolted up the steps, the heavy door banging shut behind him.

Allyssa watched him race away then turned back to me. "What was that about?"

"Trust me, you don't want to know."

She shrugged and pulled on her headphones. "Yeah, I probably don't."

---

 ho knew magic was so complicated?

I pulled my blue pen out from between my teeth and stretched my arms over my head, my back and shoulders sore from being hunched over this diary—or spellbook or whatever it was—for the past several hours. After I snuck out of the school basement, I couldn't fight the paranoid feeling of walking around with the book in my bag, and the second I caught a glimpse of Kate holding court with her followers in the middle of the hallway, I immediately turned around and rushed out the front doors headed straight for home, my stomach flipping back handsprings all the way there.

Then I read.

And read.

And read. So much so that my eyes felt like they'd been rubbed down with sandpaper after staring at the tiny words scrawled across the thin yellowed pages. But I couldn't give up yet. I'd pieced together a lot, except there were still some key things I hadn't solved. Like how to make it all stop.

A soft knock rapped against my closed bedroom door.

"Leave me alone. I'm not hungry," I yelled without bothering to look up.

The door creaked open anyway.

"You're the one who texted me to come over," Leo said, as he crept in the room. He leaned against the far wall, his hands crossed in front of him and his lips held in a tight line.

"But you never answered." I swiped my phone off the floor and double-checked that my text still sat on read like it had all afternoon. "I figured you were still mad."

His head dropped to his chest as he released a defeated sigh. "I was never mad. I just… Never mind."

"Don't do that." I pushed up onto my feet, my legs aching from sitting cross-legged, and met him by the door. I slid my hand under his chin and tipped his face up to meet mine, his eyes immediately darting away and avoiding my gaze. "Tell me what you want to say."

He turned his head away and out of my grip, then pivoted around me. "Can we not talk about it?"

"Oh. Okay, but—"

"Just stop," he demanded as he raised his hands in surrender. I shrank back and his stony expression softened. "Right now we've got much bigger things to deal with and I'd rather focus on helping you find a way out of this whole curse thing before it's too late."

"You still want to help me?"

"Of course, I do. No matter what happened, you're still one of my best friends. I'm not going to turn my back on you if you need me." He took my hand and laced his fingers between mine, then nudged me with his shoulder as a whisper of a smile graced his lips. "You're stuck with me."

The tightness in my chest eased and I nudged him back. "Thank you."

"No problem. Now tell me you've found something under all this paper, or are you casting a spell right now?"

I guided him to the center of the room, careful not to disturb the perfect arcs of notes I'd spread across the floor as I read. It probably looked more like alien crop circles than witch magic, but still creepy either way.

"I think I might have." We sat down on the carpet and I pulled Kate's book of spells into my lap and flipped to one of the pages I'd marked with a pink sticky note. "See this part here? It talks about siphon magic. Where the witch doesn't have her own magic, but she can pull it from other living things, like animals and humans and stuff. Plus, right after the first time I"—I stumbled over the words as the curse stopped them on the tip of my tongue—"you know. This is how Sunni and Astrid explained the whole thing to me."

"Maybe that explains the wolves." He leaned over the book and ran his finger down the lines as he read. "But if Sunni and Astrid told you about this stuff, do you think they're witches too?"

"They might know, but I doubt it matters. Almost everything in this book focuses on the alpha holding the power. Their responsibility for keeping the whole pack together. And Kate was the one who gave me the bracelet and pushed me to commit to the squad. Plus, she was the one mad at Sydney before she fell sick and mysteriously quit." I mimed scare quotes in the air with my fingers. "I'm pretty sure this curse is being passed from cheer captain to cheer captain."

"So if Kate's part of a long-line of magic-sucking mean girls, how come she's never just drained someone like a juice box and gone on a complete rampage?"

"That's over here." I flipped back a few pages. "They need a conduit. A magical object that helps them draw the energy out. I think she's using the bracelets because the weave pattern is drawn in the margins here"—I jumped to the middle of the book—"here"—I turned to the back page —"and here. Plus, Mrs. Danley talked about the witch's knot in the bracelets being fueled with intention. Sounds like a conduit to me."

"Then why couldn't she find new conduits?"

"Yeah, I've been trying to figure that out, but all I can think is that maybe Kate isn't actually a witch at all—or at least not one with magical powers."

Leo stifled a laugh into his fist. "That's one way to describe her."

"The book talks about everything—the wolves, the need for a pack of twelve, the bracelets, even energy transfers, but it doesn't talk about how the curse is passed down, so I'm not sure if I'm right. Except this book is super old and there are dates that go back decades. Either Kate is using it as an instruction manual or she's the oldest high school senior in the world."

"Do you think that cheer advisor, Mrs. Lochlann, might have something to do with this? She's practically a corpse and still hasn't retired."

"I already thought of that." I reached across him and grabbed a piece of paper from a pile beside him and read my notes. "She moved to Faraway from Pennsylvania in the mid 90s. Can't be her. Besides, what does she have to gain? She completely ignores the squad most days."

Leo planted his hands behind him and leaned back, tipping his head toward the ceiling. His nose scrunched up, like it always did when he lost himself in his thoughts. "Okay, so I guess the only question left is how do we actually reverse this spell and break the curse?"

I sighed. "That's the part I haven't figured out yet."

"Here, let me try." He sat up straight and beckoned with his hands for the book. I passed it over and he immediately fell into research mode, silently scanning the pages, and giving me a much-needed break.

I rubbed my hands over my face as the overhead light blurred, my eyes exhausted. All I wanted was to curl up on my bed and sleep, but even though I wanted to, I couldn't. Night had already fallen, and I'd have to head to the meeting point and pretend that I hadn't spent hours poring over plans to take Kate down. Like everything was fine.

Except I was getting tired of pretending.

Not only had I been lying to everyone in my life for weeks, I'd even been lying to myself. I gazed over at Leo reading, his teeth biting down on his bottom lip as he concentrated on the words. When he'd told me how he felt about me, I'd pretended it wasn't real. It couldn't be. Alex's attention was all butterflies and heart-eye emojis. The thrill of falling—fast and free—like a carnival ride that ends too quick and you run back in line to go again. But Leo was steady ground and I dismissed the possibility of us because it wasn't exciting and loud. It wasn't poetry. Except our kiss had played on loop in my brain all day, reigniting the warm spark in my chest as his lips pressed against mine. If it meant nothing, why did I keep repeating it like lyrics to my favorite song?

"That's it. This part, right here."

I shook my head. "Sorry, what?"

Leo shot to his knees and tapped the open page with his fingertip. "This section tells you exactly what you need to do."

I crawled across the floor and knelt beside him as I read the page. "Are you sure? It doesn't say that's what it's for."

"Yes, I'm sure. It's not like someone would put a blinking sign and arrows pointing to it. It's basically the exact opposite of the spell to create the curse. Looks legit to me."

"And how do you know what does and doesn't look like actual magic?"

He pulled out his cell phone and typed in a few words then passed it over to me. A website for the occult stared up in blood-red font, a list of similar spells written across the screen. I scrolled down and read each one, all of them eerily close to the spell in the book. "Did you seriously just fact check a magic spell on the internet?'

"Maybe." He shrugged. "I've been doing some research of my own too, you know? Besides, I told you I'd help. When have you ever known me to let you down?"

"Not once." I nudged him with my shoulder and he smiled, a pink tinge glowing across the top of his cheeks.

He eased back down to the floor. "Only one catch. This says you have to perform the reversal under a full moon."

"When's the next full moon?" I tugged Leo's cell out of his hand and swiped to the November calendar. "Of course it is." I shook my head. "The next full moon is on Friday night. The football championship."

Leo cringed. "That's not great. You could wait, though. Try the full moon in December instead."

"And then what? Spend another whole month being paranoid about what might happen to me? Besides, we don't know for sure that Kate doesn't have any magic powers. No, I have to end this before someone gets suspicious or something worse happens. I'm pretty sure Sydney was figuring things out and look what happened to her. She remembers nothing, and I can't stop the curse if I can't remember it."

"All right." He dragged the words out soft and slow. "So, you're really going to do this?"

"I have to. I need to get my life back, all of it, not just the next ten years."

My shoulders drooped and I slouched forward as the gravity of the situation crashed over me. The sheer magnitude of the task I would need to undertake to hopefully buy back my freedom. Even if Kate didn't have magic, she definitely still had power over me, and I was literally dying because of it. I closed my eyes and inhaled until my lungs ached. This was big.

Leo wrapped his arm around my shoulder and pulled me closer, his chin resting on the top of my head. "Are you going to be okay?"

"I will be," I said. "But we're still missing one thing."

"What's that?"

"We're going to need some help."

THE DOOR to the library swung open, and a trio of freshmen girls giggled and gossiped their way over to the computer lab. I checked my phone. Already 12:45. Where was she?

"Did you put rocket fuel in your water bottle this morning?" Leo laughed as he flipped through *The Complete Encyclopedia of the Supernatural*. "You told her to meet you in the library so you didn't look suspicious, but if you keep running hot laps around this table, you're going to set off the fire alarms and call more attention to yourself."

"Very funny." I stopped and scowled at him before continuing my rounds. "Lunch is almost over, and we don't have much time."

"Much time for what?"

I gasped and whirled around to see Ainsley standing behind me.

Phew.

Placing my hand on my chest, I let out a huge sigh. "It's you. I was starting to think you weren't going to show."

"Joy was having a meltdown about being Kate's new chew toy. It took me forever to lose her." She pulled out a chair and sat down. "What's he doing here?"

"He's here because we have a plan to get ourselves out of our"—I dropped my voice to a whisper—"situation."

I nodded toward Leo and he slipped a pair of over-ear headphones out of his backpack and onto his head. The muffled sounds of some rap track echoed around us as he bobbed along to the beat, giving us some very necessary privacy.

Ainsley stared at Leo then jerked her head back to me.

"You told him about the curse? How did you even do that? It's impossible."

"I didn't exactly. He followed me one night and found out on his own, then I just had to fill in the blanks." I glanced over at him as the memory of that night flashed through my brain. After all that and he was still here.

"You do know that Kate will murder you if she finds out you've been keeping him a secret, right?"

"Oh, I know. That's why I'm trusting you not to tell her anything about this. Besides, the more important thing is that I've been digging into this whole wolf curse thing and I think I might've found a way to stop all of it. No more transforming. No more secrets. For any of us."

"Are you serious?" Her eyes widened as a kaleidoscope of emotions danced across her face. "But that means no more winning too, right? How are you going to get everyone to agree to that?"

"Hopefully, you're going to help me." I gave her an uneasy grin and reached my hand toward her on the table. "You are honestly the only one I trust on the squad and I can't do this alone. Please say you'll help."

"But what about Kate? She'll definitely say no."

"Convincing Kate will be my job, but she needs to be the last to know. As the pack alpha, she has the biggest role in breaking the curse, but I need everything else to go flawlessly."

She crossed her arms and leaned back in her chair, potentially debating helping me or running out of here as fast as she could. The silence between us ticked on and I counted a full twenty-six seconds in my head before Ainsley finally sighed and dropped her arms to her sides.

"Okay fine, what do you need from me?" she said.

I poked Leo with my elbow. He paused the music and slid his earphones around his neck.

"First, I need you to keep Kate away from the locker room after the pep rally on Friday, and I need you to offer to drive her to the football game that night too." I cringed as I said the words, knowing how horribly they would probably land. "I'd do it myself, but she'd never listen to me."

"You're kidding, right?" Ainsley laughed and shook her head. "How am I going to do that? She always drives herself or gets a ride with Astrid."

"I'll talk to Astrid," I said.

"And I'll take care of her car." Leo nodded and cracked his knuckles like he'd morphed into a bad movie villain. However, slashing Kate's tires in the school parking lot wasn't exactly dangerous, but I couldn't bring myself to ruin his main character moment.

"And one last thing." Leo dug into my backpack, pulled out a white envelope, and slid it across the table to Ainsley. "Here's a bit of insurance."

"What's this?" She held open the envelope and peeked inside.

"It's a letter signed by me, blackmailing you into helping me," I said. "If things don't work out, you can give that letter to Kate, and she'll think I forced you into it. She already hates me, so she'll totally believe it."

"Blackmailed me how?"

"It says I have proof that you stole the answers to the calculus midterm and cheated your way into an A."

"But I didn't do that." She slammed the letter down on the table. "I'm just really good at math. Why would you accuse me of cheating?"

"I'm not, I just needed something bad enough that you reasonably could've done to make this plausible. I built you a safety net."

"I don't know, Melina." She leaned closer so Leo couldn't hear. "I really hate the wolf curse. My parents are constantly suspicious. I even had to break up with my boyfriend, but Kate will make my life miserable if this goes wrong."

I clasped my hands together on the table and leaned forward. "What scares you more? Kate or dying in your twenties?"

She jerked her head back. "What?"

I signaled for Leo to put his headphones back on and he obeyed. I grabbed Ainsley's hand and took a deep breath. "There are so many things I still need to tell you."

here are you, Ainsley?

I checked my phone again. We didn't have much time to pull this off before Kate would figure out that the entire cheer squad had mysteriously vanished. Fortunately, the pep rally ended early so there was more lead time before tonight's kick-off, but I didn't know how long my nerves would hold out knowing what was coming.

"We all have stuff to do, Melina. Can you please just get on with this?" Tessa said as she sat on the bench across the room and scrolled on her phone.

Everyone storming out before I could plead my case wouldn't help either.

I peeked out the door of the locker room and across the empty gym, then I stood in front of the entrance. "Just give Ainsley another minute. If she's not here, I'll start."

"Why's this such a big deal?" Melody started pacing in the center of the room like a caged cat. "You want to get a gift for Kate. Big deal. Just tell us the amount, we'll transfer the cash, and we can all get on with our lives. I'd really like to get home and eat, or did you forget that we have the biggest game of the year tonight? I'm starving."

Waiting until after the pep rally to ask the girls for their cheer bracelets was risky. I knew it. But if I'd tried earlier in the week, there was too much of a chance that someone would spoil the plan, or worse, the entire squad would start bleeding and vomiting all over the football field. Stealing them was also an option, but since everyone wore their bracelets constantly, getting my hands on them would be impossible. A well-crafted lie might've been a choice, but anything I'd come up with had sounded as ridiculous as the truth, so I figured I might as well go out with a clear conscience. I just really needed the support to sell it. "Okay, fine."

"I'm here." Ainsley burst through the door and bent over, grabbing her thighs as she panted. "We've got about fifteen minutes, max."

"Finally," Melody said.

I turned and locked the door, just in case. "Okay, everyone. I didn't actually call you here to get a present for Kate. It's kind of a present for all of you."

The vibe in the room shifted, and everyone started actually paying attention.

"How would you all like to never have to turn into a wolf again?"

The room roared with laughter.

Probably not the best start.

"Who says anyone actually wants out?" Sunni crossed her arms and jutted out her hip. "Just because you can't handle it doesn't mean the rest of us can't. Besides, it makes us champions. What's a small sacrifice compared to setting us up for the rest of our lives?"

Ainsley chimed in. "But what if the rest of your life is less than ten years?"

"What do you mean?" Sheena asked.

I stepped forward and pulled the beige folder out of my backpack. "No cheerleader who has left Faraway High has survived past her twenty-seventh birthday."

No one responded, but it was clear they weren't convinced. Some heads shook. Others went back to their phones.

"It's true." I chucked the folder in the middle of the floor, the pages spilling out. "You can check for yourself. And unless you want to be on that list of deceased cheerleaders, then I need your help."

Piper stepped forward and fanned out the pages, scanning through the list of names. "Are you being serious?"

I nodded.

"So what are we supposed to do about it?" she asked.

"That's the easy part." Ainsley gave me a nod. "All we need is your cheer bracelet."

A low murmur went through the group, a few girls grabbing their wrists.

"Look, here's the deal. I have a theory that someone created these bracelets years ago and cursed them. That's why we all turn into wolves. Then we keep passing them down year after year, to squad after squad. But it's not actually a gift, it's a sacrifice. And every time we turn, we lose some of our life energy."

Joy raised her hand. "Um, I'm not a video game character. That sounds insane."

"Trust me, I know this is completely bananas. I didn't believe it at first either, but"—I nodded to the pages on the floor—"I have the receipts to prove it. All I'm asking for is your bracelets for the next few hours and that once you walk out of this locker room, you don't talk about this to anyone until the football game starts. But it's an all-or-nothing deal. Everyone has to hand over their bracelet."

"There's a lot of dead girls on this list, guys." Piper held a few of the pages over her head and rose to her feet, her face ashen. "Does that mean that we might…"

I nodded again.

"I did not sign up for that," Piper said, her eyes glassy and her voice wavering.

"Wait a second. If everyone has to give up their bracelet, then where's Kate? Wouldn't you need hers too?" Joy asked. "Winning the state championships means more to her than anything. She's never going to agree to this, and then she's going to take it out on everyone."

"Don't worry about that. I'll take care of Kate." I strode back and forth at the front of the room, everyone finally paying full attention. "And she won't do anything to any of you because if she comes for you, you're going to take me down. She already has a vendetta against me. If I don't fix this or you don't have your bracelets back before the first snap, then you can tell her I stole them all and let her take it out on me."

"Are you concussed, rookie?" Astrid stared unbothered at her purple-claw manicure. "She will annihilate you."

I shrugged. "I'm getting used to her punishment."

"But just think about it, everyone." Ainsley walked over to Charlotte. "Wouldn't you love to go see that guy you've been dating in Cedarwood County for the weekend without having to worry about sneaking off in the middle of the night? And Nina, I know you're frustrated about being exhausted all the time. I know I'd love to stop lying to everyone in my life. Wouldn't you all risk a few hours of keeping your mouth shut and a cheap bracelet for getting your freedom back? If Melina is wrong, you lose nothing; she does. If she's right, we all get our lives back."

"Okay, so let me get this straight." Sunni's face scrunched up as the weight of the situation started to set in. "You're seriously telling us that someone cursed our squad and will eventually kill us all, and you don't know what insidious reason they have for that, but you want us to give up our cheer bracelets to keep it from happening?"

"Basically, yeah. Are you in or not?" I held out my open palm. "If I'm right—"

"Highly doubtful," she added.

"But if there is even a one-percent chance that I am, can you really afford to make that mistake right now? I'll bet you never thought you'd turn into a wolf, either, but that happened. Do you really think someone wielded that kind of magic on us all for nothing in return?"

"All magic has a price." Ainsley stepped forward and pointed at Sunni. Everyone's stares fell on her, and she crossed her arms, slinking back against the wall. "Or at least that's what they always say in movies."

"Except this isn't a movie. This could literally be life and death." I stopped myself from telling them that Kate might have magic powers. It would likely make the story too unbelievable, but I hadn't ruled it out yet. Instead, I sat in the sudden silence that had fallen over the group, clenching my fists and hoping everyone would humor me, even if they didn't believe a word I said.

Ainsley dug into my backpack and pulled out a plastic bag. She dropped her bracelet inside and handed it to me. "You know I'm with you."

I gave her a reassuring smile and held the bag out to the group. "Anyone else?"

"Well, I'm not willing to risk it." Astrid strutted across the room and stuck her hand into the bag. "I'm not saying I fully believe this nonsense, but you're right. What do I have to lose? Besides, if you're wrong, I get to watch Kate torture you, which is deliciously entertaining."

"Uh… thank you?" I said.

Astrid unlocked the door and hefted it open. "I'm pretty sure the only one dying is gonna be you once Kate finds out. But good luck, rookie."

She marched out, letting the door slam shut behind her.

"Just in case you're right." Piper crept forward and slipped her bracelet into the bag.

"Fine." Sunni tugged at her bracelet until the gold threads hung loose around her wrist. She stared down at it for a second and sighed before tossing it at me.

I lunged forward and caught it on the tip of my index finger then shoved it into my bag.

Sunni whipped her hair over her shoulder and paraded out of the locker room. I followed behind, standing near the door with the bag open as the rest of the squad filed out, dropping their bracelets in as they went.

"And don't forget!" I shouted after them. "Not a word until the game."

I exhaled as the tenth bracelet fell into the bottom of

my bag then added mine to the group. It worked. It actually worked. If I was wrong about the curse, then I'd probably never be able to show my face in this school again, but hopefully the next time they saw me they'd be thanking me for saving their lives. Or at least, I'd have been able to save my own.

39

I checked the time again then slid my phone into my pocket. If there weren't any delays I had about fifteen minutes before there was no going back. Except time hadn't been cooperating with me. The second I'd walked out of Faraway High, time sped up as the possibility that I might never return inched closer. The spells in Kate's book haunted my thoughts. The likelihood that she could actually wield magic was low, but not impossible. However, she needed energy to make that happen, and keeping her isolated would be key to ensuring she didn't overpower me. But it also left me vulnerable as the sacrificial battery.

The last gasps of sunset set the sky on fire, as if it knew what was coming and wanted to warn the world as it ran away to hide, leaving behind a blanket of night. The naked trees above us reached their clawed hands toward the rising moon and cast ominous shadows across the untouched layer of snow covering the clearing ahead of us. I pulled my arms tight to my sides as the November chill seeped under my skin, my patience wearing as thin as my coat.

Leo wrapped his arm around my shoulders and pulled me closer, his warm breath heating the side of my face. "It's going to be okay, Lina."

"Thanks, but you really should be in the car. As soon as Kate arrives, I want you as far away from here as you can get."

"You know I won't do that."

"Yeah, but I can hope that you'll listen, can't I?"

He chuckled, and it created more steam in the cold air circling around our heads.

"I'm serious. This is my mistake to fix. You don't need to get dragged into all of this."

"Hey." He rested his cold fingertips near my temple and gently swept a few stray strands of hair behind my ear. "I'm already in it."

I tucked my forehead against his cheek and closed my eyes, letting his scent surround me. Ground me. If I managed to reverse the curse, I'd definitely miss the extrasensory details my inner wolf noticed. "And you remember your job, right? If this goes wrong, I'll call you, and you run off and warn everyone about Kate. Then you bring the letter to my parents."

He swayed closer to me. "So basically, I have nothing to do, as you've totally got this."

"How can you be so confident in my abilities? You've

seen me these last few weeks. I'm a sleep-deprived, broken mess."

"Yeah, but somewhere under all that, you're still my Lina. The girl who sits through every horror movie marathon with her eyes wide open when I can't even watch. The one who stood up to Chris Jackson when he stole my bike in fifth grade and threatened to beat me up if I told anyone. The girl who always finds a way, even when everyone else has given up. That's how I know."

I gazed up at him, his emerald eyes glittering in the starlight. How had it taken me so long to understand that this boy knew me better than I knew myself? He didn't like me. He *saw* me—all of me, even the ugly parts—and I didn't have to prove myself to him. I already had. Over and over again. And I didn't even realize it.

"Leo," I whispered. "If I get through this—"

Headlights cut through the trees as Ainsley's mom's Jeep eased up the back road.

"You'll have to finish that *when* you get through this," Leo said, taking a step back toward his car hidden in the bushes.

I stood up straight and wrapped my arms around him, my head pressed against his chest. His heartbeat raced, and I knew mine matched. Probably just the fear, but maybe something more. Potentially, I would never know.

Too soon, he pulled away and disappeared into the shadows as Ainsley cut the engine on the far side of the clearing and led Kate into my sight line, her bright-white puffy jacket making her look like a human marshmallow. I pulled up my sleeve and read the reversal spell written on my arm one last time then took a deep breath. *Game time.*

"Okay, I'm out here. What's the big surprise?" Kate yelled as she walked farther into the clearing, Ainsley staying near the brush and closer to her vehicle.

"Just take twenty more steps and then you can take off the blindfold. Trust me, you're going to love this. It's amazing," Ainsley said, her cheeks flaming a telltale red even from a distance. She clearly wasn't the most accomplished liar.

"You better not be messing with me or I'm going to make your life hell."

Too late for that, Kate. You already ruined everyone's life.

Kate charged across the clearing, and Ainsley raced back to her Jeep, the tires squealing as she peeled out toward the highway.

"What?" Kate ripped the blindfold off her face and spun around. She tossed her hands over her head and screamed, "Get back here!"

I swallowed hard and rushed from my hiding spot into the clearing, making sure to keep my distance. "Hello, Kate."

She looked up then rolled her eyes and scoffed. "Oh, Melina, it's just you. Are you here to give me my surprise?"

"You could say that."

"Well, where is it?" She stomped her foot in the snow. "There's a huge football game that we're both supposed to be at right now, and if you want to stay on this squad, then hurry up and get me to that field. And where's your uniform? Do you seriously go out of your way to annoy me?"

I took a few steps closer, my hands held up in surrender. "I can take you to the game, but I need to talk to you about the wolf curse first."

"I don't have time for this. Take me to the school." Her hands balled into fists at her sides, her irritation growing by the second.

"Listen, I will take you there, but you need to break the curse first. Set us all free."

"Why would I ever do that?" She swung her hands in the air. "It's not even a curse. It's special magic that gives us all the power to be champions. It's not even a big deal."

"But is power worth all those lives? I can't let you hurt anyone else."

"Okay, drama queen. If you want off the squad so bad, fine, I'll replace you. Give me your bracelet, and I'll find someone who's grateful to be here." She shook her head and held out her hand. "I offered you everything you ever wanted, and this is how you repay me. Ungrateful."

"No. I need you to destroy the bracelets. Save both our lives and all the other girls too."

"Stop talking in stupid riddles and give me the bracelet so we can get out of here." She stepped forward, and I stepped back in tandem. Her perfectly-arched brows knit together in a puzzled V.

I stopped retreating and stood firm. "Wait, you don't know what happens once you leave the squad, do you?"

"Yeah, you forget and move on with your life." She fanned her hand in the air, dismissing the consequences.

"And then you die young."

Her head snapped back. "What?"

"Every single cheerleader coming out of Faraway High for over the past fifty years hasn't lived more than ten years after high school. They all die. You can't tell me that's a coincidence."

She paused, her angry face blanching as ghostly white as the full moon rising behind her. "You're lying."

"I have the proof, Kate. All the names of the girls who died from this. Did no one tell you the consequences when they taught you the siphoning spell to maintain the curse? Plus, it's all in the spellbook. The rules. How the energy transfers work. All of it. Did you not read it?"

"What the heck are you talking about? All I know is that all twelve bracelets need to be active or everyone gets sick. That's the rule."

"So you stole Sydney's bracelet and gave it to me."

She pointed her finger at me and yelled, "You wanted this, Melina. You practically begged me to let you on the squad. I did you a favor."

"And now you've signed both our death certificates."

"No, no, no." She grabbed the sides of her head and started pacing in small circles. "You're wrong. The bracelets give us strength. That's all. A small sacrifice for superhuman abilities. That's what Anne-Marie told me when she passed on her captain duties. I've been on the squad for three years and no one has ever said anything about dying."

"That's not the full truth. All that strength drains our bodies of life. It's all in here." I slid the spellbook out of my bag and held it up.

"What's that?" She stepped forward and reached for the book, but I yanked my arm behind me. Did she really not know or was this some kind of trick? I definitely didn't trust Kate, especially not now, but the blank expression on her flawless face gave nothing away. Or was she just a brilliant liar?

"Your spellbook. Isn't it?"

"Uh no. I've never seen that before in my life." She tilted her head to the side. "Oh my gosh, Melina, do you seriously think I'm some kind of witch?"

I shrugged and slid the book back into my bag. "Pretty much."

"Okay, embarrassing for you." Her face twisted in disgust then slowly morphed into something more like panic. "But what you said about dying—you weren't making that up were you?"

I shook my head and the light in her eyes dimmed.

"You didn't honestly think you'd get all this power for nothing in return, did you?"

Her confident exterior slipped as my words seemed to process through her brain—the harsh reality poking holes in her fantasy world. She crossed her arms, grabbing onto her biceps as if hugging herself as a cool breeze swirled around us. All of her attitude fell away as she shivered under the moonlight. "So what if you're right? What now?"

"We can still stop it. If we destroy all the cheer bracelets, then the curse can't hurt us anymore."

"If you know what to do, then why don't you just do it then?"

"I can't. It has to be the alpha, and that's you." I pulled the clump of bracelets out of my pocket and held them up for her to see. "I know a reversal spell. One of us needs to hold all the bracelets under a full moon and then you need to repeat the spell twelve times, one for each girl on the squad. That should break the curse."

She stared at the bracelets in my hand. "And if I do this, then everything will be gone, right? The strength, the power, the championships."

"Do those things matter more than your life?" I clenched my fist tighter and risked stepping closer to her.

Her shoulders slumped forward as I approached, her watery stare unfocused and scattered. "You don't understand, do you? Cheer is all I have. It's who I am. If I'm not a winner, what does that make me?"

I wrapped my arm over her shoulders and leaned my head against hers. "Trust me, I get it. All I've wanted is to get a scholarship and a ticket out of this town, and this might ruin everything. But I don't want to do it this way, and you don't have to either. You are so much more than this curse, Kate. You've just been bound to it for so long you don't even know your full potential. You don't need magic to win. I promise."

"I didn't know about the side effects, I swear." Her tears flowed harder, and she gasped. "Am I really going to die because of this?"

"Maybe not if you stop this now."

She swallowed as her body fell limp in my grasp. "Tell me what I need to do."

"Take off your bracelet and give it to me." I held out my hand and gently separated each of the bracelets from the mound of gold threads and lined them up in my palm.

Kate slid her bracelet off her wrist and added it near the ends of my fingertips.

"Now you have to take these—wait." I dug my hands into my pockets and turned them inside out, but nothing appeared. "There are only eleven bracelets here. I'm missing one." I handed the stack of bracelets to Kate and ripped through my bag, then scanned the snow-covered ground for the last one. I traced my steps back to the middle of the clearing, focusing on the ground. "I swear I had them all."

"Rookie mistake," a voice said.

I glanced up at Kate, but her mouth was closed, her eyes staring behind me.

I spun around as a figure entered the clearing from the darkness.

"Looking for this?" the voice said as the figure held her arm above her head, the last bracelet dangling from her wrist.

I gasped. "Astrid, what are you doing here?"

She swaggered forward, dressed in her cheer uniform, the glitter on her cheeks catching in the moonlight. "Ruining your little plan and getting my book back."

40

———

I blinked. Once, twice, three times, as I let everything sink in. I thought I had everything figured out, but clearly I'd missed a step or two along the way. A brisk wintry wind whipped up around us as the pieces clicked into place. I'd been outplayed.

"You're the one with the creepy altar in the school basement. You're the witch, not Kate." I stepped forward and pointed at Astrid as she strode closer.

"Yes, that room is mine, and so is that book you stole." She glanced down at my bag then wagged her finger in front of her face. "Naughty puppy. You clearly need some obedience training."

"Wait." Kate shook her head and stepped between us, her arms flailing out at her sides. "So you"—she turned to Astrid—"are a witch? And you"—she turned back to me—"were tracking her, thinking it was me?"

I nodded, and her face scrunched up, way too ugly for her beautiful face. "Astrid, this can't be true. I know you. You're, like, my best friend. How would I not know this?"

Astrid tipped her head back and laughed. "Best friends? Seriously, Kate? I've just been another accessory for you to wear. You don't even know where I live."

"Of course I do. You never invite me over, but that's not my fault."

"Okay, then." Astrid stared down at Kate. "Tell me my address. Even just the street or general area."

Kate paused, her jaw tight as she tried to access the information from some foreign part of her brain. I honestly didn't know where Astrid lived either. After all, I never really needed to, but they'd been circling in each other's orbits for at least three years. Faraway was too small not to know.

"You have no idea, do you? How much do you even really know about me?" Astrid stuck her hands on her hips and stood up straighter, the power in dangling Kate on her string seeming to charge her up. "When's my birthday? What's my favorite color? C'mon, give it a try."

"I don't…" Kate bowed her head and cringed, her shoulders folding in toward her chest. "I don't know. I never really thought about it."

"Of course you didn't. As long as I served you and your wicked cheer-queen aesthetic, you didn't even think to ask questions. Actually get to know me. It's far easier to manipulate someone when they think they are the manipulator. All I had to do was make you the alpha, and you had every one of these girls falling at your feet for a chance just to be around you. To breathe your precious air. Why do you think you were picked as captain? Because I made it happen."

Kate's mouth dropped open, but nothing came out.

Astrid strutted up to her and grabbed the back of her

neck, forcing her face up. "Oh, Captain Kate. You didn't really think you were the one in control, did you? But don't feel bad. You won't be the last girl who's too focused on themselves to see what's really going on, and you're definitely not the first. I've picked every captain for years. Girls just like you who shone too bright for their own good, while I hid in the background."

Astrid whispered something too quiet to hear as she took Kate's hand. A lavender glimmer bloomed where her skin connected with Kate's. She squirmed and turned her head away, but Astrid caught her by the wrist instead.

"All I had to do was give you the power you craved, and you'd do anything I asked. You led every single one of those girls to me. You convinced them that the wolf spell was a small sacrifice. Perpetuated the same lie I sold you and every captain before you. But every time they turned, I fed off their energy, harvesting my hard work to stay young forever, and no one felt a thing, believing they were trading up for trophies, fleeting small-town celebrity, and petty scholarship money. Rinse and repeat every four years. The old captains don't remember me or cheer-leading at all, and I come back with a new name and hair-style to do it all again. In my story, all the wolves were the real lambs to the slaughter, and you never once asked about the consequences as long as you got what you wanted. By the way, I'm thinking I might try being a redhead this time around—what do you think?"

"Let go!" Kate shouted as she shook her arm. "You're a monster."

Astrid's mouth continued to move, but I couldn't hear the words. The lavender glow returned to Kate's arm. She wavered on her feet and dipped forward as if she might fall, her hand on her forehead. A splash of red dotted the white snow as blood ran down Kate's face. She screamed, her voice echoing off the trees and scaring the crows from their perches.

I rushed forward and grabbed Kate's arm, yanking her toward me, but she stayed stuck in Astrid's grasp.

"Let her go!" I shouted, tugging harder. "You're hurting her."

"Of course I am. Thanks for bringing me all the bracelets, by the way. You have no idea how excited I was when you took them from everyone today. Do you even know how much energy I can siphon when I have all of them together? It's a total turbo boost." Astrid grabbed my arm with her other hand and threw me to the ground as easily as flicking lint off her favorite cashmere sweater. Kate slumped forward, her head bowed against her chest, her screams turning to whimpers as Astrid drained her body.

I struggled to my feet. "Stop it, Astrid. There has to be another way. Something you want. Anything."

"What I wanted was for you to stop snooping around and let me continue my plan in peace. I've been pulling this trick for nearly one hundred years, and no one has figured it out, except you. After I'm done with Kate, you're next, and I'll build a whole new squad without either of you. Everyone will forget you even existed."

"But everyone will remember you when this video goes viral." Leo raced out of the bushes and positioned himself behind Astrid. He held his hand out in front of him, a bluish-white light beaming from the end of his cell phone. He glanced over at me and mouthed, "Are you okay?"

I nodded and scrambled back to my feet. He promised he'd be far away from here in case anything happened. Fortunately, he didn't keep that promise.

Astrid spun around. "What is going on? Melina brought her boyfriend to a cheerleader-only event. What have we told you about no outsiders?" She glared at me then released her grip on Kate's arm, tossing her to the ground.

The bracelets flew across the top of the snow, each gold strand glittering in the dark. I rushed over to her side and eased her up onto her knees. Her head flopped forward like a doll's, but I did my best to hold her up. "It's okay," I whispered as I tried to keep her conscious, "but I need you to listen to me."

"Wait a minute. How exactly did you know about this? We have a very strict 'what happens in cheer stays in cheer' policy. Melina couldn't have told you if she wanted to." Astrid stormed toward Leo. With every one of her steps forward, he retreated two as he forced his cell phone light into her face.

"She didn't have to. I figured it out. I know all about the curse. About the wolves. And now you've just told me, on video, everything else. You're not as untouchable as you think you are." Leo waved his phone light right into Astrid's eyes. "So if you don't want the entire world to know about you, I'd let them go. I've been live streaming this entire thing to a friend at an undisclosed location. If you even try to threaten me or them again, she'll flip this onto every corner of the internet."

She laughed. "I doubt you'd have the guts for that."

"Do you really want to find out?" Leo straightened up

and walked forward a step. "Your entire plan hinges on people not knowing who you are and no one knowing how dangerous you can be. Once your face is out there, you lose."

"Very clever. Or very stupid. I guess history will decide."

I gathered up the bracelets in a pile and leaned closer to Kate. "Are you okay?"

"Everything hurts. My entire body. And it's all my fault," she whined as tears streamed down her cheeks. "I'm so sorry. Tell everyone I'm sorry."

"I will, but you can't let her get away with this. You didn't create the curse, but you still have a chance to stop it. You have to destroy the bracelets."

"But I don't have all of them." She stared at me with her watery eyes. The Kate I knew had shattered into splinters, stripped of her overwhelming confidence and natural audacity. She thrived on being the one in control, except now she'd lost it. "I can't."

"You're the only one who can. The alpha is the one who has to break the spell, and Astrid said herself, she made you the alpha. She picked you to be the alpha because she knew it was easier to work for you than to work against you. She needs you to keep her spell going, but you can't let her take advantage of you. You're Kate Fleming. You're a cheerleading legend. You have to end this. I'm going to find a way to get the last bracelet, but I need you to repeat after me. Okay?"

She nodded.

"What was many, now make none. The spell is cast. The deed is done."

Kate lowered her head and repeated the counter curse,

her words garbled and weak. "What was many, now make none. The spell is cast. The deed is done."

The bracelets in the pile all glowed a bright violet. "That's perfect. Now keep going. Eleven more times."

"What was many, now make none. The spell is cast. The deed is done."

"What are you doing?" Astrid screamed. She spun around, her arm glowing the same color as the rest of the bracelets. "Stop this! Stop it now."

"What was many, now make none. The spell is cast. The deed is done."

"Oh, Kate." Astrid stepped forward, but I blocked her path. It wouldn't hold her long, but I had to try. Leo joined me, creating a wall, his phone filming every move Astrid made.

"Katie, sweetie." The bracelet on Astrid's wrist glowed brighter every time Kate completed another iteration of the spell, and red darkened her cheeks every time it pulsed. "Are you actually going to listen to her? You hate her, remember? She's nothing. I can still give you everything you want. All the power we always talked about. You don't need to die like everyone else. I can teach you. We can live forever, young and beautiful and popular, for the rest of time. Just you and me."

Kate settled back on her knees, her focus switching from the spell to Astrid.

"Keep going!" I called out to her.

But she stayed silent.

Astrid extended her hand toward Kate and shuffled closer. "That's it. You know you want all this. You know you need me."

Kate pressed her hands into the snow. She shook her

head as her breathing came in short, heavy spurts. "No, Astrid, you lied to me. You used me. And you just tried to kill me. You're right. We weren't really friends anyway."

She arched her back and reared her head up as her body trembled in the frozen night. "What was many, now make none. The spell is cast. The deed is done!" she yelled at the sky.

"Fine. Enough games. I'm charged up now. I'll just get rid of all of you." She shot out her hand and grabbed Leo by the neck, lifting him off the ground. His face drained of color as his hands fell limp at his sides, his phone sliding out of his fingertips into the snow.

"Stop!" I screamed as tears poured down my face, the cold wind freezing them to my cheeks.

"Then stop the spell!" Astrid shouted back as she smashed her heel into Leo's phone, the camera light dying out in the wet snow.

My heart pulsed at my temples. This was it. We'd run out of time. If only I'd stopped Astrid from feeding on Kate, I could've fought her off myself, but now she was too strong. If I tried to save Leo, I left Kate unguarded, and all this was for nothing. If I stayed with Kate, Leo wouldn't survive. Either way, Astrid would go through me to get to them.

"What was many, now make none. The spell is cast. The deed is done."

I swooped my arm down and grabbed the bracelets, sliding them all onto my wrist. My only chance was to become something more dangerous than Astrid. Something fiercer. For the first time, I actually needed my wolf. The urge swept through my body, burning as the transformation took hold. But I couldn't wait. I rushed at

Astrid, knocking her to the side, her grip on Leo easing slightly, and some of the blush returned to his cheeks.

"You can't stop me, Melina." She laughed as she kicked me to the ground.

My stomach ached as I landed on my hands and knees in the snow. Pain pulsed through my limbs as I pushed myself up. My hands crooked into claws as familiar gray fur covered my fingers. I tipped back on my hind legs and lunged at Astrid again, except this time she toppled over onto the ground, dropping Leo beside her. She fought against me, her hands gouging at my face, her legs kicking beneath her, until she lost her breath and stilled on the ground. I stood over her, my giant paws pinning her shoulders down, my wolf eyes staring into her human ones. I expected to see fear, or remorse, or *something*, but only emptiness stared back.

"You think you're so smart. But you forgot one thing." She laughed and shook her head. "Every time you change, I just get stronger."

She raised her knee at my stomach and kicked me over into the snow, a loud crack cutting through the air. I yelped as the blinding agony shot through my body. I pushed up on my paws, but they shook and dropped me back down, my snout smashing into the ground.

"Don't tell me that's all you've got." Astrid towered over my limp body.

I raised my head, but the pain surged again. She'd likely broken a few ribs, or maybe worse.

She raised her sneakered foot above my head. "Time to put this bad dog down for good."

"Stop, Astrid. It's over. As your alpha, I'm commanding you to stop."

I flinched as the shadow of Astrid's foot faded, and I wrenched my eyes open.

"You're nothing, Kate. Don't forget, I made you. You're nothing to me."

Kate pushed herself to her feet, and her stare locked, stone-cold, on Astrid's face. Captain Kate was still in there somewhere, and she was pissed off. She gripped her hips, took a gasping breath, and screamed, "What was many, now make none! The spell is cast! The deed is done!"

Astrid laughed. "It doesn't matter. You don't have all the bracelets together."

"You're right, I don't." Kate raised her arm and pointed. "But she does."

"What?" Astrid spun around, her eyes wide. She pulled her naked wrist in front of her face and glared down at me.

I attempted to raise my head, but the world swirled too bright and too loud. Instead, I curled back the corners of my mouth, giving her my best wolfish grin and exposing the gold bracelet clenched between my teeth.

"No, no, you have no idea what you've done." Astrid rushed to get away but only managed five steps before a violet glow burst from her chest. She shrieked as she fell to her knees, the lives she'd stolen slowly draining out of her. Her eyes sank back into her skull as the bones of her cheeks protruded through her skin. A human-shaped balloon deflating before us. Decades of age and deception catching up with her in a few seconds.

An overwhelming sensation ripped through my body. A surge of energy returning to my limbs, but it wasn't enough. Everything hurt. The pain in my chest worsened as my skin suddenly froze.

"Melina, are you okay?" Leo rushed to my side, tossing his jacket over me and pressing a warm palm against my cheek.

"I think so," I mumbled, but my voice sounded far away.

"Okay, just stay here, and I'll go get help."

"No." I grabbed his arm. "Stay with me. Please."

He lay down beside me on the frosty ground, his fingers twined with mine, moonlight covering us like a fluffy blanket.

"Is Kate okay?" I asked as I tried to focus on the silver stars dotting the sky.

"She will be." He glanced over his shoulder. "She's on the phone right now. I'm sure she'll be fine."

"Good," I said. "Maybe now I'll get some rest."

He brushed my hair off my forehead and traced down the side of my cheek. "You deserve it."

I closed my eyes, and the pain started to drift away. "Thanks for being here, even though I told you not to."

"I promised you I'd help get you out of this, didn't I?"

"Yes, you did." I smiled. A true happy smile for the first time in weeks. "Maybe you really are the hero of this story."

He laughed, his breath tickling my frozen nose. "I'm pretty sure you're the hero in this one, Lina."

41

———————

I'd barely seen anyone since the night the curse was broken. My doctor insisted on rest, and Mama made sure I didn't even attempt to leave my bed until I met her standard of wellness. Fortunately, I didn't need to sneak out at night anymore. She'd even coaxed Marco into waiting on my every whim, and I honestly believed that part of him actually felt bad for me—though it could've just been his misery at having to help someone other than himself for once.

My body still ached, but at least the nightmares—images of my wolf self running through the woods—had stopped. Except the dream runs had come with a foreboding vibe, like something dark chasing me through the maze of trees and brush. Something I couldn't see but could feel. And it felt like fear.

Each day seemed to get better, though. A little less darkness and a little more light cracking through my thoughts and giving me hope that eventually this whole experience would become a hazy memory.

"Hey, Melina," a deep voice called beside me.

I jumped and slammed my locker door.

"Whoa." Alex held his hands palms up in surrender and stepped back, giving me space. "I didn't mean to scare you."

I rubbed my hand over my forehead and blinked twice, letting the real world flood back in. "It's fine. I was just thinking."

He ducked his head then gazed up at me through his lashes with those cool ocean eyes. "I know we haven't talked much lately, but I wanted to make sure you were okay. Are you feeling better? It's super strange how the whole cheer squad all got food poisoning on the same night. But I heard you had it worse than everyone else."

"Uh-huh… I'm okay."

Food poisoning? Whoever came up with that cover story was a genius. Except it wouldn't really explain why Astrid suddenly disappeared and would never be seen again. The saddest part would be if no one really noticed.

"I doubt I'll be eating at that taco place again." I patted my stomach and grimaced.

His face twisted. "I thought it was from sushi?"

"Uh, yeah. Sushi tacos. Thinking about it now, maybe they weren't really the best idea." I puffed out my cheeks and rolled my eyes before forcing a laugh.

Fortunately, Alex seemed to be buying the lie. "Probably not."

"Thanks for checking on me, though. That was nice of you." I pulled my backpack from the floor and swung it over my shoulder then headed the opposite way down the hall.

"Where are you going?" Alex called as he chased after me.

I glanced up and down the crowded hallway. "Aren't you worried that someone will see you talking to me?"

"You mean Kate?"

"Of course I mean Kate." I hadn't actually spoken to her, but I doubted her feelings about Alex had changed even if I did save her life. "You know, your girlfriend who hates me."

He waved his hand through the air dismissively. "I don't have to worry about Kate anymore. First off, we didn't get back together. That was just a rumor. Plus, she can't stop you from talking to me, because she's not cheer captain anymore."

"What?" I stopped so fast I nearly fell over my own feet. Kate wasn't captain anymore?

Alex grabbed my arm. "Are you okay?"

"Yeah, must still be a bit sick." I brushed my hand over my forehead to sell the story. "What happened to Kate?"

"After the last game, the squad voted her out. Like completely out. Off the team. I'm guessing it's because we lost and she didn't even show up, but I assumed you knew."

"No. I haven't really been keeping up with the group chat." More like I left the group chat and deleted it, but clearly I should've held on for a while longer.

"Since she's no longer a problem, I thought we could finally do something." He slid his hand into mine, the feel of his soft skin sending shivers through my arm. "Just you and me, maybe on—"

"Hey, Melina," a voice called from down the hall.

The crowd ahead of us parted, letting Sunni through

as she beelined in the opposite direction of traffic to sidle up to my side.

"Morning, Sunni. What's up?" I said as she tugged my arm, pulling me away from Alex.

"Now that you're back, I need to talk to you about the squad. I want to make sure that you are ready to train. As the new captain, I made the decision to pull out of the state championships, but we're already trying to build a strong team for next year's season, and I need you to be—"

"Can't this wait, Sunni? If you didn't notice, we were kind of in the middle of something." Alex ran a finger along my cheek and across my earlobe, coaxing my attention back to him. "So, does Friday work for you?"

"She can't Friday, or at least not until late. That's the practice when we are going to go over the new routines. Kate never let anyone else do the choreography, and now that she's been removed from the team, everyone is hoping for some new inspiration." Sunni glared up at Alex then plastered on her picture-perfect cheer smile and looked at me. "Say you'll come. We really need you."

I stepped back and banged my shoulder on the locker behind me. All I'd ever wanted since I started at Faraway High was to be one of them. The cheerleaders. The exalted ones. Now I had the entire kingdom at my feet with a charming quarterback prince by my side and the newest high school queen basically handing me a crown. All I had to do was take it.

Except it didn't seem to mean anything anymore. At least not to me.

"Melina." Sunni waved her hand in front of my face.

"Are you still in there? Can you get together at lunch to go over the routines?"

"Then maybe you might want to meet up after I'm done with my end-of-season review with Coach?" Alex smiled and placed his hand on the locker above my head, closing Sunni out. "I promise it'll be worth it."

And it probably would be. A whole evening where I got to stare at that gorgeous face. A date with Alex would be a total fantasy, but I needed a dose of reality. A firm ground to stand on that I knew wouldn't let me fall.

"Maybe another time." I ducked underneath his arm and broke free of his hypnotizing stare, heading straight down the bustling hallway. As I pushed my way through, a group of familiar faces appeared, and my pace quickened.

Leo glanced up. "Hey, Lina, you're—"

I crashed into him, lips first, and swallowed the rest of his sentence. His eyes widened, but he didn't pull away. Instead, he slipped his arm around my waist and tugged me closer. We fell back against the locker with a bang, but I simply laced my hands behind his neck and kept going. He saved my life. He didn't give up on me.

"What was that for?" Leo whispered breathlessly as I finally pulled my lips away.

"Because now that this nightmare is over, I've made my choice, and I choose you, no matter what anyone else thinks about it. But only if you're still interested?" I shrugged and planted a soft kiss on the tip of his nose. "Besides, didn't you promise that the next time I kissed you, you'd let me?"

"Well, from this angle, I thought it was H-O-T hot," Jaida said as she fanned her face with her notebook. "Does this mean that you two"—she pointed from Leo to me and back again—"are, like, together now?"

"I guess we'll have to talk about that at some point, huh?" I said.

Leo laughed and stepped back, his eyes scanning the mass of stares aimed in our direction and weighing down on my back. "Yeah. We probably should."

"I don't think everyone is happy about it." Hailey pointed back down the hall, where Alex and Sunni stood frozen in place, their jaws hanging wide open. "But we totally are. It's about time."

I nodded and looked up at Leo again. A shy redness bloomed in his cheeks. "You're right. It is."

Jaida clasped her hands in front of her, likely fighting back an excited squeal as she gazed at the two of us together, then her expression flattened. "And what do you mean, the next time you kissed him? When did you kiss him the first time?"

I rested my head on his shoulder as I touched my fingertips against his. I'd probably pushed a lot of boundaries with a public kiss. I didn't need to cause more drama holding hands too. "Long story."

"Uh-huh. Well, clearly you're going to be making time to tell it to me. If you want to, that is."

I wrapped my free arm over her shoulder. "Of course I will. And do you think there's still a spot for me at the lunch table? I quit the squad, so I might need to find another place to sit."

"I'm sorry, Melina." Jaida patted my shoulder, but her smile betrayed her sympathy. "Like, kind of not sorry, because I missed you, but I know cheerleading was your dream."

"Was," I said. "Working on getting some new dreams. Also, has anyone seen Allyssa? I need to thank her. I texted, but she hasn't answered."

Hailey shrugged. "Not sure. Haven't seen her in a few days. But I'm sure she'll turn up. Probably fell down one of her gaming marathon rabbit holes again."

Kate glanced over from her locker. Her polished shine had dulled since our battle with Astrid, but maybe it had never been quite as bright as I once thought it was. Around her, a new group of followers waited on her every move. She may have lost the squad, but she was still the same Captain Kate. I linked my arm with Leo's, and Kate shook her head with a disappointed frown. I smiled and gave her a little wave. I wasn't certain, but it almost looked like her lips twitched to smile back. But it didn't really matter. For the first time, I didn't care what she or any of them thought about me.

Leo leaned close and whispered, "Are you sure you want to give everything up now that Astrid is gone? All the popularity? Your scholarship ticket out?"

"Yeah, I'm good. I'll find another way out of Faraway, but right now I wouldn't want to be anywhere else."

THANKS FOR READING FIERCE. Be sure to check out the other books in the Faraway High Fairytales series, Falling (The Little Mermaid) and Dreamer (Sleeping Beauty).

DID YOU ENJOY FIERCE?

If you enjoyed this or any of my books, please consider leaving a review or recommending it to a friend or library. A few moments to spread a positive word can be huge for an author, plus it makes me smile :)

ALSO BY SCARLETT KOL

Never miss a new release from Scarlett Kol by signing up for her newsletter at www.scarlettkol.com.

Dystopian

Mercury Rises

Paranormal

Wicked Descent

Keeper of Shadows

Sleepless

Faraway High Fairytales Series

Falling

Dreamer

ABOUT THE AUTHOR

Born and raised in Northern Manitoba, Scarlett Kol grew up reading books and writing stories about creatures that make you want to sleep with the lights on. She believed that the treasures in her mother's jewelry box were magic amulets that would give her immeasurable power and old books could transport her to secret worlds. As an adult, not much has changed. Connect with Scarlett on social media or on her website www.scarlettkol.com.

facebook.com/scarlettkolauthor

instagram.com/scarlettkol

bookbub.com/profile/scarlett-kol

amazon.com/stores/Scarlett-Kol/author/B078RZ4PWF